Advance praise for *One for Sorrow, Two for Joy*

'While *One for Sorrow, Two for Joy* begins as a gut-wrenching portrait of injustice and abuse, it is a triumphant ode to resilience, friendship and love. Marie-Claire's spare writing sparkles, reminiscent of Adichie's *Purple Hibiscus*. You will both cry and laugh. A brave, unforgettable debut.'

Bisi Adjapon, author of *The Teller of Secrets*

'*One for Sorrow, Two for Joy* is a vivid, deeply felt exploration of intergenerational trauma, the complexities of family and the redemptive power of friendship. Stella is an utterly unique heroine who you'll find yourself rooting for from page one.'

Angela Chadwick, author of *XX*

'Wow! *One for Sorrow, Two for Joy* is an evocative and gorgeously narrated story that broke my heart and stitched it back together again even stronger by the end. I laughed and cried and hurt and healed in the course of reading Stella's deeply felt story. Absorbing and compelling, [it] brilliantly illuminates the courage and resiliency it takes to put back together a life crushed from a young age. The palpable tension on every page and the narrator's sweetness and utterly enchanting voice, even when describing the most egregious circumstances, make this an absolutely unmissable winner! Intense and beautiful and heartbreaking!'

Buki Papillon, author of *An Ordinary Wonder*

'Brilliant. I loved it! *One for Sorrow, Two for Joy* is a rollercoaster of emotions throughout. I loved how the writing grew as Stella did. From the jump I felt invested and protective of Stella and all the Stellas out there! I got lost in it and couldn't put it down. Here's to resilience and friendship!'

Jamz Supernova, BBC Radio 1Xtra DJ

Please return/renew this item by the last
date shown. Books may also be renewed
by phone or internet.

www.rbwm.gov.uk/home/leisure-and-
culture/libraries

☎ 01628 796969 (library hours)

☎ 0303 123 0035 (24 hours)

ONE FOR SORROW, TWO FOR JOY

MARIE-CLAIRE AMUAH

ONEWORLD

A Oneworld Book

First published in the United Kingdom, Ireland and Australia
by Oneworld Publications, 2022

ISBN 978-0-86154-232-1
eISBN 978-0-86154-233-8

Typeset by Hewer Text UK Ltd, Edinburgh
Printed and bound in Great Britain by Clays Ltd, Elcograf S.p.A

Oneworld Publications
10 Bloomsbury Street
London WC1B 3SR
England

Stay up to date with the latest books,
special offers, and exclusive content from
Oneworld with our newsletter

Sign up on our website
oneworld-publications.com

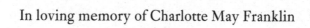
In loving memory of Charlotte May Franklin

Keep smiling, keep shining
Knowing you can always count on me, for sure
That's what friends are for
For good times and bad times
I'll be on your side forever more
That's what friends are for

'That's What Friends Are For'
performed by Dionne Warwick

CONTENTS

CONTENTS

MAGPIES

There is a poem about magpies.
No one can hear it if you say it or shout it or scream it.
In your head.

> *One for sorrow*
> *Two for joy*
> *Three for a girl*
> *Four for a boy*
> *Five for silver*
> *Six for gold*
> *Seven for a secret never to be told*
> *Eight for a wish*
> *Nine for a kiss*
> *Ten for a bird*
> *You must not miss.*

I did not know what it looked like. Before.
The Magpie.

Now.

I can hear it. Before I see it.
In my peripheral vision.

A Magpie.

Look up. On top of a chimney. A satellite dish. Perched on a tree.
Mid-flight. Telephone wire. Pylon. Branch. Landing.
Look right.

A Magpie.

Straight ahead. On the platform. Pavement. Grass. In the distance. A
field. Roaming. Free.
Look left.

A Magpie.

One Magpie. Two.
One.
One.

One Magpie.

Looking at me.
Staring. At me.

When I see a magpie, I know that something bad is going to happen. My
heart starts to race and my body becomes tense because I don't know
how bad the bad thing is going to be. I could fall off a bridge in a bus and
burst into flames. Or a tiger could escape from the zoo and chase me. If I
stop running, the tiger could kill me. Or I could basically just die. I imagine all the bad things that could happen so I can prepare. It makes my
skin tingle and my mouth go dry. Sometimes I even forget to breathe.

I am always looking. Always ready. Always waiting.
To see. And to count.

One for sorrow.
One for sorrow.
One for sorrow.

TOUCH WOOD

THE MASTER OF CEREMONIES

My dad is like Lenny Henry. He is always making people laugh. When we go to functions, he talks on the microphone and tells people when to clap and dance and eat from the buffet. People call him 'the MC'. To be an MC you have to know everyone at the party and sit on the high table. The high table is decorated with decorations that make you say 'wow' when you see them for the first time. You can only sit on the high table if you are really important. My mum sits on the high table because she is the wife of the MC.

My mum always wears lace cloth and red lipstick when she sits on the high table. She has her hair done by Auntie Joyce, with the spray that makes the picky bits lie down. I like to help my mum choose the best matching shoes and handbag to wear with her lace. I like it when she wears the colours that make you look twice, like bright orange shoes with sparkly crystals and green lace. My dad wears the same tuxedo he wore when he married my mum. I wasn't born then.

When my dad is getting ready to be the MC, nobody can be in the bathroom when it's his turn to go. Nobody just means me and my mum. If you want to test him, you can try, *boolu*. If you've used the bathroom first, you should fill the bucket with water for him out of respect. And, if you have done something stinking in the toilet, you should use your common sense to open the window, 'were you born with no brains?' By the time my dad comes out of the bathroom, we have to be ready. The worst thing to do is make him late because the MC can never be late to the function. My dad is always sweating when he comes out of the bath. It's because he can never have peace in his own house. When he is ready, we get in the car and drive to the hall.

I couldn't watch *Gladiators* on Saturday because it was Auntie Baaba's birthday party and my dad was the MC. I like Auntie Baaba because she always bakes cakes and brings me pyjamas and Polly Pockets when she comes to visit. Auntie Baaba is my pretend auntie. That means she's not actually my mum's sister or my dad's sister, but she is still my auntie. Sometimes we go to Auntie Baaba's house for sleepovers, especially when my dad's blood is boiling. Auntie Baaba lives in a place called Woodford. It's really far away and it takes a long time to drive there. When we arrive, it smells of nutmeg and cinnamon.

It's only me and my mum that can make my dad's blood boil.

My mum says I should wear my purple dress for the party. It has puffy sleeves and white polka dots and a skirt like a tutu. I get ready so quickly because my mum has already done my hair in my favourite cornrow style. All I need to do is wear my dress, and just before we leave, my shiny black shoes. My mum tells me to wear my school socks because they are white and they match my dress. She even sprays me with her perfume so we both smell like beautiful flowers. Before we go, I just need to see Wolf and Shadow run up The Wall after the referee says, 'Contestants, you will go on my first whistle! Gladiators, you will go on my second whistle!' And I really need to see Jet and Lightning do cartwheels on the podium before they do The Duel. Jet is my favourite Gladiator.

I touch wood three times so that my dad will tear his tuxedo or get shoe polish on his white shirt. He might even lose one of his shoes. When I hear him shout from the front door that we better not make him late, I run to the car. I make the sign of the cross three times as soon as my seatbelt is on and blink when I say 'Amen'. That's like saying 'pretty please' to God so He knows that you really need that thing to happen. I hope the car will not start and that my dad will have to call Uncle Papafio to pick us up. By the time Uncle Papafio arrives, I will have watched *Gladiators* almost to the end.

It doesn't work this time.

My dad puts on the Ghanaian radio station as we drive to the hall. The station crackles with every song and the DJ shouts at us when he speaks. Sometimes, when he gets to the top of his shouting, the DJ blows a horn that is supposed to make everyone feel like they are at a party. My dad thinks the DJ is so funny but his shouting voice hurts my ears.

I am singing the funfair song from *Grease* in my head so I don't have to listen to the DJ or my dad's laugh. I have watched *Grease* twelve times now, so I know all the words. The first time I saw Danny and Sandy and Rizzo and Kenickie, I knew I would have to learn all the words off by heart. My dad's laugh is like the laugh of someone you don't really know that well. I used the rewind and pause buttons on the remote so I could write them down.

> *We go together like bamalamalama kidinkydinky donk*
> *Together forever like shubop shuwody woddy ippity binky bonk*

It took me a long time to write down the words because a lot of them are words I'd never heard before. I had to listen to the video over and over again and do my best phonics to know how to spell them. When I finished, I was so happy, I felt like I was at the top of the Ferris wheel with Sandy and Danny.

When the DJ screams, '"Adwoa Yankey", coming up next!' I think about me, my mum and Sol on the carousel at Brockwell Park funfair. Sol is my brother. His real name is Solomon, but my mum and dad call him Solo for short. If you come from Ghana, you will probably say his name like this, 'Sol-lo'. When Solomon meets someone for the first time, he will say, 'Hi, my name is Sol.' I think he knows how hard it is for white people to say 'Sol-lo' and he doesn't like it when they call him 'So-low' because that's not how you say it. I call him Sol. Sol was two when I was born but now he is in Year 6. He is wearing a white shirt and black trousers to the party, like my dad, but with a blue bow tie instead of a black one. Blue is my favourite colour.

I don't think the shouting DJ is hurting Sol's ears as much as he is hurting mine. When Sol asks my dad who is playing football today, my dad says Crystal Palace and Birmingham. Sol says Crystal Palace are going to beat Birmingham 3–2. My dad looks at him when the lights go red and says, 'You wanna bet, son?'

Sol will bet £100 and his season ticket that Crystal Palace are going to win. When he says that, it makes my dad laugh with his belly and his teeth. Even if Crystal Palace lose, my dad will still take Sol with him to watch Crystal Palace play at home or away. I think that's why they are both laughing. Whenever my dad talks to Sol, he calls him 'son' and smiles.

My dad changes the radio station to BBC Sports to listen to the football. I prefer it when I don't have to listen to the shouting DJ any more but now the people talking over the football shout every time they think someone is going to score a goal. I know that my mum doesn't like the shouting DJ or the football station either but she doesn't ask my dad if we can change the station. My mum doesn't say anything until we get to the party. We just let my dad and the DJ and the football men do all the talking.

*

When we arrive at the party, we smile like it is Christmas. The balloons in the hall are lilac and silver and gold. They match Auntie Baaba's dress, which is shinier than all the Christmas tree decorations you can buy from Argos. Me and Sol sit on the children's table and clap when our dad tells everyone to 'give the birthday girl a run-of-a-plaus!' Auntie Baaba dances around the tables in the hall before she sits on the gold chair that looks like a throne.

When Auntie Baaba makes her entrance, lots of aunties leave their tables to dance behind her like a human centipede. Some people have handkerchiefs in their hands. When Auntie Baaba passes their table, they wave their hankies like they are trying to kill a fly on her shoulder. Their smiles are really big because everyone is happy to be at the function. Auntie Baaba's smile is the biggest one of all. When she passes the children's table, Auntie Baaba hugs me to her waist and we do the same big smile to each other. Auntie Baaba holds my hand until we get to the next table. When she lets go, she waves her hands in the air like a windshield wiper and everybody waves back at her with their hankies and their hands. I watch as Auntie Baaba dances to the throne on the high table. When she gets there, my dad says, 'Let's hear it one more time for the birthday girl!' The DJ plays 'Happy Birthday' by the man who is always wearing sunglasses when he plays the piano. And Sol makes the children at the children's table cheer when he does the moonwalk. Sol can do the moonwalk because my dad bought him special black trainers with silver buckles so he could have magic in his feet like Michael Jackson. They are called LA Gear. That's why Sol is so good at dancing.

Nobody knows that when my dad gets angry, it is like lightning and thunder and hailstones.

CORAL

I picked the first video tape I could find because I wanted to press record before Blanche sang 'Rydell High' over the tannoy. I wouldn't have recorded over my brother's christening tape on purpose. At least not the bit where the priest makes him cry by putting cold water all over his big black hair. That priest must not have known how long it takes my mum to wash and dry and comb our hair. Or even that she moisturises our scalp and our hair with green DAX to make it soft and shiny. If he did, I don't think he would have done that to Sol. I wanted to sing with the Pink Ladies but I couldn't find my video anywhere. I wrote my name on the sticky label between the ribbons that whizz in the machine when you press rewind. I love Rizzo so much, she's my favourite. The videos on the TV stand were lined up like soldiers. I took them out one at a time to look for my label. I looked between the cushions of the sofa and even underneath where the mice come from. I looked inside my head to remember the last time I watched it. I looked inside the video player and stuck my whole hand inside. It was empty. I scratched my hand on the inside parts of the video player as I took it out. The scratches made my skin go grey.

I asked my mum if she had seen my video. She was in the kitchen putting onions and tomatoes in the blender. She didn't let me finish my question before she said, 'I don't know, Stella.' That's when my skin started to go prickly and my chest started to hurt. Nothing felt good after that. When I went to bed, I made the sign of the cross three times and blinked hard when I said 'Amen'. I really hoped that God would help me find my video in the morning. When I went to sleep, I dreamed that Kenickie sang 'Beauty School Dropout' to me and at the end we did a French kiss. When I opened my eyes in the morning, they were still wet with tears.

I feel bad that I didn't cry as much when my mum told me that I was going to have a baby sister and she just never came. Sol wanted a baby brother. They were going to play football and Nintendo together and watch Crystal Palace play at Selhurst with my dad. I was going to be piggy in the middle and they were going to tickle me so much that I would have to say 'mercy'. I wanted a baby sister. She was going to be Sandy and I would be Rizzo. But the baby got a phone call from God and disappeared without even coming to meet us. When God wants people to come and see Him, He calls them and they basically just have to go, forever. Sometimes, they don't even get a chance to say goodbye to their family and friends, or hello, like my baby sister. I asked my mum if we could call her Coral because I really like that name. My mum said she liked it too but when her tummy went from being big and swollen to soft and saggy, we never spoke about Coral again.

I wonder what Coral and God are doing right now. I think they are probably reading or watching TV. Coral's favourite books are probably *The Very Hungry Caterpillar* and *The Tiger Who Came to Tea*. I think her favourite thing to watch is CBeebies. I want to tell God so He knows, but I don't want to speak to Him on the phone in case He wants me to go and see Him before I start Year 5.

After God called Coral, my mum stopped being able to do mum things. She would wake up crying and go to sleep crying. She wore black clothes for a very long time and when her friends came over from church, my mum wailed and wailed and wailed. The wailing shook my bones and made them hum. If I was wearing a T-shirt when it started, I would put on a jumper so the sound couldn't get through to my bones. I didn't know if the wailing could get trapped in my body once it got inside. I think it was so strong that it broke my mum's heart from two pieces into four.

I asked my mum why Ghanaian people like to have more parties for dead people than for people who are still alive. She told me to wear my headscarf and go to sleep. I lay awake thinking about my funeral. It made me excited to think that everyone would come to my house just because I wasn't there any more. There would be so many crates of Supermalt in the hallway and people would bring soft drinks, meat pies and *achomo*. I would look down from heaven and watch them like TV on Earth. It made me happy to think that all my family and friends would sit in the living room and say nice things about me over and over again. Maybe my dad would join in too. I think Sol would cry if he thought he would never be able to see me again. My mum would cry too.

Before God calls me, I would just like to ask my mum if she can make me one last jollof rice with spinach stew and plantain. I like it when the plantain is fried until it's almost black. It looks like it's burnt but it's actually delicious. I wonder if there is a kitchen in heaven for every country so that the Italian people can eat pasta, the Indian people can eat curry and the Chinese people can eat special fried rice? I think God would probably have thought about that. What if, one day, someone from Ghana wants to eat spaghetti bolognese? I hope you can go over to the Italian kitchen just to get that, or some macaroni cheese.

When I die, I don't want my mum to wear black like she did for Coral. I want her to wear pink like Rizzo and the Pink Ladies in *Grease.*

WILD TIGER

'Honour thy mother and thy father so thy days may be long!'

On Ash Wednesday, when I was getting ready for school, my dad shouted at me so loudly it hurt my ears. I tried to remember which words I shouldn't have said but he was already charging across the living room towards me and there wasn't enough time. I just heard ringing in my ears after that.

My dad used to iron my school uniform, but now that I am nine years old and 'in-so-lent', he says I can do it myself. Sol is not 'in-so-lent', so my dad still irons his uniform, even though Sol is in Year 6. When he wakes up, Sol just has to brush his teeth and wash his face and cream himself with cocoa butter. My dad hangs Sol's uniform on a hanger so it doesn't crease. Sometimes I have to wait for him to finish ironing Sol's uniform before I can do mine. I like the hissing noise the iron makes when you pour water through its nose and it makes hot clouds. If I take too long, I will make everyone late and my dad will leave me at home, *boolu*. If I go too fast, the iron could burn me. It burnt me once on my wrist and made my skin sizzle, like when my mum puts bacon in the frying pan.

When I was three years old, my dad lifted me onto his shoulders and I almost touched the sky. That is the first thing I remember about being alive. We had to write about it at school: My First Memory.

In six steps: slow fast slow, the sky is brown. My dad's fists take turns to punch my head. My mouth is screaming. The words I scream are not the words a Ghanaian child should say to her father. I must be 'craze', my dad tells me. *Boolu!* I close my eyes and imagine that he is playing the bongo drums with his fists. My dad plays the drums all over my body because I can't keep still. I wriggle the parts of my body that are free and dance to the rhythm of the beat. I hope that one day in hymn practice, Mr Hill will let us sing 'Tears on My Pillow' from *Grease*.

The percussion only stops when my mum runs into the living room with toothpaste around her mouth. Her tears rinse the toothpaste from her lips and make a white waterfall down her chin. My mum asks my dad to stop beating me because I have to go to school. I don't even know where Sol is. I am dancing on the carpet on my side when my mum says, 'Please, please, please stop beating her.' I pretend that I am at the school dance at Rydell High. I hope Kenickie will dance with me – or Danny, I don't mind. Nothing even hurts.

'Okay. We will continue when you are back from school,' my dad says.

In the car, Sol is quiet. He doesn't try to make me believe there is bird poo in my hair or a spider on my back. He doesn't even talk to my dad about Crystal Palace or Pelé, the greatest footballer of all time. I am happy that the Ghanaian radio station is crackling and that the DJ is laughing loudly at his own jokes again. My eyes are stinging but I don't want my blinking to make a sound. If I look in the rear-view mirror, I think they will be almost swollen shut, but I don't want to look, in case I see my dad.

When I see Miss Wilks in the playground, everything starts to hurt. My eyes are blinking really fast. I can hear them in my ears.

'What's the matter, sweetheart?'

When she cuddles me, I shake like Sandy's pompoms.

In class, I don't put my hand up to answer Miss Wilks's questions because ants are crawling all over me and they won't let me think. I don't know whether the ants are inside my head or on top of my head, or both. When I touch my head to make them stop, my arm is sore and tired. It's even hard to do my best handwriting. My mum says that black children don't get nits but she didn't say if they can get ants. I want to ask Miss Wilks if she will save me, but if my dad finds out, he will be like a wild tiger that has escaped from the zoo. I think he will chase me until I can't breathe, and my legs stop working. Strangers are not your family, so you have to be careful what you tell them.

At the end of the day, I want to go to Miss Wilks's house, but I can see my dad's car from the school gates. He is waiting.

In the car, I am still and quiet. Sol is looking through the X-Men cards that he traded with Theo at playtime. My dad asks Sol about his day. Sol says his day was good because he had chicken nuggets and chips with ketchup for lunch and he played football with Theo at break time. I accidentally look at my dad in the mirror. He is staring at me. My eyes are starting to sting again. I am really tired but I am also wide awake. I look at my shoes so that my dad will stop staring at me. I don't know if it is working. I hope that my mum will be home from work before us.

The handbrake makes a cracking sound when my dad parks the car. I think he has broken it. My mum drives a silver Toyota car. There are four silver cars on our road but none of them is hers. I look up and down three times to check. My mum is not home. And there is no wood to touch in the car. I make the sign of the cross three times and blink so hard that I can see Jupiter and Mars and Pluto behind my eyelids when I say 'Amen'. I ask God to please let my mum come home before my dad locks the car. He takes out his door keys but she is still not home. When I get to the front door my legs feel like jelly.

If I wash the dishes really quietly, my dad might forget what he said in the morning. My dad can't wash dishes because he is tired when he comes home from work, so he needs to relax and watch TV. Washing dishes isn't his job anyway. I open the hot tap and let the water run before I fill the bowl. It feels better when I make the water really hot, like it's from the kettle. It makes the shaking move from my head to my hands. I put lots of Fairy Liquid in the bowl to make bubbles. If you look closely, you can see tiny rainbows inside them. When I hear my dad come into the kitchen, my tummy turns upside down. The ants are back. There are hundreds of them.

'Do you know that you are in-so-lent?'

I don't know what 'in-so-lent' means. I should have asked Miss Wilks or looked in the dictionary like she taught us.

I practise an answer in my head:

Yes, Daddy. I know that I am insolent. I am sorry.

No, Daddy. I do not know that I am insolent. I am sorry.

I don't know the right answer.

He is going to explode like a firework.

I look at the ceiling. The bulb is flickering and a fly is flying in circles around it. I wish I could see the sky.

'Do you know that you are in-so-lent?'

When he asks the second time, I want to explain that the only thing I know are the words to the funfair song at the end of *Grease*. I know them off by heart. I know that my dad loved me once too. There is a photograph of him carrying me on his shoulders at Auntie Baaba's wedding. I am wearing a puffy peach dress and carrying flowers. My dad is wearing a suit and tie. My flowers are peach and yellow and white. In the photograph, my dad is smiling. I was three years old.

When I look up again, it is raining hot water from the washing up bowl. Hot water, palm oil and soggy spinach. The hot water feels like fire on my skin. I think it is going to melt me. I can't move. I am stuck to the floor like wax from a candle. My dad holds the bowl in his hand when there is no more dirty water left to pour. The washing up bowl is grey.

'Insolent child.'

I fall twice as I run.
I run as if there is a tiger behind me that has escaped from the zoo.
The tiger is chasing me.
If he catches me, he will kill me with his claws and his teeth.
My eyes are stinging.
I am blinking so hard.

There is spinach in my hair.

THE BEST GIRLS

In Miss Wilks's class, the best girls are: me, Chloe, Ruby and Zofia. That means we are the most hard-working, polite and helpful girls in Class 4. There are thirty children in my class. And everyone has a square table made of wood with a lid that hides a place where you can keep your exercise books and your pencil case. Miss Wilks's desk is a rectangle, and it has three metal drawers that slide out one at a time. They have green folders inside and so many books that I don't think she could carry them all by herself even though she is very strong. That's why me, Chloe, Ruby and Zofia sit closest to Miss Wilks, because we are her best helpers. Miss Wilks gives us jobs to do because we pay attention in class and finish our work quickly and quietly. We get stickers and stars for doing good work because we hardly ever make mistakes. I have to wear a yellow badge on my tie that says 'prefect' because I set a good example for the rest of the class. My dad has never asked me about my 'prefect' badge, but my mum says she is really proud of me.

Miss Wilks sits at the front of the class so she can see who is being good and who is being bad. She always writes the date at the top of the blackboard because every time we do a new piece of work, we have to write the day, month and year in the top right-hand corner of our exercise books. After the last break before home time, the hands on the clock above the blackboard move really fast. That's how I know my dad will soon be waiting outside in the car to pick us up. If Miss Wilks forgets to wipe the chalk from the blackboard, I always wipe it for her so it is clean for the next day.

I wish we could wear pink jackets at school, like the Pink Ladies from *Grease*, but because we go to Sacred Heart, we have to wear a school uniform. If you go to Sacred Heart, you basically have to wear a white shirt, a navy blue jumper and a grey skirt in winter with a navy blue and white and yellow striped tie. That's if you are a girl. In the summer, we wear blue and white checked dresses. The boys wear grey shorts in the summer and grey trousers in the winter. Our jumpers have a badge that tells everybody who sees us that we go to Sacred Heart Roman Catholic Primary School in Brixton. There are so many lines in our skirts that have to be folded and ironed so you can be as neat as possible. When my dad ironed my uniform, he used to make the lines really neat and tidy. It's hard for me to iron my skirt the same way my dad used to. That's because it's really hard for children to know how to iron exactly on the lines. If we were allowed to dress up like the Pink Ladies, we could wear black trousers and a black T-shirt with a pink jacket that says 'Pink Ladies' on the back. We could even wear sunglasses and any shoes we wanted, like high heels. Miss Wilks could be Rizzo and I would be Sandy, even though I've got short hair and it's always in cornrows.

When we have a supply teacher, she never knows how to say Saoirse's name when she is taking the register. Saoirse is from Ireland. We have to tell the teacher, 'It's Seer-sha,' otherwise Thomas and Tolu and Tyrese will never be able to say 'yes, Miss'. We have to be really kind to Saoirse, especially if she's sad, because she is in foster care. Saoirse has an older brother but she hardly ever gets to see him because he is in another foster home and he goes to a different school.

Saoirse can't be a Pink Lady because she doesn't always know the answers to the questions that me, Chloe, Ruby and Zofia know, but Miss Wilks still calls her 'sweetheart'. Saoirse never has to see her mum again if she doesn't want to, but only Miss Wilks knows why.

When Saoirse gets told off for swearing in the playground, Mrs Giannino tells her, 'I wash-a your mouth-a out-a with soap, you un-astan!' Saoirse says she doesn't care. Her tie is not tied properly, and her top button is missing. I am worried that Mrs Giannino is going to strangle Saoirse before they get to the sink. I am not allowed to follow them inside because it isn't wet play and I haven't done anything wrong. Mrs Giannino is a helper in the playground. She is from Italy. When she is feeling kind, Mrs Giannino gives Saoirse a carton of milk at break time even though she doesn't pay for it. I wish Saoirse would stop talking back to Mrs Giannino. And I wish Mrs Giannino would not be cross with Saoirse anymore so she can give her a bath with lots of bubbles instead.

One day, when we come back to class after a fire drill, someone has written 'S-E-X' on the blackboard in green chalk. It's Cyril. I know it is. He is laughing at the back of the class with Spencer and his hands are dirty. Cyril is always doing bad things like that. He never sits still in class and he makes Miss Wilks cross at least once every day. She is really cross when she sees the rude word on the board. That is not the type of behaviour she expects from Class 4. When Miss Wilks asks, 'Who is responsible for this?' I put my hand up to tell her that it was Cyril. That is why he has to go to Mr Whiteland's office.

Mr Whiteland is the headmaster. He is seriously scary and I don't think he likes children. Mr Whiteland has a really red face and he walks with a limp. His neck looks like it is being strangled by his tie and there are always white spots of dandruff on his suit jacket. I never want to go to Mr Whiteland's office because that means you are in serious trouble. Your mum or dad might get called into the school or you could even get suspended. Once Cyril was so bad that Mr Whiteland smacked him on his bum in assembly – in front of the whole school. When Mr Whiteland can't hear, everyone calls him Mr Tomato Face. Cyril didn't even cry.

In another assembly, as soon as we finish the Hail Mary, Mr Whiteland says, 'At Sacred Heart, we do not wear Christmas tree decorations in our hair!' Sol doesn't know why Mr Whiteland said 'we', because his head is like a shiny egg and he couldn't wear hair clips even if it was Christmas. Mr Whiteland says the word 'not' really loudly. It makes me jump even though I am sitting cross-legged on the floor. Mr Whiteland makes everyone turn around and look at Shereen's twists. Her mum puts yellow and green beads at the ends which make her sound like a rain maker when she moves her head. I don't think Shereen looks like a Christmas tree, but I am going to make sure my mum never puts beads in my hair. Sometimes, in assembly, everyone has to say 'Sacred Heart School is a very special school' at the same time, like it's a prayer or something.

'In the name of the Father and of the Son and of the Holy Spirit. Amen.'

When Shereen's mum hears what Mr Whiteland said to her, she calls him a 'bomb-o-claat'. That is a really bad Jamaican word. Shereen's mum says the next time she sees Mr Whiteland, she is going to 'run him down'. Shereen tells everyone that her mum is 'proper vex' the next day in the playground.

Sol told me that Charlene wore gold hoop earrings to school once and Mr Whiteland made her take them off and give them to him in the playground. They weren't even that big. Mr Whiteland put them in his pocket and told Charlene that if she wanted them back, her mum would have to come to his office and see him. Charlene was crying for the rest of playtime because her granny gave her those earrings for her birthday and she lives in Jamaica. Mr Whiteland found Charlene's mum in her car at the end of the day and started shouting at her as if she was in Class 2, 'Plain studs only!' All the other parents heard and turned around to look. Mr Whiteland was being so rude that Charlene's mum used the electric button to wind the car window up. Mr Whiteland's face went seriously red because there was nothing he could even do. Charlene is in Sol's class. Sol thinks Mr Whiteland is scared of the Jamaican mums, especially when they speak Patois.

I know that when the Ofsted people come to do their inspection, Mr Whiteland will choose me and Chloe and Ruby and Zofia to be the ambassadors of our class. That week everybody will have to be on their best behaviour, especially Cyril. And Shereen better not wear Christmas tree decorations in her hair. Mr Whiteland says our parents are only allowed to speak English in the playground when they come to collect us. I think he will be patrolling after school. He wants nothing less than an 'outstanding' report and everyone has to play their part.

Sometimes, when we are at home, Sol pretends to be Mr Whiteland. He walks around the living room with a pretend limp and says things like, 'We do not eat *fufu* with a spoon in this house, we eat it with our hands!' When he says the last word, he puffs out his cheeks and makes his eyes go really wide as if he is going to explode. Then he puts his hands on his hips, leans forward on his tiptoes and pretends to be cross-eyed. That's when we roll around on the floor laughing until our stomachs hurt – or my mum says, 'Stella, Sol, come and get your dinner.' Or my dad comes into the room.

Sol is always making people laugh, especially my dad. My dad laughs so much when Sol sips his Guinness and then pretends he can't walk in a straight line. Sol always says, 'I thought it was Coke, Dad!' My dad laughs even harder and lets Sol have two more sips. Sol even makes my mum laugh. Sometimes, when we are eating, Sol pretends that he has swallowed a whole *peppeh* and that his mouth is on fire. My mum gets really worried when Sol starts spluttering and choking. She rushes to the kitchen to get him water. When she comes back, she pats him on his back and says, 'Solo, are you okay? Solo? Solo?' When my mum remembers that she didn't leave a whole *peppeh* in the stew, Sol throws his head back and laughs like a clown. My mum smiles and shakes her head and tells Solo not to be so silly.

The only time my mum told me not to be silly is when she saw me giving Sol cornflakes from a bowl, and heard me say, 'Body of Christ'. Instead of saying 'Amen', Sol sang it, the way the priest does when he says the Latin mass. My mum told me to put the cornflakes back in the cereal box immediately. 'Transubstantiation is not a thing to be mocked.'

At parents' evening, Miss Wilks says that I make her proud every single day. I smile so much I feel like the sunshine. Miss Wilks tells my mum that I am 'an exemplary student' and 'a joy to teach'. 'Exemplary' means when you are the best at something and the teacher wishes that all the other children in the class were just like you. My mum's smile shines when Miss Wilks says that. I wonder if she will let me go and live with her now. My dad didn't come to my parents' evening even though he went to Sol's. I don't really mind because I don't think he would have believed all the good things Miss Wilks said about me. And he would probably have called her a 'damn liar'.

The best thing about having a square desk made from wood next to Miss Wilks's desk is that I can touch it three times before I go home every day and no one can even see me. It is the last day of term and I am not going to see Miss Wilks for six weeks. When I come back to school in September, I will be in Year 5. I don't know if there are wooden desks in Miss Montague's class, I really hope so.

I make Miss Wilks a card and draw both of us on the front cover, holding hands. We are dressed like the Pink Ladies. Miss Wilks is wearing pink lipstick and yellow hoop earrings. I draw love hearts on the border and keep all my colouring in the lines. At the end of the day, Miss Wilks kisses my forehead and tells me not to cry. She gives me a blue stone from her desk. It is shaped like a heart. I know that I will keep it forever. I want to tell Miss Wilks that I love her more than anyone else in the world.

WRESTLING

The worst part of my day is the time between when my dad picks me up from school and my mum gets home from work. That's the time when anything can happen, something bad. That's the time when I could maybe even die.

The reason my dad picks me and Sol up from school is because my mum sometimes works nights, so she has to rest during the day. If my mum works a day shift, she won't finish work in time to get to my school before the caretaker locks the gates. That means she can never come to my school assemblies, not even the Nativity play. Last year I played the angel Gabriel. I had to wear a white tunic and angel wings with a halo made from gold tinsel. When I told Mary that she was going to have a baby boy, I projected my voice to the back of the hall like Miss Wilks taught us to. I wish my mum wasn't working days that day.

My mum is a Ward Sister at St Thomas' Hospital. She works in the Neonatal Intensive Care Unit and looks after tiny babies who were born before they were supposed to be. My mum calls it the 'NICU' because Neonatal Intensive Care Unit takes too long to say. If you are born before your birthday, you are called 'premature'. My mum just shortens it to 'preemie' because she doesn't have enough time to be saying 'premature' all the time. My mum helps the doctors look after the tiny babies and run the ward. She has to keep the babies alive and make them better so they can go home. That means my mum has to know what all the sounds in the NICU mean because there are so many machines to help the babies eat and stay warm and even breathe. The machines don't stop beeping even when it's night time.

Babies don't really open their eyes much when they are preemies. They basically spend all their time sleeping and trying to stay alive. Sometimes if a baby is really premature, her mum has to go home without her at night time and come back to the hospital to see her during the day. My mum and the other nurses look after the baby so her mum doesn't have to worry about her when she goes home. Sometimes the preemies are so tiny, their skin is almost see-through. They weigh less than a bag of sugar and can practically fit in my mum's hand. Those babies need very special care because they are 'high-risk'.

My mum always talks to the babies when she is looking after them so they know she cares about them and that they are not alone. My mum normally works a twelve-hour shift, which means she starts work at 7am and finishes at 7pm. She doesn't get to sit down during her shift, not once. Not even when she is working a night shift, because she has so many things to do to keep the babies alive and to keep the ward running. Everyone relies on her, especially the other nurses and the doctors and the babies – especially the babies. If my mum was ill, for just one day, the NICU would come to a standstill. I don't think Coral ever went to NICU. When my mum comes home from work, she is really, really tired.

In March, my mum had to pick me and Sol up from school because my dad was in Ghana. One day, she was so late that she had to collect us from the reception area – even though she had swapped shifts with another nurse so she could leave work early. When we were waiting, it tasted like vinegar in my mouth because I thought my mum had forgotten us. Mr Whiteland was really cross with me and Sol. When she arrived, he told my mum that he is a headteacher – not a babysitter – and that he has a home to go to as well. I touched the receptionist's desk three times because I didn't want Mr Whiteland to shout at my mum as if she was in Class 2. The receptionist's desk is made from wood.

My dad works at KPS Autos in Brixton, 'Servicing. MOTs. Tyres. Bodywork.' It's round the corner from our school, which means my dad can drop me and Sol off and not even be late to work – unless I have wasted everyone's time in the morning. If my dad has to work late, he picks us up from school and takes us back to the garage to finish up. I don't really like being at the garage because it's dirty, and there is black oil everywhere – especially on my dad's hands and blue overalls. I think the oil has stained his fingernails forever because it never comes off. The garage smells like the nozzle of the pump when we go to the petrol station and my mum says I can fill the tank.

My dad works with Uncle Papafio at the garage. Uncle Papafio looks like he is going to have a baby soon. Sometimes when we get to the garage, he is lying on his back looking up at the bottom of the car on a big skateboard. To sit up, Uncle Papafio has to roll onto his side and use his hands to push himself up so his stomach doesn't pull him back down. When he stands up, Uncle Papafio is sweating and out of breath. He keeps a towel in his pocket and dries the sweat from his face while he catches his breath. Sol says that Uncle Papafio is the real-life Michelin man.

Sometimes, when we are at home, Sol pretends to be Uncle Papafio. He lies on the living room floor with a cushion under his T-shirt and rolls from side to side, breathing loudly and gasping for air. Every time Sol tries to get up, he falls on the floor with his arms and legs in the air like Krusty the Clown. Nobody helps him up because we are all laughing, especially my dad. He is holding his belly with one hand and his head with the other. My mum tells Sol, 'That's enough,' and begs him to stop, but she is laughing too. Sol drags himself to the sofa and says, in Uncle Papafio's deep voice, 'Please, fetch me my towel and a Guinness, *onu*.' Sol uses my dad's handkerchief to dry pretend sweat from his forehead. When nobody brings him a Guinness, Sol finally stands up and says, 'Ladies and gentlemen, a "run-of-a-plaus" for Uncle Papafio!' When she stops laughing, my mum tells Sol to put her cushion back where it belongs. My dad laughs until he looks like he is actually crying. Sol is the only person in my family who can make everyone else laugh at the same time.

At the garage, my dad teaches Sol about the different parts of the car. He says words like 'crankshaft' and 'piston' and 'hydraulics' but I don't know what they mean. Most of the time, I just sit on a stool in the corner of the garage and read my book. My feet can't touch the ground yet, but they will soon. There are plastic containers and lots of metal tools and parts in the garage but hardly any wood. So, I try to sit as still as possible and not make a sound until it's time to go home. Once, my dad let Sol help him change a tyre.

I've read almost all the books on the Class 4 reading list and my teacher says when I finish, I can start reading books for Class 5. My mum says she is going to take me to the library in Brixton when she has some spare time. And I can choose some books to take out and read at home. I'll even get a library card with my picture and my name on it. My dad has never asked me if I want to change a tyre but I don't really mind because I don't want to get oil on my hands or my school uniform.

The best thing about the summer holidays is that my mum doesn't have to go to work for three whole weeks. That means if my dad grabs me by the neck of my shirt and slams me against the wardrobe in my bedroom one more time, she can try and help me.

*

My dad slams me into the wardrobe so hard that it makes the breath go out of my body. My chest goes really tight, as if I am on Uncle Papafio's skateboard and there is a car on top of me. When my dad slams me down, it's like we are playing WWF wrestling, but he doesn't say 'ready, steady, go'. My dad is The Undertaker. I don't know which wrestler I am. I leave a crack in the wardrobe door because there are no wrestling rings to protect me. Sol doesn't say anything when my dad is choke-slamming me. He could be the referee, but he never tells my dad to stop knocking me to the ground or throwing me across the room. You don't even need a whistle to be a referee, you just need to be in the room. Sol is never in the room when my dad is beating me. My dad never beats Sol.

When you are eight years old, and from Ghana, you are not supposed to tell your dad that he is 'wrong' or that he shouldn't do something because 'it doesn't make sense'. You are not supposed to say things like that, even if they are true. Because you are only a child and your dad is an adult. Who do you think you are? Do you think you came into this world by yourself? *Boolu.* You are always supposed to remember that and be grateful. Children must respect. That is why my dad is always saying, 'Honour thy mother and thy father so thy days may be long.' That is what it says in the Bible.

When you are 'in-so-lent', your dad can lift you off the ground and throw you back down like a rag doll. My dad is so strong, he can lift me up with one hand, like the Incredible Hulk. If I close my eyes when my feet are in the air, it feels like I am flying. When I come crashing down, I always land with a thud. Flat A downstairs might even think there is an earthquake happening. If my dad would let me stand up, I could sprinkle fairy dust on him, like Tinker Bell from *Peter Pan.* That might help him think happy thoughts. But I can't stand up. I don't know if my legs have stopped working or if my dad is just too good at wrestling.

If his blood is really boiling, something can break – like a glass, or the wardrobe or a piece of me, like my arm. That's what the doctor said when he looked at my X-ray, 'a forearm fracture'. I told the doctor and nurses in A&E that I fell in the playground, otherwise they would have taken me away from my mum, and I don't want to be like Saoirse. When I said that lie, my heart was beating really loudly in my chest. I thought they might hear it and make me do a lie detector test. I saw my mum nodding, so I knew I had said the right thing, even though she looked like she was about to cry. I had to wear a cast for six weeks but it was during the summer holidays, so my friends couldn't draw pictures on it.

Three is my favourite number because there are three parts to the Holy Trinity: the Father, the Son and the Holy Spirit. That is why I touch wood three times. I touch wood so that bad things don't happen to me or my family, but mostly to protect my mum. Once when I forgot to touch wood, my dad made my mum take off her dress after he finished screaming in her face and throwing pots and pans at her. My dad said she had bought the dress with his money and if she wanted to try and make him feel small in public, she would learn what it is to feel small today. My mum had to stand in the kitchen in her bra and pants and they weren't even the same colour. When that happened, I knew my mum wished she had bought her own dress. And I knew I should have touched wood when I woke up that morning.

When I touch wood, it makes my dad not explode like a firework and it stops his blood from boiling red hot. If I want something good to happen, I make the sign of the cross three times and blink when I say 'Amen' at the end. It's like saying 'pretty please' to God. If I have to choose between stopping something bad happening and making something good happen, I always choose to stop the bad thing from happening. That's because good things don't really happen to me. When I make the sign of the cross, my friends sometimes ask me, 'What are you doing?' But it's basically a secret between me and God.

GHANA

I am going to the NICU. My mum is taking me and Sol to Marks &
Spencer in Bond Street before our trip to Ghana. We stop at the
hospital before we go shopping so she can show us where she works.
I have never been to a place like the NICU before. My mum says the
preemies can pick up infections really easily. Infections are caused
by germs brought in from the outside, so we can only stand by the
door. I don't want to go near the babies anyway because they aren't
cute and cuddly; they are really scary in real life. They look more
like aliens than the kind of babies I like. The NICU is not the sort of
place where you can talk loudly or laugh because everyone there is
not really smiling. Some people are even crying. I think they are the
mums of the babies in the plastic boxes.

The babies live in see-through boxes so my mum can see them all
the time. Each box has two holes that she can put her hands through
to touch them. Some of them have wires in their noses, which makes
me want to sneeze. The wires are attached to the machines that don't
stop beeping. Sometimes they make funny noises that make you
want to put your fingers in your ears. Everyone in the NICU wears a
hairnet and blue pyjamas called 'scrubs'. My mum wears them when

she is at work, but because we are going to Marks & Spencer, she is wearing jeans and a purple polo neck. Me and Sol don't talk until we leave the NICU and get back on the bus.

My mum is taking me and Sol to Ghana for the first time. She is paying for our plane tickets herself because she doesn't know what my dad does with his money. Or why they have been in the UK all these years and still not bought a house. She is always saying this on the phone to Auntie Baaba. My mum shows me and Sol her bank statement so we can see how much it costs to go to Ghana; it's a lot of money. My mum has to pay for everything herself and she is only one person.

My dad takes us to Heathrow airport in the morning. He doesn't know what he is doing on the day we fly back to London because he cannot see into the future. If he is busy, we will have to take a cab – or the tube, like other people do. We have to wake up early and wear the new clothes that my mum bought us because we are 'travelling'. The lady at the check-in desk asks my mum lots of questions before we are allowed on the plane. When she asks my mum if she is carrying items in her luggage on behalf of anyone else, my mum says 'no'. I think she has forgotten that Auntie Baaba gave her a mobile phone to take to her brother and some money to give to her mum. I saw my mum pack the mobile phone in the green suitcase. The money is in a white envelope in her handbag so no one can steal it. You can never trust the baggage handlers. That's why we had to put padlocks on our suitcases. I think my mum has also forgotten that Auntie Maame asked for salmon. My mum packed the frozen salmon in a different suitcase so our clothes won't smell of fish. When I tap my mum's arm and say, 'But Mummy,' she gives me a look that tells me to be quiet.

British Airways give us pretend jollof rice and stew to eat on the plane. There is salad on the side and a slice of cold plantain on top. The air hostess keeps asking us if we want something to drink. My mum asks for two glasses of red wine and presses a button on her seat that makes it go back before she takes her first sip. I love the way everyone claps when we land at Kotoka airport in Accra. Outside the airport, the air is hot and sticky, and the soil is like red clay. There are so many shiny faces looking at us as we push our trolleys towards the crowd at 'Arrivals'. My uncle works in the airport and tells anyone who offers to push our luggage for us to 'get away!'

'They push for you and ask you to pay them to push. Is it by force?'

Auntie Maame is waiting for us at the front of the crowd. She waves with both her hands and cries '*Akwaaba!*' at the top of her voice. That means 'welcome' in Fante, that's the language my mum speaks with her sisters. Auntie Maame squeezes us so tightly, we can hardly breathe. She hugs us one at a time, and then starts all over again. '*Akwaaba, Akwaaba!*' Auntie Maame and my mum look so alike, they could even be twins. Auntie Maame is very happy to see us. My mum is really happy too. She keeps saying, 'Eiiiiiii Maame!' My mum sprays us with mosquito repellent before we go outside so we don't get bitten. Two cars have come to collect us and our luggage; it's like we are famous.

When we get to Auntie Maame's house, it is night time, so my cousins are asleep. That means it's night time in London too because there is only a one-hour time difference. I don't think about my dad for one second. Lots of people come to help us with our bags. When Auntie Maame tells them what to do, they say 'yes, ma'. When they have finished doing that thing, they come back and wait for more instructions. 'Do Something' is the smiliest of all the helpers. His real name is 'Do Something With Your Life'. When Auntie Maame needs him to come quickly, she calls him 'Do'. Auntie Maame has our rooms ready for us and tells us that we are 'home'. She wants us to 'feel free' and she wants to feed us, all the time. If we want a drink, we are not supposed to ask for permission, we should just go to the fridge and help ourselves or ask one of the 'house girls' to get it for us.

The room I am going to share with my mum has its own bathroom, which is called 'en suite'. Sol is going to share a room with Ekow because they are the same age. Ewurasi is a year older than me but I want to sleep in my mum's room because I have never met her before. My mum says we should have a shower before we go to bed. Auntie Maame cannot believe that my mum brought towels with her from London to Ghana. She has plenty of towels for us. If she cannot give her sister towels, what can she do for her? Before I fall asleep, I hear Sol and Ekow giggling from their room down the hall.

In the morning, I am the last person to wake up. I put on my *chale wote* and follow the sound of laughing outside to the courtyard. *Chale wote* are basically flip flops, that's what we call them in Ghana. I like wearing them because they make your toes feel free and happy. When you walk in *chale wote*, they make a sound like they are slapping the soles of your feet, but it doesn't hurt. Auntie Maame is wearing red lipstick and a really big smile. She is dressed in a *boubou* like the one my mum wears at home. The colours make me think of the aurora borealis. Auntie Maame says I look just like my mum when she was younger but with more hair. Sol is playing football with Ekow and Ebow. Ebow is Ekow's big brother. He is fifteen years old and very tall. They are my cousins. Ewurasi asks me if I would like coconut or sugar cane with my breakfast. I've never had those things before so I don't know. When Auntie Maame hears me say that, she calls Do Something and tells him to prepare coconut, sugar cane and mango for me and Sol.

If you try to read Ewurasi's name, you will definitely get it wrong. That's because you have to pronounce it 'Eh-reh-si', which would confuse a lot of people. Do Something chops the coconut with a big knife called a machete and Ewurasi gives me a straw to drink the coconut water. The coconut water tastes like water with sunshine in it. It makes my mouth smile and it makes me happy to be in Ghana.

Once you have finished drinking it, Do Something chops the coconut in half so you can eat the white bit inside. The white bit doesn't really taste of anything but I don't like the way it feels in my mouth. Ewurasi loves it, so she can have mine. You can't eat the green skin on the sugar cane, so Do Something chops that bit off and cuts the sugar cane into sticks. You have to chew and suck the white sticks of the sugar cane until there is no sugar juice left, 'like this'. The mangoes are my favourite. Ghana mangoes are so soft you can peel the skin off with your teeth. They are small compared to the ones in Tesco's and the skin is yellow not green. If the juice gets on the floor, hundreds of ants will appear from nowhere, to fight the sun for the juice. When I have finished eating my mango, Do Something takes the seed away for me. When I have had three mangoes, my mum tells me that I shouldn't eat any more, otherwise I will have a running stomach. That's when you can't stop going to the toilet. Even though we have never met our cousins before, it's like we are already friends. I think I'm going to sleep in Ewurasi's room tonight. Tomorrow we are going to go to her friend's house for a birthday party. Ewurasi's friend is called Lady but you say it like this, 'Lay-dee'. She is going to be ten. At lunchtime, we hear Auntie Maame's voice across the courtyard, 'Come and eat!'

My grandma is called 'Mama'. This is the first time I have met her. My mum said when I was born, Mama came to London to help look after me but I don't remember that. When we go to her house, Mama is so happy to see me and Sol, she can't stop smiling. When she smiles, Mama has lots of gaps in her teeth. She wears fake teeth called dentures that she keeps by her bedside table. Mama wears a pink T-shirt and a patterned wrapper around her waist. I can't see her hair because she is wearing a headscarf. It is tied in a bow on the side of her head. Underneath the scarf, Mama has short grey hair, like a boy. I understand a bit of Fante because sometimes my mum says things to me in that language, so sometimes I understand it when Mama is

speaking. If I don't, my mum has to tell me in English. Sol likes practising words with Mama in Fante. He's not even scared to say the
hard ones. I don't really sound like I'm from Ghana when I try to
speak Fante and I'm too shy to try any more, even though I know
Mama will clap for me if I do.

Mama is cooking a big meal for us in the courtyard. It's called
banku and okra stew. Mama does all her cooking outside. She has four
cats. They look really skinny and they lie in the shade all day. I want
to stroke them a little bit, but I'm scared. When Mama finishes eating
fish or meat, she gives the cats the bones to eat. I don't think they
have Whiskas cat food in Ghana. The cats don't have names.

Mama's living room is small and peach. There is a black and white
TV in the corner with an aerial that looks like a hanger for clothes.
At the other corner, there is a black and white photo of Mama and
Dada with all their children. My mum has two sisters and four broth-
ers and she knows all their birthdays off by heart.

In the photo, Dada is sitting next to Mama. The youngest children
are sitting on the floor and the older ones are standing up. I never
met Dada because he died before I was born. In the photo, he is wearing a military uniform with a funny cap because he was in the army.
I can't tell the colour but I think his uniform was probably green and
his cap was black. You have to guess the colours that everybody is
wearing in the photo because it is black and white. Dada has four
medals on the left side of his jacket and a coin on his cap. I don't
know what he did to win the medals but I think he was very brave
because he fought in the Second World War. If a soldier had killed
him, he wouldn't have married Mama, or had any children, and I
wouldn't even be alive. My mum says, 'Dada was a military man.' His
real name was Laurence.

Dada used a cane on his children if they were naughty. My mum
says that he was loving and kind; firm but fair. If Dada gave you the
cane, he would give you Calpol afterwards so you wouldn't get a

headache from crying. My dad never does that. I don't think that Dada was really fair or very nice because one day when my mum didn't come straight home from school, Dada cut off her hair with scissors when she was asleep at night. My mum couldn't stop crying when that happened because she had the most beautiful hair you could ever imagine. It was so thick and long.

Dada was very cross when my Auntie Mansa had my cousin Araba because she was very young and she didn't have a husband. But when baby Araba started to smile, Dada started to love her very much. He never used the cane on her, not once. When Araba was born, Dada was even stricter on Auntie Maame and my mum. One day, when she was in secondary school, my mum went to a disco with her friends. I think she probably forgot the time because she was dancing and having so much fun. When she was late coming home, Dada went to the disco and pulled her off the dancefloor by her ear. I think my mum would have been really sad that Dada did that in front of other people, especially if she was wearing nice earrings.

When Dada retired from the army, he became Vice Chancellor of Cape Coast University in Ghana. The university gave him a big white house on the campus so he didn't have to drive a long way to get to work. In those days, Dada didn't actually have to drive anywhere because he had a driver who opened the car door for him every time he got into and out of the car. Dada had two offices: one at the university and one at home. Both were filled with books and paperwork. Dada loved to read and learn. My mum says that Dada was 'an academic'. He didn't like to repeat himself because he was always clear first time round. Instead of 'house boys' and 'house girls', Dada had butlers and maid servants to do the cooking, cleaning, chores and gardening. The butlers wore white tunics and black trousers, not like Do Something who wears brown shorts and a T-shirt at Auntie Maame's. And the maid servants wore blue dresses. When they entered the house, they had to take off their shoes so they didn't bring dirt from the outside indoors with them. Dada liked the white house to be 'spick and span'. If he ran his finger along the door frame and found some dust, somebody was going to get into trouble. The AC was always on inside the white house. If it was really hot outside, you would look forward to going inside just to feel nice and cool. The AC also helped to keep the mosquitos away. AC stands for air conditioning.

My grandma is called Anna Maria, but everyone calls her 'Mama'. Mama was a lot younger than Dada. She doesn't know when she was born because she does not have a birth certificate. But Mama's mum told her that she was born at the beginning of the Second World War, so my mum says she was born in, or around, September 1939. I don't think Mama has ever had a cake or a party, or that anybody has ever sung her 'Happy Birthday', though. Mama loves cooking and baking and knitting and sewing. She used to be a seamstress before Dada started working at the university. She loved to buy a big piece of fabric and make matching clothes for her children, like the lady in *The Sound of Music*.

Mama was so good at sewing that women would travel for a long time to come and see her. They would ask her to make dresses for special occasions, like weddings and birthday parties. Mama made beautiful wedding dresses for the bride and the 'mother of the bride', because she has to stand out too. Mama made a lot of money for a woman in those days. But Dada asked her to stop working when he started his job at the university. Dada was 'a traditionalist' and he earned more money than Mama could ever earn, even if she made a wedding dress for every day of the year. Mama stopped working to spend more time at the white house and to go to functions with Dada, as the wife of the Vice Chancellor. Dada was always going to functions. When he died, Mama started sewing again.

Mama is always going to church. She loves to pray the rosary and read the Bible. In the evening, her friends come over for Bible study and gossip. On Sunday, Mama takes us to Christ the King Church for morning mass. We drive past lots of shops on the way to church; they are all called things about God and Jesus. At the first set of traffic lights, there is a shop called Blood of Jesus Supermarket, it's a bit like a small Tesco's – if Tesco's had a tin roof. Across the road, there is another shop called God Is Merciful, which is like KPS Autos at home. At By His Grace, you can buy bottled water or mineral drinks, like Coca-Cola, Fanta or Sprite. If you don't want bottled water, you can buy water in a small plastic bag from people who shout 'ice water, ice water' at the traffic lights. You tear the plastic bag with your teeth and drink the water from the bag. My mum says she will never buy bagged water because it is unhygienic. Mineral drinks are basically fizzy drinks, they just come in glass bottles instead of cans in Ghana. At Only Jesus Can Do It, there are four women sitting at sewing machines, with a hundred patterns of colourful fabric at their feet. We drive past a church called Ultimate Heaven Prayer and the sound of tambourines, singing and clapping follows us down the road. Mama says that church is too 'happy clappy'.

The church service at Christ the King lasts for four hours. That is almost as long as it takes to get from London to Accra on the plane. I have never been to church for that long before. To stop myself from falling asleep, I think of all the ways that Christ the King Church is different from Sacred Heart Church at home. The biggest difference is that Christ the King Church doesn't have stained-glass windows because it doesn't have *any* windows. You can walk in from the back of the church or the sides because it is all open air. I think that's because people would get too hot if the breeze couldn't flow through. There is no AC at Christ the King, so some people come to church with fans. There are a lot more priests on the altar here than at home, and the altar boys don't giggle when the priest blesses the congregation with holy water. Jesus is crucified on a bigger cross in Ghana too, but He is still white. When it is time for the collection, the ushers pass around a basket for people to put money in, not a red pouch. So everyone can see if you only put in £1 or five cedis. The money people use in Ghana is called cedis.

Everyone in church is dressed smartly. Not one person is wearing jeans. The priest asks us to kneel down and stand up again and again and again for blessings. Sol says it's worse than doing the bleep test. I am wearing a dress that Auntie Maame bought me. It is made from Ghanaian cloth and it has patterns of yellow and blue all over. It makes me think of the sun and the sea all mixed together. I think it must be really difficult to keep kneeling down and standing up if you are wearing *kaba* and *slit*. That's what most of the women in church are wearing. Instead of just saying 'peace be with you' and shaking the hand of the person next to you, everyone moves from their seat to shake hands with their friends, even if they are sitting seven or eight rows away. The priests walk down the aisle to shake hands with the congregation before 'peace be with you' can be over. Sol whispers in my ear that if the priest tries to shake his hand, he will give him a fist bump instead. I try not to laugh because the worst thing you can do in church is get the giggles. At the offertory, people carry baskets of food and toiletries to the priests, not just money. It's a big procession.

When the service is over, it's still not over because we have to wait for Mama to speak to her friends. My mum says there is no need for any church service to last that long.

My mum takes us to Cape Coast so we can see where she was born. It is quite far from Accra, which is the capital city of Ghana. We visit a place called Cape Coast Castle where a tour guide shows us around and tells us what happened there many years ago. Cape Coast Castle was a castle for slaves.

When black people were slaves, they were kept in dungeons and treated worse than anything you can ever imagine. Hundreds and hundreds of slaves were squeezed into the dungeons with no food or water or air because there was only one window. I don't know how they could even breathe. Or how they could stand or sit or stretch because the dungeon is so small. I close my eyes to imagine it.

I can't see outside, so I don't know if it is daytime or night time. It is really dark, so I can't see my mum or Sol either. I can't read my book or play with my friends. I can't even go to school. Everyone in the dungeon is sad because they have been separated from their family and friends. I don't know when to sleep or how to sleep because there is no space. People are sitting and standing on top of me. I can't move. I have to sleep standing up because there is no room to lie down on the ground. Everyone is tired and weak because there is no food or water. It is really dark in here, like midnight with no moon or stars. There is no toilet. It smells like the gutters on the street. My mum says they contain open sewage and that they are a public health risk.

The slaves wear handcuffs and chains on their arms and legs so they can't run away. When they are caught and made to be slaves, they are not allowed to take any clothes with them. They have to say goodbye to their family and friends because they will never see them again. The white man who owns the castle uses a hot poker to write his name on the slaves so everyone knows they belong to him. He holds it over the fire for such a long time that it starts to glow red before he puts it on their skin. The poker sizzles like when you put a match in water as soon as you've blown it out. It is so hot that it melts their skin. If the slaves scream too loudly or do anything that the white man does not like, he will whip them until they are whipped to death or die from being whipped. Once the hot poker touches their skin, it leaves a mark that will never ever come off. I look at Sol when the man says that because I don't know if people are allowed to do things like that. Sol doesn't look back at me because he is wiping something from his eyes with the back of his hand.

The white man likes the slaves because he can sell them and become rich, but he actually hates them more than he likes them. I think the white man thinks that the slaves are animals instead of real people with brains and hearts and feelings. But I don't think people are even allowed to be that mean to animals, especially not dogs and horses. The only reason they are slaves is because they are black.

I feel shaky, so I have to open my eyes. I don't know why the slaves had to be locked in the tiny dungeons all the time because Cape Coast Castle is really big. They could have sat outside or even walked to the beach to watch the fishermen fish. If you are lucky, you can see the fishermen pulling in the big nets with the fish they have caught that day. There are nine men on each side of the net pulling it in from the sea. I think they will all have fried fish for dinner.

In the family picture, Mama is wearing a headscarf and a body wrapper which I can tell is *kente* because of the pattern. *Kente* is a beautiful Ghanaian cloth which you wear on special occasions. It is really colourful, like Joseph's technicolour dreamcoat but better. Mama's wrapper looks like a towel that you wrap around your body when you come out of the bath, but it is actually made from two pieces of cloth. One goes from her armpits down to her waist, the other goes from her waist down to her ankles. Mama has lots of beads on her wrists and around her neck. I wish I could see what colour they are. She is wearing *oheneba* slippers, which are like really special *chale wote*. My mum says that the markings on Mama's body and the bodies of the girls in the photo are made with chalk. It is painted in lines along their arms and across their chests because it is part of Fante culture. Maybe it was a special occasion, like Dada's birthday, or maybe they just wore it for the photograph.

My mum is the tallest of all the girls and boys in the photo because her afro is really high. I know it's my mum before she even tells me, because she looks like me; we have the same eyes.

Mama lets me choose beads for my waist from her cloth bag. She makes them herself and gives them to her friends to give to their grandchildren. She gives them away to people at church too. Mama says the beads will help to shape my waist as I grow. I choose the beads that are shiny green, purple and blue. Mama fixes two sets onto my waist. I don't even have to take them off when I have a bucket bath or go to sleep. If I shake my hips, I look and sound like a human maraca. Ewurasi takes off her yellow beads so Mama can fix green and purple and blue beads for her too. Now we look like twins. The beads sit just above my hips and are hidden by my clothes, so Mr Whiteland won't be able to see them and make everyone look at me in assembly. When I wear my beads, I feel like being Ghanaian is the best thing in the world.

In Ghana, I never have to touch wood, or make the sign of the cross or say 'Amen' and blink. Not even one time.

SUDBOURNE

My mum says that I should be a barrister when I'm older. It's because I try to stick up for us when my dad says we make his blood boil. Like when he emptied the food shopping from the carrier bags onto the floor and told my mum to pick it up. 'That's not fair!' I said it without even thinking. And it came out loudly by accident, like a shout. When he bent down, I thought my dad was going to clean up the mess he had made, but he picked up a tin of baked beans from the floor and threw it at my head instead. I think he would be really good at playing darts because it hit me in the middle of my head, right between my eyes. Bullseye. I can't remember if the scream came from my mouth or my mum's mouth, or from both of us, but it made me jump. My dad stood in the doorway and watched while me and my mum picked up the shopping. We didn't talk; we just picked. When he left, my mum left the lettuce, cucumber and tomatoes on the floor and wrapped herself around me like a warm blanket. She touched the bump on my forehead really gently and blew soft air on it to make it stop burning. My mum said that she doesn't want me to try to protect her; and that I will only get hurt. But that's what barristers do, argue for people. I don't know anyone who is a barrister, but if you are Ghanaian, your parents will be really proud if that is your job. Or you can be a doctor or an engineer; that will make them proud too.

My mum says that there are no good secondary schools in our area, so she is going to send me and Sol to a private school. You have to pay to go to a private school and it's really expensive. Basically, you can only go to a private school if your mum and dad are rich and you live in a big house and have a cleaner. We live in a two-bedroom maisonette in Brixton and me and my mum do all the cleaning, so I don't know how we are going to afford it. We are in the top flat, so we don't have a garden but it's okay because me and Sol can walk to Brockwell Park in ten minutes, five minutes if we run. I've never been swimming at the Lido because we go swimming at Brixton Rec. The Rec is warmer because it's indoors; the Lido is an outdoor pool. When my dad is in a good mood, he takes me and Sol swimming, but he doesn't come in the water with us. I wear a swimming cap because I don't want my hair to get wet, but it always does. I can hold my breath for thirty-nine seconds underwater – if I count quickly. Sol can hold his for forty-eight seconds. At Water Palace in Croydon, they have a real wave machine, but we've only been there once. Before you can go to a private school, you have to pass an entrance exam.

Sharon lives in the bottom flat with her three children, DeShaun, Dion and Danisha. They are Flat A and we are Flat B. Sharon is white and fat. She wears round glasses and dark coloured clothes and she is always smoking. Even though her children are mixed race, Danisha's hair is not really that nice. I don't think she even uses DAX because it is greyish brown and never shiny. Danisha's dad is called Lloyd. He doesn't live with them any more because he is mad. Me and Sol always see Lloyd on Rattray Road and Kellett Road. He always has a can of beer in his hand and he can never walk in a straight line. Winston says Lloyd is banned from his off-licence. Sometimes me and Sol see him in the hallway banging on Sharon's door. He bangs and swears but no one lets him in. Sometimes, the police come and take Lloyd away. When my dad is in a good mood, he takes us to Winston's after school and we are allowed to choose a packet of sweets or crisps or a fizzy drink as a treat.

My mum doesn't like it if me and Sol play outside with DeShaun, Dion and Danisha and we are not allowed inside their house. Once we saw inside when Sharon was standing in the hallway talking to the police. When we got upstairs, my mum said it looked filthy and she doesn't know how anybody can live like that. It's a pigsty. That's probably where the mice are coming from. My mum says there is no way that me and Sol are going to the same school as Sharon's children. She prays that God will bless her sufficiently to allow her to provide for her children, and give her the strength to find a way out of this godforsaken marriage.

If you want to go to a private school but you can't afford to because your family doesn't have any money, you can get an 'assisted place'. That's when the school basically feels sorry for you and says you don't have to pay as much money as the families who are rich. That's how Sol got into Jacobson Secondary School, an independent school for boys and girls. He's going to play sports like rugby, hockey and tennis and maybe even go skiing in Year 8. Sol is the only boy from Sacred Heart who is going to Jacobson. He is going to make friends with boys called Melchior and Caspar and Balthazar. He isn't even nervous that he won't know them on his first day at school. I don't know what it will be like when Sol is not in the playground when I start Year 5. But I am happy when my dad says that I can walk to school by myself. He is going to be dropping Sol at school in the mornings from now on. My mum speaks to Chloe's mum on the phone and they agree that we can walk to school together. Chloe only lives two roads away from me.

My mum says she can't afford to pay Sol's school fees and my school fees by herself, so she will pay Sol's fees and my dad will pay mine. My mum takes us to John Lewis in the West End to buy Sol's new school uniform. He has to wear a blazer in a colour called 'forest green' with a white shirt, black trousers and a green, black and white striped tie. Sol has to try everything on in the changing room so my mum can make sure it is big enough to last for at least two years. She is not going to be able to buy another uniform anytime soon. My mum has to buy Sol a PE kit and a hockey stick too. When she pays for his uniform at the till, my mum says it costs more than her ticket to Ghana. I feel really bad because I wish she could spend that money to go and see Mama and Auntie Maame again.

Before I take the entrance exam to Sudbourne, I touch wood every time I hear someone say my name. I keep one of my mum's rosaries in my pocket because it's made from wood. That means I don't have to worry about being next to a wooden table or thing all the time; I just have to wear clothes with pockets to keep the rosary safe and close. If my dad calls me, I touch wood before and after I make the sign of the cross. And at night time, I keep the rosary under my pillow. It's the last thing I touch before I go to sleep and the first thing I touch when I wake up. There is no way I'm going to fail that exam because I am not going to the same secondary school as Danisha.

The entrance exam is in the assembly hall at Sudbourne and there are about two hundred and fifty girls taking the same exam at the same time as me. We have to do exam papers called verbal reasoning and non-verbal reasoning. I've been practising for months and months at home. My mum bought me practice test papers to help me prepare. Even though I've done so many practice questions before I get there, my hands are sweaty and shaky on my pen when the teacher says, 'You may begin.' Even though every girl is going to try her best, not every girl is going to get into Sudbourne. There are only seventy-five places and two hundred and fifty girls.

The letter came on a Saturday morning in a white envelope that said 'Sudbourne' with the school crest in a red stamp. My hands were trembling as I opened it, but I knew as soon as I saw the words 'We are delighted . . .' that I was going to make my mum so proud.

I really like my new school uniform. It is navy blue like my Sacred Heart uniform, but the jumper has black and white lines along the 'V', and a crest that lets people know I go to a private school. My skirt is 'A line' and not pleated like my old one, so it is easier to iron. My shirt is white and I don't have to wear a tie. My mum buys me a blazer, a new winter coat and a purse belt for my lunch money. I like the way it makes a sound when I clip it at the front of my skirt, and how smart it makes me look. If they haven't been to my house, people will probably think I have a cleaner and a driveway.

When I start Sudbourne, I get the bus from outside Boots in Brixton to the hill a short walk away from my school. It takes about an hour and fifteen minutes in total, depending on the traffic. Walking down the hill in the morning is always easier than walking up the hill at the end of the day. If you can afford it, you can get the school coach, which picks you up from near your house and drops you off at the school gate. Sometimes, I go to the Body Shop after school. I love to smell the bath bombs and body butters before I go home. You can put the 'tester' cream on your hands to take the smell home with you. I like going to Morleys to look at the shimmery eyeshadows at the MAC make-up counter and all the different colours of lipstick. I rub the eyeshadows on the back of my hand so I can imagine what it would look like if it was actually on my eyes.

I have to pass the men outside the betting shop on my way home. There are usually about five or six of them and they always shout comments at me as I walk past.

'Pssssst! Oi, you!'

'Wagwan, princess? Look at dat walk!'

It happens almost every day. I cross the road so I don't have to walk right in front of them because it makes me feel so uncomfortable. I don't know if they are going to get angry at me for not answering back. Or if they will follow me home. In winter, I run home because it's dark and I'm by myself. Sol has after school sports and activities, so he usually gets back after me. My dad picks him up from school and they get KFC on the way home, or Subway.

The worst thing about going to Sudbourne is that every time I ask my mum for something, like new shoes or clothes, she always says the same four words: 'I can't afford it'. I don't ask my dad for anything. Sometimes he doesn't pay my school fees on time and we get a letter in the post with red writing that says if he doesn't pay within fourteen days, I won't be allowed to go back to school. When my mum shows me those letters, my chest goes tight and my hands get sweaty. I don't know what will happen to me if I can't go back to school. It's the one place I love to be more than anywhere else in the world. My mum would pay my school fees as well as Sol's if she could because she hates asking my dad for anything. But she shows me her bank statement and all the minus numbers in it so I know she has no spare money and that she even has to borrow some. I wonder if God would mind if my mum stopped putting £5 in the collection at church, so we can use it for food instead.

The best thing about Sudbourne is my friends.

THE FAMILY PROTECTOR

My mum said to my dad that it would be good if we could buy a house because she doesn't want to rent from the council for the rest of her life. My dad isn't sure what money he is supposed to have after paying my school fees to use to buy a house. My mum has had enough of the mice. My dad puts traps behind the cooker, the fridge, the washing machine and the sofa in the living room but we still can't catch all of them. They just keep coming no matter what we do. They make my skin prickle when they run from behind the cooker or the sofa like a horrible surprise. One day my dad catches four mice behind the living room cabinet where we keep the *Encyclopaedia Britannica* that my mum bought me and Sol. He kills them with his shoe. In the morning, even if I don't see a mouse, I know it has been in the kitchen overnight because it leaves droppings all over the cooker and the kitchen counter. It makes me feel sick. My mum has to clean the mouse droppings up and spray the cooker and kitchen counter with bleach before she can start to cook. We can't leave any food out overnight because that will make them come even more. One day, I look at a mouse inside the trap even though it's so disgusting. I scream at it in my head to leave us alone and stop coming to our house. I can't wait for my dad to throw it in the bin. I have had enough of the mice too. My mum asks the council to give us a bigger house so me and Sol can have our own rooms.

Our new house is on Nursery Road in Brixton. It's a terraced house. We don't have anyone above or below us any more and, best of all, we don't have any mice. I love it so much even though we don't have furniture in every room yet. My mum will have to buy most of the furniture herself because if she doesn't, we will eat our dinner on the floor for the rest of our lives. And if we are going to do that, we might as well be in Africa. Another great thing about our new house is that we have a garden. My mum says when she has enough money, she will make it really nice for us, with a patio and flowers.

One day, when I come home from school in Year 7, my dad doesn't live with us any more. It's Easter and my mum says that she is finally free. She doesn't know why she didn't divorce my dad years ago because her marriage has been a sham from Day One. She has suffered like no woman should ever have to suffer. God have mercy on her. My dad has to move out as part of the divorce. He moves out the week before Easter. On Good Friday, the Ghanaian Choir wear black cloth and sing mournful songs at church, as if they are really at Jesus's funeral. On Easter Sunday, they wear white to celebrate Jesus's resurrection and sing joyful songs at the top of their voices. The songs are about kneeling before God and giving Him all the praise and glory. The ladies in the choir dance all the way down to the floor, swaying their knees from left to right. This year, I join in with them and sing the 'Alleluia' chorus with every part of my body. You don't have to have a good voice to be in the Ghanaian Choir, you just have to be Ghanaian and you have to be able to sing really loudly. On Easter Sunday, my mum makes lamb with roast potatoes and Bisto gravy for our lunch. We are celebrating the resurrection of Jesus Christ and peace in our house now that my dad has gone.

We have apple crumble and custard for dessert. There is enough for seconds.

My mum says she should have known to manage her expectations when my dad was late to pick her up from Heathrow airport when she arrived from Ghana. He was not what she expected he would look like or be like – not in the flesh. How could somebody whose father was the Director-General of Ghana Broadcasting Corporation, and enjoyed all the benefits of his esteemed position, not aspire to equal greatness? How could the son of the father, who went to such lengths to woo her on his behalf, not want to shower his wife with flowers and kindness, perfume and love? How could he be so quick to anger and strike, to humiliate and terrorise?

My dad has taken all his things from our house. I don't know where he lives now. Sol is the only one who misses my dad. He stops making jokes and starts talking in a deep voice after my dad leaves. Whenever I try to speak to him, he just tells me to leave him alone. Sol has grown patches of black hair around his mouth that make him look like my dad. When my mum is on nights, he stays out really late after school. Sometimes, I wait at home alone until he gets back. When he comes home, he doesn't say hello to me. He just goes straight to his room.

When I lived with my dad, I had to touch wood all the time because there were so many bad things that could happen to me or my mum. I had to protect my mum more than I had to protect myself, that was my job. Sol didn't need protection. He doesn't know about protection. He is not The Protector of our family, I am.

When my dad leaves our house, it feels like heaven. I don't have to worry about all the things I could say or do that will make his blood boil. Or how much he hates my mum and how much I have to protect her. But that doesn't mean I can stop touching wood. If I do, the worst thing that could happen is that me or my mum or Sol could die. Or, we could come home from church one day and find that there are a hundred mice in our living room. And they are eating baby Coral before we have had a chance to say hello to her or to see her beautiful face.

Sometimes, I have so much to remember and so many things to do that I can never have a moment of peace in my house.

THE BUS CRASH

If my dad wants to see me and Sol, he waits outside our house in the morning to drive us to school. He drops me off first because you pass my school before you get to Sol's. I have to say 'Good morning, Dad' when I get into the car, otherwise he won't speak to me. After I say 'Good morning', my dad tells us stories about the customers who have come into the garage and the party he went to with Uncle Papafio on the weekend. Sol laughs at all the right parts of the story but I don't know how to. Everyone thinks that Uncle Papafio is my dad's brother but they are just friends, best friends. Sol does most of the talking. My dad never remembers to put cocoa butter on his hands. I think he has thrown his wedding ring in the bin.

My dad still lives in Brixton. Sol says it takes eight minutes to walk to his flat, but I have never been there. My dad rings the doorbell to our house anytime he wants to see Sol. He rings it in a special way, so Sol knows it's him, like a code. I try not to open the door but if he rings the bell too many times, my mum gets upset. When I open the door, I just say 'hi', and then I call Sol. My dad normally gives Sol money when he visits. He offered me some money once, but I said, 'No, thanks,' even though it would have been good to have £5.

Sometimes my dad gives Sol trainers like Air Jordans or a Nike tracksuit instead of money. Other times, he brings him rice and stew in a Tupperware which he says he made himself. I have never seen my dad cook, but now that he is divorced from my mum, he says he cooks for himself all the time. On the weekends, my dad and Sol go to watch Crystal Palace play at Selhurst.

In September, my dad comes back from holiday in Gambia. He doesn't ask me or Sol if we want to go with him. Even if he did, I would have said, 'No, thanks.' My dad is taking us to school. When he turns left out of Nursery Road, I notice that he has a new ring on his wedding finger; it is silver instead of gold. When I ask my dad why he has a silver ring on that finger, he tells me that he is married – to a new wife. Her name is Auntie Coumba; she is from Gambia. I have never met Auntie Coumba before but Sol has. Once I heard my mum say to Auntie Baaba that 'that Coumba woman' is my dad's girlfriend.

When I ask my dad if he had an affair with Auntie Coumba, he slams his foot down on the brakes and shouts from the front of the car, 'What do you mean?!' I feel like time stands still when he does that. The traffic lights are green, but my dad doesn't care about traffic lights. He won't stop staring at me in the rear-view mirror. The car behind us is beeping, but my dad won't move. It reminds me of the time he was driving me home to pour palm oil and hot water and spinach all over me. I don't want to see his furious eyes. I look outside my window and whisper-say, 'Nothing.' My dad is becoming a beast, again, from the front seat of the car. He won't stop shouting at me. I don't know if I am ever going to get to school. My dad says that I am 'rude' and that I 'don't respect'. When he stops the car outside my school, he is still shouting horrible words at me. As usual, Sol is busy looking out of the window as if he can't hear what is happening. He sinks lower and lower into his seat to try and make himself invisible. Sol is five foot ten inches tall and silent. He never sticks up for me.

He has never stuck up for me, not once in my life. He has never asked my dad to stop shouting at me or beating me or making me wish I was never born. And I know my dad would listen to him. Sol says he 'hates confrontation'. I don't know what that means or why it is important when it comes to sticking up for what is right. I can't wait to get out of the car and get to school. I slam the door without saying thank you. I know that I am never going to get in my dad's car again.

That is why I am in an ambulance on my way to King's College Hospital. Ever since the day my dad shouted at me for the last time, I wake up early to take the bus to school. Sol waits behind for my dad to give him a lift.

The bus is climbing the hill like a rollercoaster at Chessington before the big drop where everyone screams with their hands in the air. Two more stops. I am thinking about the word 'brinkmanship'. Mrs Wardell taught us that word. Mrs Wardell is the most glamorous teacher at Sudbourne. She teaches history and is the head of middle school. Mrs Wardell's nails are always painted red. If there is not silence in class and she is waiting to start the lesson, she taps her nails on the table to make a 'rat-a-tat-tat' sound that makes everyone be quiet. We love it when she wears her bright blue leather skirt. It's basically electric blue. In winter, she wears really expensive cashmere jumpers and pashminas. After assembly, everyone says, 'Did you see Mrs Wardell's shoes?' Mrs Wardell drives a Porsche. Her husband gets her a new one every year. She calls 'history' '*her*story' and teaches us how to write in shorthand. Mrs Wardell says this is a 'skill' that we will use for the rest of our lives. When she talks about the girls in middle school, she calls us 'my girls'.

Brinkmanship is when you push someone to the point where they might break. I think my dad is good at brinkmanship. He pushes and pushes and pushes until you feel like you are going to explode into a million pieces that scatter so far and wide that no one can put you back together again and make you whole. You're not even sure you know what it feels like to be whole. Or whether being alive makes any sense. I feel like I don't want to be Stella any more when my dad sends me to the brink. Even though I don't like brinkmanship, me and Kemi find this word funny.

Kemi is one of my friends at Sudbourne. We laugh every time we say 'brinkmanship'. Mrs Wardell thinks we are being silly. This makes us laugh even more. Kemi lives in Catford. She is from Nigeria and she gives me a reason to laugh every single day. We really want to know who built the big cat outside the Catford shopping centre and why it has been there for so many years. Tomatoes are disgusting; the jellied pips make us shudder. We would never eat a soft banana with black spots all over it because that is gross. The smell makes us want to throw up in our mouths. On her birthday, Kemi brings in *puff puff* to share. *Puff puff* is basically the same thing as *bofrot* but that's what Nigerian people call it. *Bofrot* is a type of Ghanaian doughnut; everyone loves it. We surprise her with a sponge cake from Marks & Spencer: vanilla buttercream and raspberry filling. *'Oruko mi ni* Stella' means 'my name is Stella' in Yoruba. That's what Kemi is, Yoruba.

The bus does not stop at the top of the hill where it is supposed to stop. It does not stop at all. Instead, it hits an oncoming car: a red car. I hear the sound of crumpling metal and see how awful it looks up close. Everyone screams as if we are watching a horror movie. Everything happens really slowly and really quickly after that. The only thing I can think about is the man driving the crumpled red car. We need to call 999 and ask for an ambulance for the man who is dying in the red car. I am at the back of the bus but I wish I was at the bus stop in Brixton or asleep in my bed instead.

The bus driver is screaming, 'I tried to bank it, but it won't stop!'

He is Jamaican. I don't know what 'bank it' means or why he won't stop the bus. I think he is supposed to slam the brakes really hard like my dad did when I asked him if he was having an affair with Auntie Coumba. The bus is crashing into a wall made from bricks. I think when you look down from the brick wall, there is a railway track below. I am falling. Free falling. Like a drop of rain from the sky. There is no wood to touch. And I cannot make the sign of the cross. The blood is rushing around my body and my heart is trembling in my chest. We are falling. In the bus. Over the bridge. Onto a railway track. I am screaming and bouncing around the bus. Why are buses red? I don't know when the bus will stop falling, or how. We are going to die. In a few minutes. Or seconds.

When it stops, the bus lands on its right-hand side, like a toy that has been flicked over by a little boy's finger. I have to get out of the bus before it bursts into flames. I've seen that happen on TV, and then you die from burning. If God calls me now – before the fire gets me – I can go and see Coral and I won't have to feel the power of the flames. I can see her face for the first time and we can be sisters. Everything looks strange inside the bus because it is on its right-hand side, not upright like it's supposed to be. I can't see her, but I can hear her. A woman is talking.

'It's okay, everyone, just keep calm. Keep calm and try and find a way out.'

'Miss Wilks?'

Miss Wilks helps me to stand up and stay upright by holding my arm with hers. She guides me slowly and carefully to her house. Coral is waiting for me inside. I can hear her. She is calling my name. Miss Wilks tells me that I'm okay; it's okay. She can see the wreckage of the bus from her living room window if she looks but she doesn't. She looks only at and after me. I am bleeding on her blue carpet, but she doesn't even care. Her carpet is the same colour as her eyes.

There are no straight lines when I finally open my eyes, just blurred shapes against a confusing background of colours. I have to blink slowly, open my eyes wide and concentrate before I can understand. There are so many houses around us and lots of parked cars. But the bus finds a space that God made especially for it. It landed next to, but not on, the houses or the cars or the children's play area. In the news, the reporter will say it fell forty feet.

A lady who held a pole as we fell looks like she has walked on her knees in smashed glass for a mile. I don't try to help her. I am trying to understand where I am in the sideways bus. A boy who was sitting in the front has broken his leg. He is trapped. I don't try to help him. I don't even see him. I am just trying to follow the sound of safety. A girl who was coming down the stairs when the bus started to fall is badly injured. She is screaming as if she is already on fire. I don't hear her. The only screaming I hear is my own. I climb over the Perspex sheet that covers the driver to get out of the bus. His front window is smashed; it is the new exit. Lots of people come out of their houses to see the wreckage and the commotion. Some of them are wearing dressing gowns, others are dressed for work. I am out of the bus. I am running so the fireball won't catch me. I fall. I get up again. I am running. And falling.

'An ambulance is on its way.'

'The bus driver is okay and there are no fatalities, thankfully.'

The doctor says that I have a kidney contusion, caused by blunt force trauma to my lower back, but it will heal. I have been incredibly lucky, and I will be okay. I don't feel lucky. I don't feel lucky at all.

My mum and dad both come to the hospital. This is the first time my mum has seen my dad since he got a new wife. She is calling her friends on her mobile to tell them what has happened. She tells them that Sol is fine because my dad drops him to school but he makes me take the bus. She makes sure my dad can hear her when she says this. I want them both to leave the room. My dad says that he will take me to school from now on and that I won't have to get the bus ever again. I am purple and yellow and blue and green all over my body. Even though I almost died, that is not going to make me get into my dad's car because I am fed up of brinkmanship.

Because I almost died, everyone is so nice to me, especially my dad. He rings the bell and asks for me when Sol opens the door. He has brought me a bag of pick 'n' mix sweets from Woolworths and some DVDs. He will come again to see me tomorrow. Sol is being the best big brother. I hear him on the phone to his friends. His little sister was in a bus accident and she almost died, so he's not going out this weekend. He wants to stay home so he can look after her. He doesn't go to rugby or hockey or tennis practice for a week. My mum can't stop shaking her foot when she sits down and tells her friends that her daughter almost died in a bus accident. She can't stop praying the rosary either.

When I get the bus to school again after half term, I have a new phobia of rollercoasters. Every time the bus climbs the hill, the things that happen to me are: my blood turns to Tizer – after you shake the bottle – my heart shakes in my chest, my skin prickles and my blinking gets really loud. Every time the bus climbs the hill, I am scared that the driver will say he can't 'bank it' and that we will start to fall. I never hold on to the pole because I don't want to be like the woman who walked on her knees in smashed glass for a mile. Every time the bus climbs the hill, the accident plays like a video over and over again in my head but the ending is different because I die. Every time the bus moves, I squeeze my bus ticket tightly. Paper comes from trees. Trees are wood. Touch wood. I always make the sign of the cross. And I always blink hard when I say 'Amen'.

My dad parks outside the house very early so I will see him when I leave for the bus stop. He says, 'Good morning, Stella. How are you?' without waiting for me to say it first. I say, 'Fine, thank you,' and carry on walking. My dad asks if I am going to get in the car, when I say no, he says that I am being 'defiant'. Sol doesn't want to carry his hockey stick on the bus. He doesn't understand why I won't just come in Dad's car.

After I almost die, my mum has to pick me up from behind Morleys in Brixton at 5.30pm every day after school. That means she has to change her shift pattern at work so she can leave early. She has been given special dispensation by Dr Gates, Consultant Neonatologist and NICU Lead, in these 'exceptional circumstances'. He saw the bus accident reported on the news and he can only imagine the impact on me and the whole family. I can't walk home from the bus stop on my own because I am too shaky. Even though I did it before the accident. Even though nothing can happen to me. And even though it's only a ten-minute walk from the bus stop to my house.

I am standing outside Morleys waiting for my mum but she is not here. My watch says that it is 5.36pm and she is supposed to be here at 5.30pm. At 5.42pm, I am a statue. I cannot move. I am shaking and frozen, both. She has forgotten me. And I have forgotten my way home. I cannot control my blinking. It is so loud. There are so many people in the street. Too many people. Brixton feels like Cape Coast Castle in the open air. But there is not enough light. I cannot move because the fishermen have cast their net over me. I am their catch of the day. A concrete statue beaten by the waves. They will watch me die on the busy shore. Gasping for air like a fish. I don't know where she is. 'Mummy, where are you?' She is supposed to be here. To pick me up. That's what she said before I left home this morning.

'See you at five thirty behind Morleys. Have a good day, Stella.'

When I see my mum's car, it is 6.04pm. I slam the door as hard as I can when I sit down. My mum jumps.

'Sorry, Stella. One of my preemies was very sick today. We thought we were going to lose her and I had to stay a little later than planned. Sorry I'm late. How are you?'

I say words that a Ghanaian girl should never say to her mum. I am The British Bulldog and I wrestle her with words from my mouth. She does not even know about WWF wrestling and she does not know how hot my blood is right now. I play the bongo drums on the dashboard of the car with my fists and wet it with my tears.

My mum is sorry. She will never be late to pick me up again.

We drive home in silence.

After I almost die, I can choose if, and when, I see my dad. On my birthday, he knocks on the door and asks for me. He can't ring the doorbell any more because my mum has disconnected it. She has had enough of him trying to control her life from outside her home. Ringing the bell six times a day, or more, to deny her peace, to harass her. My dad doesn't usually remember my birthday but when I come to the door, he gives me a card. My lips are really stiff when I try to move them to say thank you. My tongue rests against my teeth and won't move. There is a £50 note inside the card. It is big and pink and crisp. It has never been folded before. If I take it, my dad will think that I will come to the door the next time he knocks, or that I will let him take me to school in his car, but I won't. Because you can't pay someone to make them forget all the things you did to them when they made your blood boil.

'Thank you.'

THE GIRLS

BEST FRIENDS

If your dad beats your mum and pushes her down the stairs and makes her nose bleed so that she has to go to hospital in an ambulance when she is pregnant with you, your mum is probably going to spend her life thinking she should have married someone else. She would have married someone else if Papa had not sent *bofrot* and *kele wele* to 37 Military Hospital and told her that he would marry her to his second-born son in London. She could have married someone else, anyone else, because she was the most glamorous nurse in the whole hospital, and so many men wanted to marry her. She could easily have married a doctor.

If your dad beats your mum and pushes her down the stairs and makes her nose bleed so that she has to go to hospital in an ambulance when she is pregnant with you, the nurses at the hospital might ask your mum if she wants 'a termination'. If your mum decides not to have a 'termination' and you are born, and your dad decides to beat you too, you can have something called 'childhood trauma'. That means you are going to grow up feeling sad and shaky most of the time. You will always wonder what is wrong with you but never know for sure. You won't know about 'childhood trauma' until you get older.

*

The only place I don't feel sad and shaky all the time is at school. I love going to school and being at school and learning. Last term, I joined the Debating Society. To be a good debater you have to be able to put yourself in someone else's shoes and imagine the world from their perspective. You also have to be able to persuade other people to agree with you on different topics and issues. That can be hard because you might be arguing in favour of an unpopular idea, or one you don't believe in, like the death penalty. It's a great feeling when you can persuade someone to change their mind on something based on the strength of your argument. In my first debate, I had to argue that race isn't the most important factor in adoption. I managed to change the minds of six people, who started out believing that couples shouldn't be able to adopt children outside their race. Next week, the topic is: *global warming is the greatest threat to humanity*. I am arguing against this proposition, which is going to be really hard. I love debating because you can say things in a debate without worrying that someone is going to call you 'insolent' or 'disrespectful' or 'rude'.

I'm also part of a group called Amnesty International. Amnesty International is a human rights charity. We try to raise awareness about human rights abuses and atrocities around the world. Last week, Miss Sellu told us about a woman who had been charged with 'inciting prostitution' in Iran because she refused to wear a veil. She was sentenced to ten years in prison. It's completely unjust and so unfair. I got everyone in my year to sign a petition to the government of Iran against the abuse of her human rights. I really hope that we can make a difference.

There are lots of other teams and groups at Sudbourne: the netball team, the gymnastics team, the chess team and my team, The Girls: Eimear, Farah and Kemi.

Eimear is one of my best friends. She is kind and caring and beautiful; she makes me think of sunshine. Eimear has two sisters, one older and one younger. They are identical. If they are walking in front of you, it's really difficult to tell who is who. I can tell the difference but that's because I know her really well. Eimear and her sisters all go to Sudbourne and not one of them is on an assisted place. She is really close to her sisters and her parents. Her dad has never shouted at her or hit her and her mum is her best friend. When she was little, Eimear's mum used to chase her up the stairs with a baguette and smother her with kisses at the top. On Sundays, they play Celine Dion in the kitchen and cook together. Whenever someone in Eimear's family has a special birthday, they throw a big party at Castle Court Hotel and invite all their family and friends to celebrate. Eimear invited me, Farah and Kemi to her mum's fiftieth birthday party in April and we had a sleepover at her house afterwards. Eimear's family is from Ireland, so they like to have 'the craic'. That's something they say in Ireland; it basically means to 'have a good time'.

Eimear's mum picks her up from school every day in a green Mercedes that is big enough for seven people: two in the front, three in the middle and two at the back. The Mercedes has a number plate which says their surname: K3LLY 4. Mrs Kelly is never late to pick Eimear and her sisters up from school.

Eimear plays 'C' in the netball team, which means she plays Centre. To play Centre, you have to be really fit because you can go practically anywhere on the court. The only place you can't go is the goal circles, but you basically spend the entire match running up and down. Eimear is on the badminton, hockey and tennis teams too. She even plays hockey for a local club on Saturdays. Eimear's dad is a businessman. He comes to as many matches as he can to watch her play and he always cheers loudly from the side lines. After a netball or hockey game, Mr Kelly drops Eimear's friends home so they don't have to get the bus. I call Eimear 'Eim' for short.

When she invites me to her house for a sleepover, it's the first time I have ever been to Beckenham. My mum has to look it up in the A to Z so she knows how to get there. I only have to ask my mum if I can go to Eimear's house once because now, when I'm at home, there is a switch inside me that can make me get very angry very quickly. When it's on, nothing can switch it off. It can make my lungs fill with hot air. And it can make me roar. My mum says she thought she would be free when my dad left but she is still a prisoner in her own home.

Eimear lives in the biggest house I have ever seen in my life. In the driveway, there is a black Mercedes with a personalised number plate: P K3LLY – that's Eimear's dad's car. Next to it is a dark blue Jaguar, which her dad gave her mum for her fiftieth birthday: K3LLY 5. I think it's a sports car. He surprised her with a red bow on the bonnet. The silver Volkswagen Golf is for Eimear's older sister. She's just passed her driving test. When Eimear passes her test, her dad will probably buy her a new car too. And then, there's the green Mercedes that her mum uses for the school run.

Eimear has a dog called Stanley and two cats. Kemi is terrified of cats, so when we go to Eimear's house, her mum puts them in the laundry room so Kemi can relax. In Eimear's house, the washing machine and tumble dryer are in the laundry room, not the kitchen. There's a 'wellie rack' in there too. That's where they hang their Hunter and Barbour wellies, upside down. When Eimear's dad comes home with Waitrose shopping bags, she unloads the shopping with her sisters, and her dad helps. I've never seen a Waitrose in Brixton and Eimear doesn't know where the market is in Beckenham, so I'm not sure where her mum buys meat and fish. Eimear and her sisters are wearing Adidas leggings and her dad's shirt is Ralph Lauren. When we go to the park, her dad gives us £10 to buy ice creams. We buy Magnums and sit on the swings.

Eimear has a conservatory in her house and a granny annex where her nan lives, so she sees her nan every single day. If I could speak Fante properly, I would call Mama on the phone at least once a week. I wish I could do that instead of having to rely on my mum to translate our conversations. Eimear's house is so big, she can have a sleepover for more than ten people at a time. There are three floors and a gym. The top floor is a loft conversion. Her garden is the size of a football pitch and full of flowers. I think my mum would love a garden just like it. Unless you've been to her house, you would never know that Eimear has four cars in her driveway, or that she goes on holiday three times a year with her whole family – including her nan. Eimear doesn't talk about things like that. She cares about her family, her friends and her pets.

On her fourteenth birthday, Eimear had a 'murder mystery' party. We had to dress up as if we lived in America in the 1920s. That's when *The Great Gatsby* is set. We're going to read it in English after we've finished *A Streetcar Named Desire*. Sometimes I feel like I can relate to Blanche because we are both shaky, and little things make us jump. At the murder mystery party, everyone had different instructions that we had to read in secret. During dinner, Rebecca Smith 'died', and we basically had to act out our instructions before we could guess 'who dunnit'. In the morning, Eimear's mum made us breakfast before we went home. Croissants, crumpets and 'eggs to order': scrambled, fried, omelette or poached. And freshly squeezed orange juice with bits, from Waitrose.

When you have a lot of feelings and you can tell when other people are sad at school, it means you are 'deep'. Farah is really deep and she can do amazing eye make-up. Farah has an American accent because she went to an international school in Saudi Arabia before she came to Sudbourne. That's where her dad lives, he's a surgeon. Farah is part Egyptian and part Sudanese, but she grew up in Saudi Arabia. She tells us things about life in Saudi that are really hard to believe, like women aren't allowed to drive cars there. And they aren't allowed to vote. It scares me when she tells us that in Saudi, a woman can be controlled by her father, her husband and even her sons. I don't have to imagine how awful that could be because I think I know. Farah's dad didn't want her to live a restricted life because of her gender. He wanted her to have the same opportunities as her brothers and to realise her full potential. That's why she moved to London with her mum and two brothers when she turned eleven. She speaks to her dad almost every day and goes back to Saudi during school holidays to see him.

Farah is my first Muslim friend. She's not allowed to eat pork, and at Ramadan she fasts for a month. Fasting looks really hard. Basically, you can't eat or drink anything from sunrise to sunset, which is approximately fifteen hours a day. Farah breaks her fast at sunset but she has to wake up again to eat before sunrise so she has enough energy to get through the day. The only time you don't have to fast is if you are a woman on your period, or if you are sick. Farah breaks her fast by eating something simple like dates before she has something more substantial. As a Muslim, you have to pray five times a day. And before you pray, you have to wash your hands and face in a special way. Farah has been to this place called Mecca in Saudi with her family. It's a really holy place, like Lourdes for Catholics. If we are sharing sweets from the vending machine at break time, we always make sure they are not made with gelatine because gelatine comes from pigs and is basically another form of pork. We never eat in front of Farah when it's Ramadan because that would be out of order and we don't want to make fasting harder for her than it already is.

Farah lives in a detached house with a red door in Dulwich. Her house is symmetrical and from the outside you would never be able to tell how big it is inside. Her living room is so big, you can do twelve cartwheels and a round off from one end to the other. Farah has lots of furniture from Saudi Arabia in her house. When we drink tea, it's not PG tips with milk, but mint tea made with real mint leaves. You don't add milk or sugar to mint tea because that would ruin it. We drink our tea from small gold-rimmed glasses with gold and green patterns. There is a matching jug to pour; it's really pretty. The carpet in her bedroom is cream and fluffy and there is a red rug in the middle of her living room called an antique Persian rug. It makes her house feel like a home from home to her. It makes it feel like a palace to me. Farah plays the violin in the orchestra. When she plays at the Spring Concert, I stay behind at school with Eimear and Kemi to watch her. Her solo performance is amazing because she has practised and practised and practised. Farah and I go to Amnesty International meetings together every week.

The Arabic alphabet is really beautiful but I think it must be really difficult to learn as an adult because it's made entirely of symbols called Arabic script. And instead of reading from left to right, Arabic people read from right to left. Farah switches between English and Arabic all the time and she dreams in both languages. When she is with her mum, Farah speaks Arabic. Sometimes, she'll be speaking Arabic and we'll have no idea what she's saying, and then she'll just say an English word, like 'ketchup'. So, we know she probably wants McDonald's. '*Walahi*' means 'I swear' in Arabic, to show that what you are saying is the truth.

Farah's mum wears a headscarf called a 'hijab' when she picks her up from school. When we go to her house, she takes it off because we are girls. You only wear a hijab to hide your hair from men so they don't lust after you; and to protect your modesty. When Farah's mum takes off her hijab, she is like a beautiful secret. Her hair is brown and wavy with a reddish tint. I feel very lucky to see it. Farah doesn't wear a headscarf; it's her choice.

One day Farah's mum makes us pasta soup for dinner. When she says it is 'bird's tongue', I spit it into my bowl and across the table. I imagine how many birds' tongues are in my bowl and it makes me feel sick to my stomach. I am so upset with Farah that she would let me eat birds' tongues because she knows how much I hate pigeons and that it's something I would find disgusting. Farah and her mum are laughing hysterically.

'It's not *real* birds' tongues. That's just what we call it – it's pasta!'

I can't eat pasta for a long time after that!

In Farah's room, we talk about the boy she loves called Eesa. He just 'gets' her spirit, you know. She plays music by 2Pac like 'Life Goes On'. We know all the words and when we sing them, it just comes from the heart. Because we are so deep, me and Farah.

Sometimes we organise charity events in school to help people who are less fortunate than us. In Year 9, we decide to have a cake sale because that way people can 'bake or buy'. When Kemi says, 'I put weed in the chocolate brownies, *walahi*,' we know that she is not even joking. We sell six brownies to Dr Jagessar who puts a £20 note in our collection box. He is going to try not to eat them all at once and to save at least one for Mrs Jagessar, who loves chocolate almost as much as he does. We ask Dr Jagessar to 'try at least one' brownie as soon as he buys them and clap when he takes his first bite. We are smiling because we are so happy that he is supporting WaterAid and because we are helping children in Africa. When he leaves we are LOLing and holding our stomachs.

'How much weed did you put in, Kemi?'

'Two ounces!'

We are wild with laughter. At the end of the cake sale, we share the leftover brownies between us, and sit through Latin, high as kites. *Walahi.*

At break time, we use our hockey sticks to sweep the bottom of the vending machine for coins that have rolled underneath. The most money we ever got was £2.40. We bought Tooty Frooties, a Kit Kat and purple Nik Naks to share. If we buy something and it gets stuck in the vending machine while it's rolling out of the spiral, we take turns to bump it with our hips until it drops. It's called 'the hip shake'. We love it when people who don't know about 'the hip shake' abandon their sweets, crisps and drinks mid-spiral, because when they go to the Admin Office to ask for a refund, we add their treats to ours. My 'hip shake' is the strongest.

We love writing letters to each other to let the other person know how much we love them and how important their friendship is to us. We hold hands when we walk around school at break time and we don't care that there are no boys in our school. In fact, we prefer it.

In Year 10, me, Kemi, Eimear and Farah spend pretty much all our time together because we are in the top maths set and we've all chosen double science for GCSE. Mrs Gamon teaches chemistry, which we hate because it's really hard. She teaches us rhymes for the periodic table 'to help' us. Does she think we're in nursery or something? Mrs Coelho teaches physics. She's my favourite science teacher because she just explains things really clearly. Mr Edwards teaches biology. He looks like a sixth former and whispers when he speaks, so no one really takes him seriously.

I am rocking backwards and forwards on my stool in physics with my lab coat over my head. Mrs Coelho is talking about atomic structure and I'm struggling to concentrate. My finger is in a tub of Vaseline because we hate having dry lips. When I lean too far back, I fall backwards onto the floor. My stool falls on top of me and I land with a thud. The Vaseline lid takes ages to stop spinning before it makes a clanging noise on the ground. There is a lump of Vaseline on my finger; there is a dent the shape of my finger in the Vaseline tub. Eimear, Farah and Kemi can't stop laughing. I am on the floor with my blue lab coat draped over my head. I am laughing too. Mrs Coelho tells The Girls off for laughing and not helping me. She gives me her hand and settles me back on my stool.

'Are you okay, darling?' That makes us laugh even more.

After that, everyone says I'm Mrs Coelho's favourite.

When Mr Edwards says, 'Today we are going to dissect a sheep's heart' in Year 10 biology, I think of Brixton market on a Saturday, buying meat and fish with my mum. When the butcher touches the mutton with his hands, it makes me shudder. There are some types of meat that you can't even tell what animal it came from. My mum says it's called tripe and offal. I would never eat that in a million years. I can't even eat ox tail because I don't know why anyone would want to eat meat that comes from near where the animal goes to the toilet. When I look closely at the giant snails, I can see that they are moving, really slowly. The crabs are alive too. They will die – instantly – when my mum puts them in boiling water to make stew. She makes sure the water is boiling first so they don't suffer.

Me, Eimear, Farah and Kemi are in the same group for dissection. We have to use a scalpel to cut the sheep's heart in two and identify the 'atrium' and 'ventricles' on the left and right sides, the 'bicuspid' and 'tricuspid' valves and the 'apex'. We are wearing gloves, but I hate the way the sheep's heart feels in my hands. I don't want to hold it: 'It's cold!' I throw it to Eimear. Eimear doesn't want it, she's a vegetarian. Eimear throws it to Kemi, overarm. Kemi thinks it looks disgusting. She throws it to Farah. Farah cannot hold it for another second. Mr Edwards is writing on the whiteboard with his back to us. Before we know it, we are playing ball – with Baa Baa Black Sheep's heart. It lands in Eimear's hands as Mr Edwards turns around. There are tears in my eyes. I didn't know that laughing could make you cry.

At Sudbourne, I'm a different Stella to the Stella my dad thinks I am. For eight hours of every day, I try to block out his voice in my head telling me all the things that are wrong with me, the things I don't know and can't do. When I am learning and laughing with my friends, it's hard to think about anything else. The reason I want to stop touching wood is because it's hard to touch wood without people seeing you. If they see you, they will ask questions like, 'What are you doing?' And it's really hard to know what to say. It's the same if you make the sign of the cross. The reason I can stop touching wood is because Farah, Eimear and Kemi are always with me. They remind me that good things can happen in my life.

ZOMBIE

I wasn't born when my mum was pregnant with me and my dad beat her, but I feel like I was there because she tells me about it all the time. Instead of buying sweets, why doesn't he help with your living costs? Will your school shoes buy themselves? Another red letter has come; my dad is late paying this term's fees. Do I want to see the letter? She cannot give me money to go shopping in Bromley with Eimear, Farah and Kemi, because she has none. Do I know how much she spends each week on food shopping? How much gas and electricity costs each month? She pays the bills by herself, and she is just one person. Come and look at her bank statements. Look, she has reached her overdraft limit for the month and there are more than two weeks left until she gets paid. She does not know how we are going to survive. She is trying her best, but she gets no help from my dad. And, on top of that, she has two teenage children, and not one of them knows how to wash dishes. I close my ears so I don't have to listen.

If I ask my mum to do something and she ignores me or doesn't do it properly, I roar at her and I can't even control it. My mum and Sol won't listen to me when I shout. My mum is sure that none of my school friends speak to their mums the way I speak to her. I don't think their mums take them through their bank statements every week either. We never have any money to do anything.

My mum says that people in the UK are very fortunate because we have a 'welfare state' and the government will always try to help people in need. When you are poor in Ghana, you literally have nothing. If you are Ghanaian, and there is rice in your house, your mum will always say there is food at home. My mum cooks with Tilda Basmati rice. With Tilda Basmati rice you can make jollof rice, rice and stew, rice water and ground rice. When I have to eat rice for two days in a row, I don't want to eat it on day three. I ask my mum if we can have a Chinese takeaway for dinner. When she says, 'There is rice at home,' my heart starts to beat in an angry way. I have had enough of rice and I don't want to eat it tonight. When I raise my voice, my mum gives in. She gives in a lot these days. Sol thinks I'm my mum's favourite and that I always get what I want. He thinks I'm lazy because I fall asleep in front of the TV and lie-in on weekends.

In Year 11, the reason I always want to sleep is because I am exhausted all the time. I can barely keep my eyes open in class. I have to pay attention because this is my GCSE year and there is so much to learn. I feel like I am carrying a basket filled with plastic bags of ice water on my head, like the women at the traffic lights in Accra. Instead of water, I am carrying equations, information and diagrams, and conjugated French verbs. The basket is really heavy and I want to set it down but I have to look in the direction I am walking and carry on. I have lost my appetite and my mum says that I am losing weight; she is worried. Auntie Baaba reminds me that Ghanaian girls are supposed to be curvaceous.

'We like bottoz and breasts, not bones bones bones.' Even though she is laughing, I know it's not a joke.

I know something is wrong with me when I have to lie down to brush my teeth because my hand is really weak in the mornings. I spend my lessons with my head in my hands resting on my desk because all I want to do is sleep. When I'm really tired, my words come out slurred. I know something is wrong with me when I try to run for the bus after school and the screen goes black as my legs turn to jelly. I can hear people laughing as I open my eyes. I am on the floor of the bus. School children, I think. They are laughing at me. I wake up in front of the driver's door. I saw a magpie at lunchtime on the Astroturf at school. When you see one magpie by itself, it means that something bad is going to happen. I think that's why I feel like I'm trying to stand up in a sideways bus that has just fallen off a bridge. That's why I've fainted, again. A lady who looks like a mum helps me to pick my things up from the floor and stand up. My legs don't work properly after that.

Sometimes my fingers hurt so much, I can barely grip my pen. If I'm writing an essay, my handwriting looks really neat at the beginning, but by the end, it looks like I've just learned how to join up. In exams, I get extra time 'to put me on the same footing as everyone else'. Mrs Wardell says it's nothing to be ashamed of, it's called 'equity'. I'm allowed rest breaks whenever I need them but I just wish I could sit in the main hall with everyone else.

Dr Gordon says I have something called Addison's disease. Now I feel like I have something wrong with my body *and* my brain. It's so rare that only eight thousand people have it in the UK. It's so rare that it takes a long time for anyone to know what is wrong with me. I have to have something called a 'synacthen stimulation' test to check the cortisol levels in my body. Cortisol is basically a natural steroid that your body makes. It helps to control the blood sugar in your body as well as your circulation. It also helps you to deal with stress. I've never really thought about 'stress' before but when Dr Gordon explains a bit more about it and how it can affect the body, I realise that I've had a lot of stress in my life. When Dr Gordon speaks through this part of my diagnosis, my mum wrings her hands together and looks at the floor. I can't see her eyes, but I know that they are filling with tears. I also know that we won't talk about it when we get home because we never talk about things like that.

Dr Gordon tests my thyroid gland to see if it is working properly. When you have Addison's disease, your body doesn't always produce enough hormones. Dr Gordon says I have an underactive thyroid gland. Addison's disease is an 'autoimmune condition'. An auto-immune condition is one where your body attacks itself. That is why I have to take tablets three times a day, so I can replace the hormones in my body – and brush my teeth.

There is only one person I know who can understand what it is like to have Addison's disease. God sent Kemi to the same school as me and put her in my year. That is what our mums say. We have to wear medical alert bracelets so that, in an emergency, people will know why we have fainted or why we are sick. Kemi is in my form class. We sit together in French and in double science with Eimear and Farah. We get on so well that we understand things about each other without having to explain them. Kemi has to tell the teachers how to pronounce her name. She finds it annoying because it's really not that hard. Kemi can make me laugh by just looking at me. Her mum says I can come to her house whenever I want. She makes jollof with Tilda Basmati rice too.

Kemi's mum is called Auntie Monilola. Everyone calls her Moni for short. Auntie Moni and my mum think it is a miracle that we have each other. What are the chances? Auntie Moni wears rings that are so sparkly they make you want to wear sunglasses. She is my first Nigerian auntie. When I'm at her house, I make her call me by my pretend Nigerian name, 'Titilayo'. She calls me 'Titi' for short because it makes me laugh. Auntie Moni loves to keep fit. Before Kemi was diagnosed with Addison's disease, she would go spinning with her mum every Saturday morning at the gym. Now, they do Pilates together instead but only if Kemi feels up to it. Auntie Moni says, 'It's always good to try – you never know, you might surprise yourself.' Auntie Moni also says that God is a Woman and that women rule the world. She teaches me Yoruba.

'Kemi, is that your boyfriend?' I am giggling too much for her to take me seriously.

'Stella, that's my dad!'

Kemi's dad gives her a big hug when he picks her up from school as a surprise. He is really pleased to know that her friend thinks he is young enough and cool enough to be his daughter's boyfriend. Kemi is an only child. If anyone asks her dad if he wishes he had a son, Kemi's dad answers, 'I have everything I want and need.' When Kemi smiles, she looks exactly like him. At home, Kemi's dad plays Fela Kuti and they dance to the Godfather of Afrobeat. When Kemi was diagnosed with Addison's disease, her dad told her not to worry. Now they understand the problem, they can work around it; there is nothing she cannot achieve if she puts her mind to it. Kemi's favourite Fela song is 'Zombie'. She is a daddy's girl. If she calls him 'Dad' by accident, Kemi's dad reminds her, 'I'm not your dad, I'm your daddy.'

I am going to the Jazz Café with Kemi and her parents. Uncle Obi bought four tickets and told Kemi to bring a friend. Auntie Moni and Uncle Obi pick me up at 6pm. Kemi and I are wearing jeans, black tops and gold earrings. Uncle Obi says we look like sisters. Auntie Moni tells him that's because we are. Doesn't he know that he has two daughters? Uncle Obi says it was remiss of him to forget. In the car I want to make myself really small, but Uncle Obi won't let me. He keeps asking me and Kemi questions. When he speaks to us, he glances at us in the rear-view mirror and smiles. If you give an answer, he wants to know the reason for your answer. It makes me feel nervous because I don't know if he is trying to trick me or what will happen if I get the answer wrong.

'Stella, what is your favourite Fela song?'

'I don't – I don't really know any of his songs.'

I think, but don't say, that everything I know about Fela Kuti is what Kemi has taught me. When Uncle Obi slows the car down to a stop, I don't see the red traffic light because my heart has jumped to my throat and the skin on my arms has gone cold and prickly.

'You don't have a Fela favourite?!'

The indicator is ticking to turn right and for something bad to happen. I know I have said something wrong and that it is too late to take it back. I know that tears are rushing to my eyes because they are blinking hard and fast. I am looking for two magpies outside the window of Uncle Obi's car, but it is too dark to see. I know because I am looking. With my blinking eyes. No one can hear it if you say it or shout it or scream it in your head – the poem about magpies. I want to get out of the car before the lights turn green. Before we get to the Jazz Café. Before the car falls forty feet off a bridge. Before it's too late. Uncle Obi is staring at me through the rear-view mirror. His eyes are wide; they have forgotten how to blink.

'Kemi, what is the correct answer?'

'You're supposed to say, "Zombie O Zombie".' Kemi rolls her eyes and laughs at the same time. That is the cue for Auntie Moni and Uncle Obi to join in.

'"Zombie" is the ultimate anti-establishment song. Dance to the beat of your own drum. That's what Fela is saying. Don't let other people make decisions for you or tell you what to do. Don't be a follower, don't be a zombie. It's such a great song. I want you to learn the words before we get to the Jazz Café.' Uncle Obi is laughing again. Auntie Moni says she also loves the song 'Lady' and that she can't wait to hear it tonight. Did we know that Fela Kuti's mum was a women's rights activist? What they did to that woman was wicked. Uncle Obi agrees before he turns up the volume to Track Six. I try to smile and stop tears from flooding the banks of my eyes as we drive in the direction of Camden.

*

I keep fainting. At home in the morning. Between lessons during the day. On the bus after school. When I miss my bus stop and end up in Vauxhall, my mum says we need to go back to see Dr Gordon. I have lost too much weight. My purse belt is sitting really low on my hips and my bra has grown too big for me. Dr Gordon says that I am having an Addisonian Crisis. She admits me to hospital and puts me on a drip of corticosteroids, saline and sugar. I am so tired. In and out of sleep. When I wake up, Kemi is here with Auntie Moni, my mum and Auntie Baaba. The adults look at me with worried eyes and take turns to reassure each other, 'It is well, thanks be to God.' Kemi has brought flowers, magazines and a mix-tape with all my favourite songs, and hers.

'"Zombie" is the first track,' she says with a smile.

She arranges the flowers in a plastic vase borrowed from the nurses' station and holds my hand. Whenever I open my eyes, Kemi is there. She stays until visiting time is over.

SOL

When Sol comes to prize-giving with my mum, his deep voice and dimples send the girls in my year into a frenzy.

'Oh my God, your brother is so fit!'

'He looks like that model, Tyrese!'

'Has your brother got a girlfriend?'

Now that Sol is in sixth form, my dad doesn't drop him to school any more. If I am not ready by 7.15am, Sol leaves for the bus stop without me. He doesn't say 'goodbye' or 'see you later', he just goes. If I wasn't his sister, I don't think Sol would want to be my friend. He says that my mum lets me get away with anything and everything, but Sol doesn't have Addison's disease, so he doesn't even know what he's talking about. In my birthday card last year, he wrote:

> *Happy Birthday, Stella. I hope you have a good day.*
> *Try not to use Addison's as an excuse.*

His handwriting is like spider's scribble. I don't think he meant the 'Happy Birthday' bit.

*

When Sol starts to grow a moustache and muscles, I start to like him less and less. He doesn't ask for things, he just takes them: my nail scissors, my hairbrush, my space. When I am getting ready to eat, he comes into the kitchen and takes the chicken drumstick from my plate. He has already eaten half the chicken that my mum made yesterday and there are only wings left. I don't like the wing part of the chicken. He bites the drumstick in front of me: one mouthful, two mouthfuls, three. Demolished. He saves the crispy skin for last. Everyone knows that is the best bit. He smiles at me as if it's a joke. That is when a wild thing inside me starts to stir. A beast whose name I do not know and whose face I have never seen. It thrashes against the bars of its cage, fighting for freedom and chicken. It is loud and uncontrollable and angry. Our voices clash in the air; a battle with no rules. My voice gets louder as his steps get closer. Until there is a knife in my hand. The sharp one that my mum uses to cut chicken and dice beef. I hold it next to Sol's face when he gets too close. That's when he knows that he shouldn't have taken the chicken from my plate. My mum is on days; she will be home soon.

'She's not just crazy, Mum. She's dangerous!'

He says it loud enough for me to hear from my bedroom. I hear my mum on the phone to Auntie Baaba as I lie in bed at night. She doesn't know what to do with me. She is exhausted. She has tried her best. My dad has ruined her life, and mine. She should have left him a long time ago. I think of all the reasons why I hate my brother. Now that he has muscles and a moustache, he looks exactly like my dad. That makes me hate him even more. I wish my life had been as easy as Sol's. He doesn't know what it's like to be me. He will never understand. When she switches off her lamp, I know that my mum is shaking her foot and praying the rosary. I wish Sol lived with my dad.

I have to write Sol a letter to say sorry for holding a knife to his face. I don't know what happened to me in that moment or why I did it. I am really sorry. I promise that I will never do anything like that again. I am trying really hard to be a better person. Please can he be my brother again? He doesn't speak to me for four weeks. Sol says I need to 'Get. A. Grip.'

In the summer, my dad takes Sol to Ghana for a holiday with Auntie Coumba. Sol goes into my mum's vanity case to get his passport. My mum cries when he tells her the day before that he is going to Ghana with his dad. She would have expected a responsible father to at least discuss such a thing with his child's mother. Would that have been too much to ask? And she doesn't know whether my dad is encouraging his son to steal by taking his passport in that way or what. My dad doesn't ask me if I want to come. They are gone for four weeks.

When Sol comes back, he has 'holiday blues' and spends all his time on the phone talking to his friends, old and new. He now speaks Pidgin English.

'Chale, how far? What dey happen?'

'Chale, I dey oo, I dey!'

I wonder what the person on the other line is saying and if they even understand the language Sol is speaking.

Sol has had 'the sickest time' and talks non-stop about his holiday. Alessandro is Italian, but he's lived in Ghana practically all his life. His dad imports Italian food to Ghana and owns a restaurant called La Cucina in Osu. Bea lives in Surrey but her dad works for Ashanti Goldmines. They have 'the most incredible' house you have ever seen in Cantonments. She goes to Ghana every half term, Easter and summer holiday. Flies business class every time. She's a really sweet girl. Finlay's dad owns the Black Star Hotel. He is the coolest guy and a seriously good polo player. He plays at Accra Polo Club; 'White jeans are a serious look, cuz.' Sol got the hang of it after five minutes. He must have 'played a pony' in another life. Sienna is Finlay's sister. She is absolutely beautiful. Their mum is English but their dad is from Ghana. Everyone in Ghana knows the Bannerman family. I can tell from the way he talks about her that Sol loves Sienna.

Sol, Alessandro, Bea, Finlay and Sienna spend the summer lounging poolside at the Black Star Hotel, chilling at the polo club and eating at La Cucina. I study their pictures and retake them. I am sandwiched between Sienna and Bea at Labadi Beach, bikini babes, our toned abs on show. I am on Alessandro's shoulders in the pool, our wide smiles made brighter by the glare of the midday sun. I am cheering for Finlay in a game of polo, three inches taller in wedged heels, looking like I belong. I imagine what it would have been like to have been there, part of their holiday, their memories and their lives.

I don't invite Eimear or Farah or Kemi to my house over the summer. My house is really small, and I don't want them to feel claustrophobic. Also, I don't know what I would do if we were in the living room and a mouse ran out from under the sofa. I think I would literally die. Eimear says almost every house in London has mice, even hers. She says it like it's not a big deal. I don't tell The Girls what it's like to live in my house and to be a part of my family. Or what it was like to live with my dad before he left us alone to try and make sense of our lives. I don't tell them that my dad is really different to their dads and that I'd love to play 'Family Swap' for a day or a week or forever. When I'm with them, I just want to feel this way forever, happy and free. Sometimes, I meet Eimear, Farah and Kemi for lunch at Pizza Express. My mum doesn't say no when I ask her for money, not when Sol is in Ghana.

When he comes back, I don't tell Sol that I spent the entire summer telling my mum that I wished I was in Ghana instead and how much I hate living in this house.

DAMIAN

I don't think boys fancy me. Whenever someone asks, 'What's your type?' there are only two options: blonde or brunette. I don't think white boys even see me. I don't know what black boys think of me. I dream about my first kiss. Will I know what to do and how to do it? Will the boy whose lips are locked with mine be able to tell that I've never been kissed before? Should I tell him? No one ever looks at me. No one ever looked at me until I met Damian.

We have planned Eimear's birthday party to the last detail and down to the purchase of Alka-Seltzer, for the morning after the night before. Her parents are in Spain for the weekend and she has a free house. They trust her to be responsible. We have decorated her Olympic-size living room with helium balloons and banners to celebrate her 'Sweet 16'. Pink, silver and gold, a joint effort. There is alcohol and there are boys. Damian is one of them. He is tall and handsome, with eyes two shades of brown lighter than mine. His hair is low cut. His ego, inflated. Damian is more than confident, he is arrogant. Not self-assured, as much as self-congratulating. He offends, without knowing or intending. I watch him with disbelief and finish my second bottle of Archers as he approaches.

Damian assumes that I am from the Caribbean. I look at him blankly.

'My family is from Ghana.' His family is from Jamaica.

I am wearing too few clothes and too much skin. A red corset – Lipsy, or something similar. The Girls have given me a false sense of confidence and encouraged me to 'show off' my 'amazing figure'. Pictures will record that my make-up is inexpertly applied, and my outfit, a mistake. But standing next to the vodka-spiked watermelon, I am Naomi Campbell herself, catwalk ready, confidence filled. I give monosyllabic answers to Damian's questions. I thought I would be excited to speak to a boy. I didn't think I would feel shy. I didn't think it would feel – like this.

Garage music provides the soundtrack to the night and the smell of weed laces the air. Nathan doesn't disappoint when he turns up with canisters of nitrous oxide to enable our transformation into chipmunks. The lights are low. We have learned to rave, God bless us. When we hear the intro to So Solid Crew's '21 Seconds', we reach a new height of ecstasy. We migrate from various corners of the dimly lit living room and congregate in front of the fireplace. We are amped up. 'Ha ha ha what you laughing at?' Hyped. As we become: So So Solid. We are Megaman and Asher D and Neutrino. DJ run the track! 'Two multiplied by ten plus one. Romeo done.' I peak at 2.47am. The hardcore ravers last till 4am.

Some girls have a Quinceañera or a Bat Mitzvah, others mark their Confirmation. At Sudbourne, we 'Danced till Dawn at Eimear's Sweet 16' and we came of age. We speak about the party for days and weeks after. When we start Year 12 in September, we are still reliving the highlights. My path crosses with Damian at weekends: a gathering at Eimear's house, a trip to the cinema with Kemi. Damian gets as close to me as I will allow him. When I agree to give him my number, he calls it.

Damian likes to talk. He talks a lot about aikido training. He has been training since he was eight years old. He talks about it as if he is the Karate Kid himself. 'Yes, Sensei,' I say. He grew up in Catford and lives near Kemi and the Catford Cat. His dad lives in Jamaica. Damian likes to talk about meaningful things like life, love and the meanings of dreams. He asks me questions and listens to my answers. He mistakes his red Alfa Romeo for a Formula 1 racing car and offers to drop me home when we've been out, even if it's out of his way, especially if it is. When he parks, I don't always get out of the car straight away. We talk for thirty minutes, an hour, more. When I get indoors, he calls me, and we speak into the early hours of the morning. One night, after parking, he gives me a sheet of paper.

A handwritten poem.

'I wrote if for you. You can read it now if you want.'

'I do, want.'

I read out loud a poem about a beautiful flower called 'Poison Ivy'. It is surrounded by an unbreakable mist; a shroud of black protection. The roots of the flower, once pure and graceful, have been tarnished by some invisible force. To touch it is to rekindle a past pain so powerful that its branches will bear fruit of poison. The flower is to be admired from afar. However, if you take time, pleasure and love to watch the fruits of the flower blossom, you will know the feeling of true love, passion and fulfilment. At some point, he starts calling the flower 'she', that's when I realise that 'Poison Ivy' isn't a flower at all, it's me.

It is the most beautiful thing I have ever read. And I can't believe he wrote it for me. I didn't know that boys wrote poetry. I didn't know that seventeen-year-old black boys from Catford wrote poetry like this. He wrote it for me and about me, Poison Ivy. For the first time, I notice the veins along his arms. They are sexy – he is.

'Damian, why do you have a tattoo that says "Sweet and sour prawns Hong Kong style" on your arm?'

It's easy to make him laugh. Guided by the streetlights, our lips find each other. His kiss is soft and gentle.

I dance a dance of retreat and defence around Damian. When I feel scared that he is going to hurt me in some indescribable way, something inside me stirs, an angry thing. I know how much a man can hurt a woman. If he doesn't hit her, he can humiliate her. He can destroy her dreams and break her heart. He can push her down the stairs and make her wish she was never born. I shout at him. I tell him that I don't trust him. I don't want to spend time with him. I want him to leave me alone.

If I let him, he hugs me until it stops. Or suggests that we speak again when I have 'calmed down'. I have never seen Damian angry, the veins in the side of his head pulsing with rage. He has never raised his hand to me or his voice. If I talk over him, he says, 'Please, let me finish,' until I allow him to speak. We laugh before we kiss because we are friends, not this, whatever this is. What are we doing? I'm not sure. Damian is good and kind, if not occasionally annoying. More than that, he makes me feel safe. If he is a boy when I meet him, he grows into a man when I am with him. I don't know anyone else like Damian. So, I don't know what to do or how to be when we cross the boundary of friendship into some unknown place. I do not do what I say, or say what I mean, when I tell him, 'I can't do this with you.' I don't know what 'this' is or why I can't do it. I oscillate between friend and 'something more'. I confuse him. Emotionally. He is fed up.

*

I don't know that I have built a fortress of protection around myself until Damian tells me. I am not scared of him but I am scared of something. The fortress has been carefully constructed, of wrought iron and fast-setting concrete. I have built it over time, subconsciously and deliberately, both. To protect the most delicate of organs that is buried deep within its walls, my heart.

'I don't want to ruin our friendship,' I tell him.

Because I don't know better, because I am scared, I push him away.

BUSTED

Farah is not sure about red lipstick, but she is sure that if her mum finds out, she will literally ground her for the rest of her life.

'It's all about the eyeliner anyway.'

We take turns for Farah to apply black liquid liner to our upper lids, sitting still like mannequins, our mouths resting in perfect pouts. With her expert hand, Farah sets down the eyeliner and takes up a small brush dusted in shimmery lilac.

'Close your lid, don't squeeze it.'

I exhale to relax my eyelids as she glides the brush over them to 'complete the look'.

'My turn!'

We are tickled by the fact that the same eyeshadow looks completely different against Eimear's pink skin to the way it does against mine. It transforms her eye colour from a familiar green to a sky blue. She chooses a purple top to match her sparkling eyeshadow, and bronzer over blush for her cheeks.

'You're a pro – thanks, Farah.'

*

Eimear's parents think she is having a sleepover at Kemi's.

'It's totally fine, they trust me.'

Kemi looks amazing in a figure-hugging dress. Her parents are 'chilled' but the less they know, the better. 'A birthday party in Brixton,' if they ask, 'Erin's, from school.'

Farah agrees that Kemi was right to ignore her advice, the red on her lips looks showstopping. 'And it's matt, not glossy.'

I don't have to answer to my mum, my dad or Sol but I don't want to share that.

'My mum is on nights, so she'll never know.'

We dance to 'getting ready' music as we take turns to look in the mirror. Eimear has prepared a sickly-sweet cocktail that is as strong in colour as it is in taste. I have abandoned my cornrows and tamed my thick hair into a chemically straightened style, side parted. Kemi wears her naturally soft hair in gentle twists styled in a half up half down do. We turn simultaneously and suddenly when Auntie Moni knocks on Kemi's bedroom door and walks into her room. She takes a deep breath when she lays eyes on us.

'Wow, you girls look . . . amazing! I can't believe how grown up you all are!'

We smile in unison and tilt our necks from left to right as Auntie Moni spritzes us with expensive perfume.

'Let Daddy know when you are ready. He is waiting to drop you.'

Kemi maintains her mum's gaze as she gently pushes a bottle of Archers out of view with a heeled foot.

'It's fine, Mum, we'll get the bus. We're going to uni next year!'

Auntie Moni and Uncle Obi concede to our maturity and to public transport as they wave us off in the direction of Erin's birthday party in Brixton.

*

The man who takes a seat two rows behind us on the top deck is handsome at a glance. He is also 'a Morleys fried chicken eating, bus pole holding, no volume lowering' weirdo. He wants us to know that 2Pac is his 'homeboy' and that he is very much alive. Farah straightens her back as if preparing to write down 2Pac's new address. Yes, 2Pac is alive and well because they were 'chillin' together and bunnin' weed' last night. It is only at the mention that he is on his way to meet his 'boys, Biggie *and* Pac' that the fallacy is confirmed. Farah's shoulders relax. And guess what, the feds are never going to find out who killed Pac. He knows but he ain't telling. Do we know why? We do not. 'Cos stitches get snitches. Dats wats up.' I can tell from the way Kemi has narrowed her eyes that she is fighting an urge to correct the expression: 'snitches get stitches'. Eimear pleads her into silence with wide, unblinking eyes. Irony hangs in the air with the smell of unwashed clothes as the Morleys Fried Chicken Man gifts to the top deck his enthusiastic rendition of 'It Was All a Dream' by the Notorious B.I.G. Spitting bars on the m.i.c. for real as chicken and saliva escape his mouth during his impassioned performance. Eimear, Farah, Kemi and I manage a wordless conversation, communicating entirely with our eyes. We are trapped between a place of fear and uncontrollable laughter. We succumb to laughter as the Morleys Fried Chicken Man interrupts his impromptu performance to disembark at the Hootananny stop – but only when the bus doors have safely closed.

When the bouncer waves us through the entrance to the club, we exchange wide smiles of triumph and delight, explanations of forgotten ID shelved for the night. We choose the dancefloor of the RnB room over the cloakroom to store our coats. The cost does not justify the hanger, we agree. Eimear's dad gave her £50 for a sleepover pizza which she redirects to the bar.

'Three rum and Cokes, one with Diet Coke, please, and a plain Coke. Can you add a slice of lemon to each? Thank you.' What Farah lacks in alcohol consumption, she makes up for in nicotine inhalation. We take turns to accompany her to the smoking area at the entrance of the club. Farah is concerned that there is a man who keeps staring at her from across the dancefloor.

'The one who looks like Ron Weasley!'

Eimear decides that he is 'off his face' and that we shouldn't make eye contact with him.

The smoke machine transforms the dancefloor into a clouded utopia as we dance around our coats to Blackstreet and Ginuwine and Dru Hill. On cue, and channelling Kelis, we lean into each other to confirm that it is *our* milkshake that brings all the boys to the yard, 'and they're like, it's better than yours'. Missing all but two glacé cherries to make our performance MTV worthy. When the chorus of the next song drops, I turn to ask Farah whether she can pay my telephone bills, can she pay my automo'bills? And then to Kemi, 'I don't think you do'. Eimear's gestures mirror mine as we tell each other with conviction and resolve, 'you and me are through'. Each of us reaching for our inner Beyoncé as we sing and dance on our clouded stage.

Ron Weasley is having a fit. He is going to have a fit on Kemi. OMG is he okay? A frantic look for help. Help for Ron. With a look of terror on her face, Kemi braces to catch him – until she realises that Ron Weasley is not having a fit at all – he is challenging her to a dance off. Ron Weasley's dance moves are ... dangerous. He does not know about Kemi's dance moves – or personal space. He thinks that he is body popping; we know that he is not.

'When I say oli, you say oi. Oli—'
    'Oi.'
    'Oli—'
    'Oi.'
    'Oli oli oli—'
    'Oi oi oi!'

*

Kemi announces over the noise of hedonism that we should go to Ibiza next year! To confirm it as the best idea ever, the DJ sounds a piercing horn and emits a gust of smoke across the dancefloor. The smoke spreads like a field of clouds and makes our feet, strained in high heels and discomfort, temporarily invisible. Mr Kelly is invisible too as he approaches us on the dancefloor on a no-nonsense mission. The 'no hats no jeans no trainers' dress code temporarily suspended to allow him entry to the club to retrieve his daughter and her friends from its premises. Mr Kelly having informed the bouncer that he had 'reason to believe that there are four under-aged girls – descriptions given – in this club right now'; and having secured confirmation from said bouncer that he had failed to ID said girls.

Our shock in seeing Mr Kelly on the dancefloor causes Eimear to direct her question – 'don't cha wish your girlfriend was hot like me?' – to her dad, her volume disappearing with the smoke from the dancefloor. We lower elevated arms, straighten dancing feet and sober girlish laughter, our mouths agape. The sight of Mr Kelly's face makes something that was very funny not funny any more. The smoke, now disappeared completely, adds clarity to the fact that we have been well and truly busted. We collect our coats in silence. Our dancing quartet, disbanded until further notice, is escorted off the dancefloor by Mr Kelly and a burly security guard. At the exit, Ron Weasley winks at us. He has a gold tooth, and his flies are open.

Mr Kelly drives us home to Eimear's house because it is 'too late to knock on your parents' doors'. Mr Kelly is cross and serious but he does not shout. He is going to trust us to tell our parents the truth about tonight: a lesson in accountability. Eimear, in the passenger seat, focuses on the early morning revellers outside her window to avoid eye contact with her dad. They stagger in a way that alcohol-inspired revellers do. In the back seat, Farah and Kemi exchange looks that teenagers who have no idea what they are going to tell their parents exchange. Sandwiched in between them, I can't get over how much fun I had tonight: Eimear making cocktails; Kemi hiding the bottle of Archers from her mum who was literally standing right in front of it! Farah doing our make-up; the crazy man on the night bus; Ron Weasley! I had the best time ever. I wish we could do it all over again.

Mr Kelly doesn't tell Eimear off in front of us; I don't know if he is going to tell her off at all. Eimear's mum still makes us crumpets with eggs to order in the morning before Mr Kelly drops us home.

DECISIONS

I am a straight A student. Six A*s and three As at GCSEs. I am satisfied, content. I know how to hate myself for the things I am bad at and
the things I can't do, but I don't really know how to 'celebrate' when I
do things right or well. I got the grades I had to get. My mum is really
proud of me. My dad says he is proud of me too, but his words bounce
off my ears as soon as I hear them. I think this is the first time in my
life that my dad has told me he is proud of me. I'm not sure how I am
supposed to feel. I imagined it would make me feel like I had won
The Prize of Life, but I don't. I don't feel anything. I don't celebrate, I
go home and sleep. I am relieved, satisfied and exhausted.

I tell Mrs McIntyre, Head of Sixth Form, that I want to study
Home Economics at A Level. She tells me not to be silly. Mrs
McIntyre won't allow me to study Home Economics because my
life's journey will not lead me to the catering profession. I choose
English, History and Classics.

I know that I don't want to go to Oxford or Cambridge, but I don't
know why. I know that I won't fit in, but I don't know why. I know
that I should take the open day seriously, but I don't. A number of us

are 'selected' to visit Magdalen College in Oxford. The 'bright' and the 'gifted'. I don't approach the visit with an open mind or see the opportunity for what it is. I spend the day walking around on tiptoes and speaking out of the left side of my mouth, pretending to be 'posh'. I am full of judgement, determination and decision.

Our reception room is decorated with pictures of the college's lauded alumni. They are all the same: old white men. The carpet is immaculate. It makes me think of the Bayeux Tapestry. We are served drinks on arrival. When Farah accidentally spills hers, the comedians among us howl with laughter. We move an ugly antique armchair a few inches to the left to conceal the spillage. Miraculously, a crack on the right arm holds firm. We are encouraged to raucous laughter by our good fortune and genius thinking. The day has not been a complete waste. I have laughed myself into a defiant frenzy.

I do not include the universities of Oxford or Cambridge on my UCAS application form.

I know that I don't want to go to university in London, but I don't know why. Sol is in his second year at Exeter. He is having 'the time of his life', naturally. When people ask me what my brother studies, I think but don't say, 'Girls. He studies girls.'

'Computer Science,' the unconventional African Dream.

'It's the future,' Sol assures my mum.

He is my dad's personal IT support desk and mobile phone advisor, 'Android over Apple, Dad, every time.'

I don't include any universities in London on my UCAS application form.

I know that I don't want to go to the University of Warwick. They don't have a Topshop in the city centre. You have to travel to Coventry to go to Topshop. In the twenty-first century? How and why? I list Warwick as my fourth choice. Bristol as my first.

I choose Bristol, 'Posh Boy Province of the UK', to go to university. I can imagine myself touring St Michael's Hill with straight hair, an Addison-resistant gait and a gaggle of girlfriends, laughing loudly into the night. I can picture myself with a hot date at Mr Wolfs, sipping cocktails with confidence since Damian taught me how to kiss. The start of a love story that begins 'we met at uni'. In Bristol, I see them and they see me on open day, two magpies. They parade proudly to the right of Royal Fort Gardens on the Clifton Campus, iridescent and beautiful in the early autumn sunshine. Two for joy. I choose Bristol because I know I will be happy there. I choose Bristol because the magpies tell me to.

In my personal statement, I make a case to study history. I am a sixth form scholar. Intelligent, ambitious and hard-working. I am Head Girl. I am in the Debating Society, an advocate of student welfare and a member of Amnesty International. I am determined. I have overcome adversity: Addison's disease and an Addisonian Crisis. My predicted grades are: English (A), History (A), Classics (A). I do not include that I have overcome the adversity of domestic violence. That has no place in a UCAS application form; it is not an achievement per se.

In our Year 13 yearbook, The Girls write:

> In 10 years, Stella is most likely to be working in the City as the most successful and highly paid journalist;
> Stella is most likely to be found in Brixton;
> We will be grateful to Stella for being a true friend, giving never-ending support and advice; and for being a loud-mouthed comedienne.

Dressed up in loud eighties clothes, we paint our faces in offensively bright make-up, and sing 'Hevenu Shalom Alechem' and 'Jerusalem' for the last time in assembly. When we say goodbye, we cry until our eyes are puffy and our make-up is ruined.

Sudbourne Class of 2007. Born in the eighties. Friends Forever.

PLUM DROP

I arrive at Kennard Hall of Residence, Bristol, in mid-September 2007. A catered hall, fifteen minutes' walk to campus. I am nervous and shy. I am only fifty per cent Stella. My mum and Auntie Baaba walk me to my room. A bed, a desk and a wardrobe. I think of ways to make it cosy; my new home. I take pictures from my bag. The Girls: our last day at Sudbourne, Eimear's murder mystery party and Sweet 16, our infamous night out in Brixton. My mum and Auntie Baaba are on a cleaning mission. My mum attacks the table, window-sill and sink. Auntie Baaba scrubs the inside of the wardrobe.

'You don't know who was here before you.'

'Or how thorough the cleaners are.'

They came armed with cleaning products, a Ghanaian deep clean – with bleach. I try to familiarise myself with my new surroundings as we walk around the residence. I wish the magpies were here to help me. I look out of my bedroom window and the windows in the common room. I look in every window I pass. There is only one magpie. He is on the grass outside my bedroom window. He has no friends. And he will not move.

*

I am the only black girl in a hall of two hundred people. There is one black boy, Nigel. He is Eritrean or Ethiopian, at a guess, and from the Midlands. I am from South London. I have never been the only black girl anywhere. I don't like the way it feels. I wonder if my mum and Auntie Baaba have noticed.

'Stella, don't worry about it. They are not looking at you and saying, "Look, she's the only black girl here." You are beautiful and intelligent and gifted. Please, banish that thought from your mind.'

Auntie Baaba tries her best to reassure me, her big breasts pointing proudly like cones. If I assume the assertiveness of her posture, I know I will be fine. She squeezes my hand and makes it warm with love. I try to think about other things, like Freshers' Week and making new friends. My mum finds it surprising that we have been here for two hours, and we have not come across 'any blacks' other than Nigel. She thought that Bristol would be 'more culturally diverse'. Auntie Baaba thinks it is extraordinary, 'in this day and age'. The campus is beautiful, though. My mum wishes I had applied to Oxford or Cambridge. She would have been so proud.

My mum and Auntie Baaba bless me with the blood of Jesus Christ and anoint me with the power of the Holy Spirit before driving in the direction of the M32. God is in the driving seat of my life. He has already decided my success. He will send forth His angels to illuminate the path before me. He will strike down any enemies whose evil forces conspire to obstruct my path. He will lead me to a success far greater than that which I could ever imagine for myself. Auntie Baaba goes to Pentecostal church. I wait for her to start speaking in tongues. Instead, she makes the sign of the cross on my forehead with such force that I stumble backwards – in testament to the power of prayer. I can tell from the way my mum says 'Amen' that she wishes she had led the departing blessing. She steps forward to hug me. I am still locked in her embrace when it is time to say goodbye. I wave until the car disappears from view, until they can no longer see me in the dark or my falling tears as I stand.

I think of my mum's preemies in the NICU, asleep in their plastic incubators. Their whole world of monitors, feeding tubes and ventilators enclosed in that tiny space. When their mums go home to sleep, mine watches over them. She talks to them so they know that they are not alone. So fragile and delicate that if you took the incubators away, they would die, within minutes or seconds. There is no one to watch over me here in Bristol. I am alone and scared. I am at Cape Coast Castle in the late afternoon. I cannot move because the fishermen have cast their net over me. They are carrying me home from the sea. To fry me in hot oil. Rigor mortis has set in. To leave my gaping mouth wide open. They will fry me and eat me. Until all that is left of my body are a few bones. And the debris of my carcass. There is not enough light. I stand at the entrance to Kennard Hall as the waves engulf me. I am overwhelmed. By a powerful and distinct feeling of aloneness.

Week One.
'So, how do you make those plaits stick to your hair? Do you have to sew it on?'
I step back before a physical examination can take place.
'No. You just braid the hair onto the scalp. They're called cornrows.'

Week Two.
I am about to make a new friend but then she opens her mouth.
'I've never had a coloured friend before!'
If I wasn't 'coloured', I'm sure she would have seen me blush. I don't know how to respond.

We walked around Sudbourne like representatives from member states of the United Nations or a United Colours of Benetton ad. Nobody was different because we were all the same, ignorant South Londoners, labouring under the falsehood that every fifteen-year-old girl shared our experience of cultural diversity. I don't want to be different, not like this. I don't want the notoriety. I don't want to have to 'teach' people about the black experience or to be the voice of 'blackness'. I want to be back at Sudbourne giggling on the swings with Eimear, listening to 2Pac with Farah, learning Yoruba at Kemi's house and eating weed-infused chocolate brownies with my friends. I don't want to be here thinking about the fact that I am black; the only black girl in Hall. I miss my mum's Tilda Basmati jollof rice.

Week Three.

Friendship groups have formed. The blondest girls with the bluest eyes have extricated themselves from the masses and formed a Made in Chelsea Confederation. The Jack Wills Ambassadors have similarly identified themselves and united in a Public School Boy Fellowship. Among them is Henry Foskitt. Together, they are the 'elite', privileged and self-assured. They will elect from their numbers Earl and Countess of Kennard Hall by Week Four, I am sure.

My first encounter with Henry Foskitt is on the floor of Jasper's dorm room. I have a two-week-long friendship with Jasper. He is intelligent and friendly. I enjoy his company and conversation, platonically. The door is open as we chat before bed. Innocuous chat, light humour, some normality. I do not enjoy it when Henry Foskitt staggers into the room uninvited and drunk. He operates under the influence of too many Snakebites, I can only assume, when he lifts me off the floor. I don't know why, or how, in fact. I don't know what he is thinking. Can he not hear me shouting, 'Get off me! Put me down!' over and over again?

He is wearing brown desert boots. The kind of shoes that Indiana Jones would wear on a night out in St Michael's Hill. I struggle from his grip and fall. I am on my knees in front of Henry Foskitt because that is just how I land. Regrettably. My eyes are level with the zip of his navy blue chinos. Some six inches away. God help me. Time speeds up slows down speeds up again. As he unzips his trousers in front of me. Time slows down, slows down and causes paralysis. As he removes his penis. And testicles. From his undergarments. He waves them. In front of my face. He is laughing and audacious. I am stunned into stillness and silence. I cannot find my voice. I run. As if I have hot water and palm oil and spinach in my hair.

It is the first time I have ever seen an uncircumcised penis. It is the first time I have ever seen a white penis. It is wrinkly. And shrivelled. And disgusting. It is the first time I have ever not found my words. I feel lava inside me. Rising.

I call Kemi from my room. Through my sobbing, punctuated with confused and urgent words, Kemi is able to understand that something terrible has happened. She says I need to do two things: first, tell someone in Hall what has happened; second, get on a train back to London as soon as I can. She will meet me at Paddington station. In the morning. The earliest train I can get. I sit down with the Hall Warden. I am embarrassed. It is embarrassing to say what happened out loud. I don't know if my reaction is proportionate – or normal – for someone my age. I am telling him because Kemi said I should. I agree. I think someone should know what has happened. I do not want the Warden to do anything for now. I do not know what I want. I just thought I should tell someone. I wonder if the magpies are still by Royal Fort Gardens.

The familiarity of Kemi's face, her smile and her voice provides the kind of comfort that only a friend of seven years can offer. She gives me a kiss on the cheek and a big squeeze to let me know that I am okay. We walk with arms linked. Kemi is cool and effortlessly chic. She is wearing a dark green faux fur coat, cropped jeans and black Chelsea boots, real leather. Kemi's love of shoes borders on the extravagant. Storing them is a challenge. Her dorm room at LSE is a respectable shrine to her first love. Pinned to her wall and scattered across her table – recently moved from the floor – are flow charts and study notes indecipherable to the unknowing eye; penmanship that Kemi understands but I cannot. Papers upon papers, books upon books. A politics student with style. Fairy lights adorn her window and bottles of nail polish feature around her sink. The smell of blue Lenor drifts from bedding and newly laundered clothes throughout the room. It is both chaotic and cosy. It feels like home. We remember the red platform shoes her mum bought her for her twelfth birthday. Such a little tart! She has them somewhere, she is sure. I don't need to worry that I left Bristol in such a state that I forgot my Addison's medication; she's got enough for the both of us. Kemi makes having Addison's disease look easy. She is content and with likeminded people.

'You should have bitten it off!'

I try to explain the full-body paralysis caused by Henry Foskitt's disgusting willy. I am filled with regret of the 'shoulda woulda coulda' kind, so angry with myself that I didn't do more. Like bite it off. And spit it out. Between his brown desert boots. I spend my entire undergraduate degree wishing I had. No, I haven't told Sol because I don't know what he would say – it's complicated. I haven't told my dad because I don't want anything to do with him. Since forever, Kemi. My mum? I could tell her that I really understand what it is like to be humiliated by a man and to forget your words, I think but do not say. That we are so alike, she and I, more alike than I have ever realised or we would ever want to discuss. But she would just pray the rosary and ask if it is too late to transfer to Oxford. I don't think that would help, not right now.

'I told the Hall Warden. You're the only other person I've spoken to, Kemi.'

We order pizza because I don't feel like leaving the safety of Kemi's room and Kemi wants to do whatever makes me feel comfortable. Hearing her discuss toppings and garlic dip over the phone makes me think I am hungry and that I can eat. I press the green button under Damian's name as she collects our delivery from the doorstep. I want to hear his voice. Damian is furious that anybody would do that to me. Do I want him to come to Bristol, right now? I don't but I know he would.

'I'll be okay, thank you.'

My heart is heavy on Sunday evening as I prepare to go back to Bristol. It is hard to say goodbye. Kemi is going to visit me as soon as she has finished her coursework. She hasn't spoken to Farah for a week or so, but Eimear was in touch yesterday. Shall we go for dinner when we are all back for Christmas? That would be so nice. She'll send a message to The Girls now. Let's get a date in the diary. Something to look forward to. She gives me a kiss on the cheek and a big squeeze before I board my train. She waves from the platform until my train pulls out of the station.

My effort to downplay the seriousness of a stranger waving his willy in my face is not reciprocated by the Hall Warden. Henry Foskitt is hauled before him and the Head of Pastoral Care to explain his actions. I am invited to the meeting. I would rather eat the tongue of a real bird, while stroking a dead pigeon, than look Henry Foskitt in the eye. I am already seated when he enters the room. Head down. He is shorter than I remember. And his face is a unique shade of scarlet – I think it is called shame. An aerospace engineering student, whose underdeveloped brain orbits his penis. He apologises 'for any offence caused'.

'I was playing a game called plum drop.'

Henry Foskitt is from Richmond. Perhaps this is a game played in its most affluent parts. His apology is inadequate. I want the ground to swallow me. When will this meeting end? I study an ornate clock on top of a cabinet to the left of Henry Foskitt's chair and decline the opportunity to explain to him how his actions have made me feel. But, thank you.

The Vice Chancellor of the university is unfamiliar with the game 'plum drop'. The matter has been escalated notwithstanding Henry Foskitt's 'apology'. He is informed that he will have to move halls or face suspension. This is a very serious matter. I know now that I should have taken the Oxford University open day more seriously I wish I had approached it with an unbiased and serious mind. I wish I had at least considered staying in London. I should have known that the location of Topshop is not a determining factor when choosing an institution for higher education. I could have avoided this.

Plum Drop Gate. The Made in Chelsea Confederation and the Jack Wills Ambassadors close ranks. Their stares follow me from the hall corridors to the hall canteen. At breakfast, lunch and dinner. I sit at the furthest end of the dining hall wishing my five foot eight frame into a smaller existence. My cutlery is loud, theirs is silent. I can hear my eyes blinking. I wish they would stop talking about me in front of me.

'She reported him to the Hall Warden!'

'Can you believe it?!'

'He was only playing plum drop!'

'How pathetic is that?'

'Can't she take a joke?'

I decide to eat in my room from now on.

On the fourth night, Jasper brings his dinner up to join me and takes my tray down with his. I wonder, but cannot bring myself to ask, why did you not do anything when Henry Foskitt waved his willy in my face?

The walk from Hall to lectures is fifteen minutes. I leave forty-five minutes early every day so I can look for the other magpie. I only ever see one. It patrols the lawn in front of the Arts Complex. A bold exhibitionist. It is there every single day.

I write to the Vice Chancellor to explain that if Henry Foskitt is made to leave Kennard Hall, it will have such an adverse impact on my university experience – and life – that I will end up being punished instead of him. Henry Foskitt has apologised. I accept his apology. I acknowledge the role that alcohol played in his conduct that night. I plead with the Vice Chancellor to let him stay. I do not say in my letter that my university experience has already been impacted. That I am already being punished. That I have no friends in Hall. That everyone is always talking about me. In front of me. And behind my back. That I am stared at in the corridors. In the dining room. And everywhere in between. That I am known as 'Plum Drop Girl'.

The Vice Chancellor commends me for the maturity with which I have handled the situation. It is an experience that no young woman should be exposed to. Intending no pun, I am sure. He has considered the contents of my letter with care. My best interests are his primary concern. With that in mind, he will honour my wishes and permit Henry Foskitt to remain in Hall subject to the strictest conditions of continued residence.

I don't make anyone laugh in Bristol, not like I did at Sudbourne. They laugh at me but not with me. I try to keep it moving, my university life. Whenever I see Henry Foskitt, I study the parquet floor of the common room or the green carpet of the corridors with interest. I have never spoken to the Made in Chelsea Girls or the Jack Wills Ambassadors. They don't know anything about me.

I stay in touch with The Girls by text. I don't have pictures to share but I comment on theirs. I have put on a stone during my first term. I cannot make eye contact with the girl in the mirror and I do not want anyone else to have to look at me or to see my shame. There will be no cocktails at Mr Wolfs with anybody, let alone a hot date. There will be no love story that begins 'we met at uni'. I hate the things I feel and the decisions I have made. I hate that the sight of Henry Foskitt or the mention of his name makes me jump in my skin. I hate that the idea of being in a relationship makes me feel anxious and scared. I hate that while everyone around me is finding love, I prefer the safety of solitude. I hate the person I am.

I do not deign to face the hostility of the dining room. I stay in my room and count magpies. I don't know if it is the same one I am seeing over and over again or a different one each time. When Eimear, Farah and Kemi caption their pictures #uninights! #best-nightever, I always put a heart emoji. I miss them so much. I go home every other weekend. My mum sends me back to Bristol with Tupperwares of jollof rice and chicken. I can heat them up in the microwave.

TRIALS AND TRIUMPH

CONFRONTATION

I leave for New York on a wing and a prayer. I am twenty-three years old and, unlike The Girls who are flourishing in their personal and professional lives, I have no idea what I am doing in mine. Eimear works in shipping, undeniably a man's world but she is forging her own path and holding her own. A bona fide ship broker with unstoppable ambition. She travels constantly for work and found Sean, her #dreamboatboyfriend, en route. Sean is sweet-natured and kind. And he makes a real effort with Eimear's friends, which has earned him serious brownie points.

Kemi has landed her ideal job as Assistant Private Secretary to the Minister for Education. When she is not working her 'PAYE' job, Kemi works as a mentor to local children born on the wrong side of opportunity. She hates the word 'underprivileged'. 'Education is everything', her mantra on repeat. Kemi's energy levels, spin class attendance and permanently bright mood belie the fact that she has Addison's disease. When I grow up, I want to be just like her. Farah? Farah has just qualified as a doctor. She works in A&E at St George's Hospital and will soon train to be a surgeon. There is no time to have sex in the storage cupboard and she doesn't work with anyone who looks like McDream, so it's not exactly like *Grey's Anatomy* but close enough, she indulges us. The hours are long and gruelling. Our pride knows no bounds; Farah saves lives.

The Girls are hard-working and formidable and trail-blazing. They think I am too, but we aren't the same. I feel, but find it hard to explain, that everything I do is a struggle. From getting up in the morning to getting dressed to getting the train to work. Their affirmations, praise and encouragement cannot fix me. On Nursery Road, I search my pillow, my duvet and my mind for motivation to get out of bed every single day. Is that normal? Mornings are the hardest. Instead of sleep, my eyes fill with tears. Something is wrong with me.

The Langman Internship Programme – a 'unique postgraduate experience'. I will work in the Events Department at the British Consulate in New York and study for a Diploma in International Business Practice, accredited by the University of Cambridge. A retrospective gift to myself. I go because there is no reason for me to stay. America: home of the brave, land of the free.

It is early September and I am overwhelmed. I direct Sol to Heathrow Terminal 1 instead of Terminal 3, in error. He promises that he will get me there on time – in his brand-new Audi sports car. He has explained his job to me several times but I still don't have a clue what he does.

'It sounds really complicated, Sol.'

We settle for buzzwords: data analysis. Algorithms. Optimisation. Something about Artificial Intelligence. His official title is Senior Engineer, Google Search Ads. He is on track to become a Principal Engineer before his thirtieth birthday. He works hard and plays hard. He is generously rewarded and generous.

My mum is fussing in the passenger seat. Rummaging through her bag for nothing in particular and checking the time every few minutes. She offers me her Bible and her wooden crucifix. 'Thanks, Mum, I'm okay.' She puts them back in her bag. She tells Sol to slow down and warns him that I will miss my flight in the same breath. Yes, I have my passport. My travel insurance is sorted but anything Addison's related won't be covered. Dr Gordon gave me enough medication for three months. And you can bring some more when you come to visit. Eimear is going to fly out at some point before spring for work. And Sol says he has a stag weekend in Miami at Easter. He will go home via New York. So, I think between you, Sol and Eimear, we will figure it out.

Sol takes the lead with 24kg of my life's possessions, packed as neatly as possible, to the check-in desk. Easiest to access are the things I need to run. If this feeling flies with me, across the Atlantic Ocean, I will put on my trainers and run. To where, I don't know. But if I stay on top of my medication, and my Addison's does not betray me, that is what I will do.

'Have you told Dad you are going?'

I have learned not to discuss my dad with Sol. Because we end up speaking, with raised voices, about two different people. I know my father's wrath and his fury, his rage and his beatings. The damage that he can inflict with his hands and his words. Sol does not know that person. Sol knows a dad who bought him trainers so he could dance like Michael Jackson. A dad who took him to Crystal Palace matches every other weekend. A dad who taught him how to fix car tyres and dropped him to school every day. Sol does not know what it is to have hot water and palm oil and spinach poured over his head. Our father is an unholy trinity: father to me, dad to Sol, and the man who ruined my mum's life.

For a brother who never once stuck up for me as a child or teenager, Sol has developed an incredible ability to advocate on behalf of my dad: I wasn't the easiest daughter to parent. They had similar interests. He tried his best. He wanted to have a better relationship with me. I never let him in. Remember the time I held the knife in my hand? Sol is passionate in his new role of advocate. And incredulous. We have very different recollections of our childhood experience. And it is difficult for me to listen to his testimony. When Sol says he hates confrontation, I am not sure whether he is drawing an inference that I like it. In any event, the conversation is a painful visit to a past that very much lingers in our present.

I think of the fairy-tale figure that Sol has created and wonder if my dad would recognise himself described in my brother's words. I try once over a birthday dinner, organised by Sol to celebrate my father's fifty-four years. To explain. To my dad. How difficult it has been. For me to forge a relationship. With him. As an adult. He is so happy that I came. He wasn't sure I would because I didn't reply to his text. That I had tried. But struggled. He smiles from ear to ear, a view of the waterfront before him. I came. With hesitation. Thai Boat in Battersea at 7pm. Because of what he did to me. As a child. The power station gives me the courage to continue. It affected me. It affects me. Uncle Papafio directs his attention to his Chang beer as I speak. I wonder. What I would be. Who I would be. Battersea Power Station, rising one day from its ashes to become a millennial's residential and cultural paradise. If—

Sol is caught off guard by my monologue. He declares that it is neither the time nor the place to have this kind of discussion. A tear escapes from my dad's eye as my voice starts to crack. It is the first time I have ever seen him cry.

The waitress brings out a chocolate cake. Two candles, '5' and '4', centre the 'Happy Birthday' written in white icing on top. We sing a tuneless 'Happy Birthday' before Sol helps my dad to blow out the candles. My rendition is particularly monotonous and uninspired. Uncle Papafio says something about the waitress's 'Thai buns' to bring us back to ourselves and our status quo. My dad and Sol laugh with Uncle Papafio as they cheers with Chang beer.. I look at the power plant in the distance and pour another glass of red wine to finish the bottle. And the evening. By myself. Sol gives the waitress his card when she brings the bill. Whatever the cost of the evening, his Amex card will absorb it.

'Yes. I called him last weekend and told him.'

'Good. That's good, well done.'

I stand in front of the departure gate at Heathrow, Terminal 3. J-1 Visa and passport in one hand, fear in the other.

'If you don't like it, Stella, you can come back. You can always come back.'

My mum's words encourage me through the gates. I look back with blurry eyes before we lose each other from sight.

'Love you, Stella.'

'Love you, Mum.'

NEW YORK

New York is delight and distraction. It is everything that London is but more. Busier, brighter, louder. The sky is more blue, less grey. Every landmark, from every New York-based film and sitcom I have ever seen, is within sight. At the Wolcott Hotel on 4 West 31st Street, between 5th Avenue and Broadway, I meet sixty-nine other interns from the September intake. We are from England, Scotland, Ireland and Wales. A twelve-month adventure to embark on. Together. We learn to navigate the Manhattan Grid Map. We enjoy the view from the Empire State Building. We shop in Bloomingdale's and wander through Central Park. We visit the Museum of Modern Art and go to concerts at Madison Square Gardens. We watch baseball games at the New York Yankees stadium and stand in silence at the Ground Zero Memorial. We ride yellow taxis around the city and take pictures with obliging NYPD officers. Together, we discover the magic of the city.

New York takes on a different character with every passing season. That is the beauty of the city. Every three months, separate and distinct. In autumn, I enjoy the warm days and the changing colours of the leaves. The spectrum of oranges, reds and browns, a gift from nature. A beauty to behold. On the weekends, we go apple picking upstate – because we can. The New York Halloween Parade is entertaining and theatrical, if somewhat alien to me. A pagan festival, never really marked in our household. It forces a memory of Eimear's mum opening the front door to trick or treaters, a witch's hat on her head, their black cat on her shoulder.

In winter, I discover the power of the wind tunnels that whistle through corridors between tall buildings. The city drops to temperatures that I have never before known. Running over Brooklyn Bridge carries with it a warning of black ice. My heart aches for the homeless who shiver outside the subway stations, missing teeth and shelter, frozen fingers and toes. The disparity between wealth and poverty is so extreme – too extreme. I eat pumpkin pie on Thanksgiving and enjoy the elaborate window displays of the department stores at Christmas. No expense or effort spared. New York knows how to do 'festive'. It is just like the movies.

In spring, the city reveals a vibrant palette of colour. Flowers blossom and beautiful window boxes appear here, there and everywhere. The sun shines brightly and constantly, making sunglasses an essential accessory to every outfit. The city's temperature normalises pleasantly and I enjoy brunches and walks and outdoor markets. On Easter Sunday, I visit St Patrick's Cathedral, alone but not lonely. I thank God for this incredible year so far. It is in spring that I start to consider, seriously, a career in law. I am working and studying and socialising in this city, and I am surviving! New York has energised me. I will apply to study the law conversion course when I get back to London. I submit my application online.

Summer establishes itself with heat and humidity, oppressively so. Air-conditioned buildings provide intermittent relief. A unique moment when rooftop bars offer their space for cocktails and incredible views of the city. Pool parties, barbecues and outdoor cinemas, a few of the pastimes indulged in these months. Central Park, Bryant

Park, Prospect Park, they all come alive. Outdoor concerts and festivals draw fun-loving crowds of which I am now a part. The highlight of my summer? A Café Wha? boat cruise along the Hudson River. Live music, an intimate venue. The rhythm gets me as I dance the night away. The sun refuses to set. I want this feeling to last forever.

In New York, there is not one single magpie lurking in any background, foreground or in plain sight. At the top of any apartment or commercial building, on any sidewalk or subway station platform. It does not sit on telephone wires, electricity pylons or tree branches. I do not think the magpie inhabits this city at all. Its absence makes me feel alive and free.

I leave my heart in Williamsburg, Brooklyn. But it feels so good to be able to say that my year in New York was the #bestyearever.

A BARRISTER

With a barrister's confidence, I would go far. Stereotype: white male, middle-class, middle-aged, Oxbridge-educated, three-piece suit, last button undone. Fortunate beneficiary to bank of mum and dad, city home, country home. Stands to inherit: a property or properties, in due course, and substantial funds. Family signet ring, left pinky. Confident. Self-assured. Belongs.

'Hi. I'm Virginia. Ginny for short.' She pronounces her words in a way I don't. 'Ver-gin-nyah.' We meet at a RealLaw Prisons Training Session. A pro-bono programme, student-led and delivered to prisoners and ex-offenders on topics of legal relevance: Stop and Search law, housing and immigration. I am the Student Director of the programme and motivated by the work. In training sessions, I talk students through the process of volunteering to present. Female students should not wear low-cut, cleavage-revealing tops or heels. Don't talk down to the men. Prisons are restricted environments, so the men are generally very grateful that you have taken time out of your day to come and speak to them. They are interested to hear what you have to say and to learn. Don't make assumptions. Don't ask them why they are in prison. Don't ask personal questions. Basic common sense. I want to add 'but for the Grace of God', we could be in their shoes and vice versa, but I keep it simple and secular.

My first visit to HMP Pentonville is memorable. I have followed the prison's protocol to the letter. I present my driving licence on arrival and take a photograph for my ID badge – to be worn at all times – and visibly. I walk through D Wing with butterflies in my stomach.

'Just be careful you don't lean against that red panic alarm behind you by accident, Miss Sai. It runs all the way around.'

Most of the men are dressed in unbranded grey tracksuits. They are intrigued by my presence. There is a snooker table in the middle of the landing. The lights are an offensive shade of yellow and it is noisy, grey noise. Chatter. Inmates talking. Wardens talking – distinct. Shouting. TV channels in conflict with one another. Laughter. Banging against steel. I want to see inside a cell. The cell doors are open – if not, ajar. The rooms are basic but personalised. Family photos on the walls. Bunk beds. An open toilet – in a shared space. I smile gently and try not to prolong eye contact as I am escorted through the wing.

I have a class of pre-release prisoners enrolled in the prison's education programme.

I have prepared and memorised an icebreaker:

'Hi. I'm Stella. I'm a law student. I'm studying to become a barrister. I'm originally from Brixton, so I'm not used to being on this side of the river. I'm really pleased to be here with you today and I hope we can have a useful discussion on the subject of housing law. I would like to share with you some information that I hope you will find useful. I'm very interested to hear your views and experiences in the two hours we have together this afternoon. If you have any questions at all, please feel free to ask. Before we start, I would like to know everyone's name and something about you. So, if we start from this side of the room, can you tell me your name and something you are good at?'

'Miss, my name is Jerome. I work as a chef in the prison, and can I just say, I would love to cook for you.'

The laugh leaves my mouth before I can stop it.

'Wow. Thank you, Jerome.'

The ice has been broken, and from that moment, working with the men is without fear and purposeful. They have so many questions for me.

'How long they can keep me after I finish sentence? They want deport me.'

'I'm being released in three weeks and I've got nowhere to live, Miss. Can I still see my kids?'

I answer what I can and promise to research the answers I don't know. I will feed information back through the Education Coordinator. My mum arranges a collection of unwanted books through Sacred Heart Church to donate to the prison library, for which the men, and I, are immensely grateful. After each session, I feel that I have done something good in, and with, my life.

Virginia stays behind after the training session. She really enjoyed my talk and would love to give a presentation when a slot becomes available. I glance at the list of registered students. She has a double-barrelled surname with multiple syllables. She wears a signet ring on her left pinky, bearing a family crest. I didn't know that women wore signet rings. She would have been at home at Kennard Hall. She is too enthusiastic. We talk – just friendly, I decide. She has a nice smile. My suspicion dissipates. We agree to go to a dining session together. As she says goodbye, I notice on her left hand, fourth finger, a diamond-encrusted pearl ring.

I have to complete twelve 'qualifying sessions' before I can be called to the Bar. Qualifying sessions are designed to complement the Bar Vocational Course, we are told. Tonight's session is an educational talk at Gray's Inn on 'The Rule of Law'. It is my first time dining at the Inn. Custom dictates that we must wear to dine what we would wear in court:

A dark suit, shirt and a dark tie or blouse. A dark dress or skirt of appropriate length and worn with a jacket. Gowns will be provided and worn during dining.

We look like Harry Potter Hopefuls. There is reference to a 'Loyal Toast', proposed by the Inn and drunk when seated. I have no idea what it means. We are to sit in groups or 'messes' of four. I know what a group is. A 'mess'? I have no idea. I feel like one.

The Student Barrister nearest the top of the table on the right-hand side of each mess is the Captain. The Captain serves himself first and then passes the food anti-clockwise. The Junior, who sits beside the Captain, serves himself last.

It sounds like a posh man's game of 'Pass the Parcel'.

I meet Ginny outside Gray's Inn. Her enthusiasm is unabated. She gave a presentation on Stop and Search law at Wormwood Scrubs this morning. She has thought of an update to the presentation pack and she is keen to share it with me. I have compiled the presentation packs with care. They are sufficiently detailed and comprehensive, I am sure. I listen, half intrigued, half insulted, as Ginny shares the details of her prison visit experience with me:

'Er, Miss?'

'Yes, Billy.'

'When they search me—'

'Yes?'

'Can they ask me to roll back my foreskin?'

'I'll have to get back to you on that one, Billy!'

'Stella,' she says, giggles surfacing, 'I couldn't find the answer in the pack!'

We are doubled over with laughter that will not cease and

disturbed by the image. Our laughter carries across Gray's Inn Fields and accompanies us into the dining hall.

I am still laughing when the Loyal Toast is given. The kind of laughter that quietens and is triggered moments later by eye contact, expressing itself in stifled snorts and giggles. It is not until the session speaker approaches the lectern that I notice the silverware laid neatly in front me. I count my cutlery in silent horror: three forks, three spoons, two knives and three glasses. When my mum makes *omo tuo* and groundnut soup at home, we eat it with our hands. Mercy. I forget the customs I have studied in preparation. When the soup starters are served, I still don't know if I am the Captain of the Mess. Pea and mint. I find it difficult to settle. I watch Ginny, carefully, as she works her way through the silverware in front of her, from the outside in, with comfort and ease.

She tells me a story about her grandfather. An Air Marshal in the RAF. At a formal dinner, just like this. Attended by senior officers. Among them a junior officer, looking extremely nervous. He starts to eat his peas – with a knife. Laughter, laughter, lots of laughter. His face takes on the colour of beetroot. What does Grandpa Air Marshal do? He puts his fork down and starts to eat his peas with his knife, the most senior person at the dinner. That is how she defines good manners.

Ginny doesn't hint that she senses my nerves. She comes from a kind family, I conclude.

The dining experience passes without further complication and I am relieved that I have shared it with Ginny. She is the only person I know to receive pupillage offers from every Chambers she applies to. Ginny is hard-working and well deserving. A rare combination of humility and grace. A lady with a pinky ring. I want to expand RealLaw Prisons to work with female prisoners and ex-offenders, a project. My grin mirrors hers, as we laugh once more across the table. Oh Billy! You little goat.

THE BAR

I am called to the Bar of England and Wales in July 2016. My mum wears a beautiful *kaba* made from *kente*. Patterns of purple and yellow and black. Complemented with her finest gold jewellery. She playfully tries on my wig. My dad wears a striking *kente* of maroon and orange, yellow and green. It is carefully draped over his left shoulder. He wears a white undershirt and green shorts, *chokoto*. I want him here. I invited him. To see what I have become not because of him but in spite of him. I want him to know that I did not choose insolence, I chose advocacy – or rather it chose me. And that I have emerged, full circle. He may have ruined my mum's life, but he has not ruined mine. That they arrived wearing *kente*, separately and without communication, is testament to the symbolism of this moment in their lives. In wearing *kente*, they communicate without words, in colour and pattern.

Kente is a traditional Ghanaian woven fabric, rich in symbolism and craftsmanship. The cloth is beautifully woven in geometric patterns, each with its own meaning. The patterns relate to the history and beliefs of the Ashanti people, a proud people, from where this regal fabric originates. My mum wears the '*Akokobaatan*' pattern: 'mother hen'. It is a symbol of motherliness, parental care and tenderness. The purple is a symbol of feminism. The yellow, an expression of richness, royalty, prosperity and wealth. The black, as she wears it, represents maturity and spiritual energy. Her heart is bursting with pride and it makes me happy to see. I understand her hard work and sacrifice. I know the cost she has paid to see me here. I want her to live this feeling twice, as my mum and then vicariously through me. Dreams of 'should have, could have, would have' materialised in this moment. Alongside a new chapter of opportunity and prosperity.

My dad wears '*Obi nkye obi kwan mu si*': 'To err is human'. It is emblematic of forgiveness, conciliation, tolerance and patience. The maroon is a symbol of mother earth and healing. The green, as he wears it, represents spiritual growth and maturity. My dad is beaming from ear to ear. I know that he will speak about me to his friends and customers, as if he had some hand in my success. His temper has disappeared, it seems. Years away from forces of provocation and greyness of the beard will do that to a person. He has widened at the waist and softened in the brow. And he shows me the deference of one who bows before a person more learned. I recognise that he is proud of me in the way he clasps his hands in front of him, no longer in a power stance at his hips. To make him proud today is to know a new feeling in my heart. It makes me believe that I have forgiven him without the need to understand. Oh, Happy Day. Perhaps what his heart is, is not what his hands did. It is possible, is it not? All things are – I am proof.

A *kente* weaver must know not only the different patterns but how to create them. It is a timely and costly labour. Traditionally worn by kings and queens of Ghana, it is woven by men and sewn together by women. We are, after all, the thread that weaves the fabric of life. A masterpiece in textile design, reserved for the most special occasions.

Sol wears a bespoke suit: navy blue, orange lined. A matching pocket square and socks. His watch is Swiss. His cufflinks, expensive. He has taken a day off work to celebrate my achievement and to celebrate me. Principal Engineer and N16 resident. He alternates between his role as his mother's son and his father's son with dexterity. A gulf of resentment, anger and pain separates one from the other. It is a relief to have him here. He mingles with my peers, their parents, the Bar and the Judiciary with the ease of someone who knows what it is to feel comfortable in his skin. He is the proudest big brother in the world. He shows it with an expensive gift. A substitute for words I think he feels but cannot say. A Pandora's package of Mulberry bags. I undo the black ribbon of the gift container and untie protective cloth to unwrap my present. A beautiful bag, black, grained leather, gold fastening.

'I thought you could use it for court.'

I struggle to believe that I own my very own Mulberry bag, a real one. When did we arrive at this place of luxury from whence we came?

'"Started from the bottom now we here!"' Sol does his best Drake impression. It makes us laugh because no other words could explain our journey to this point.

I think of 'dual consciousness' and admire my new bag.

'Sol! It's amazing. I love it! Thank you so much.'

'It's a belted Bayswater.'

Neither Sol nor I know what a 'belted Bayswater' is. In any event, I know he didn't choose it alone. It was chosen by a woman for a woman. From Brixton to the Bar via Chancery Lane. Who even are we?

My mum has bought me a wig tin from Ede & Ravenscroft to keep my barrister's wig safe and intact. It is engraved in gold letters: 'S. A. Sai'.

'Thank you, Mum. That's really kind of you. I love it.'

We pose for pictures in Gray's Inn Fields. My mum and dad receive compliments on their traditional outfits. And the magpies come to celebrate with us. They fete from the trees, the lawns, the telephone cables and across the green. Each in the company of a friend. I am so happy that they are here. With me, with us, my family.

*

The '*Fathia fata Nkrumah*' *kente* cloth – 'Fathia is a befitting wife for Nkrumah' – was created to honour the very first First Lady of Ghana, Fathia Nkrumah, wife of Ghana's first president, Kwame Nkrumah. I love it in pink and green and yellow, predominantly pink. My mum explains to me its origin. Nkrumah led the country to independence in 1957 and the Gold Coast became Ghana. His marriage to Fathia, a charming Egyptian woman, was considered to represent the unity of African people on the continent. Some say that in wearing the '*Fathia fata Nkrumah*' cloth, we honour the first ladies in our lives: wives, mothers, sisters and aunts. I want to have a *kaba* made in this pattern the next time I go to Ghana. I like it, the colours.

I don't reserve tickets for my mum and Sol to dine at Gray's Inn after I am called to the Bar. I should have been more organised. My mum wishes the celebration could continue over lunch. She would have loved the formality of it all: dining in hall, the privilege and esteem of the experience. That she could have charmed some old judge with tales of Ghanaian history and *kente*, in her heels, wine-coloured lipstick and floral perfume. The most glamorous nurse at 37 Military Hospital-cum-domestically abused wife-cum-proud mother. Her daughter's place, rightly earned in this historical setting. Stella, a lawyer. My dad is relieved, I am sure, to go back to his comforts and overalls. He reminds me, before he leaves, that my MOT is due next month. He will sort it out for me.

Ginny and her family are less focused on the photography of this event for posterity than mine. They are proud of her success, but I can tell that they have seen this kind of achievement before. One step ahead of me, Ginny has organised tickets for them to attend the celebratory lunch and emailed Gray's Inn in advance to ask for us to be seated together. We look at the seating plan and make our way to the top table to take our place with the Benchers of the Inn: silks, judges and other esteemed guests.

Before he leaves, Sol asks me to give him a call when I've finished with the Patriarchy. He's got a meeting at the Rosewood; he'll be just around the corner.

The entrance to the Rosewood is so beautifully lit it cannot but keep the joy of the day bright. I am a barrister! It is both reverie and fact. Walking past the iron gates of the courtyard, I know that I am crossing a threshold that divides my future from my past. I consume the artwork of the Cocktail Room as I walk in the direction of opulence and extravagance. My eyes are momentarily confused to see that within its design, the room's decor includes the beaming faces of Farah, Kemi and Eimear alongside Sol, his girlfriend Sienna and two of his closest friends.

'Congratulations!'

My confusion gives way to a surprise so effervescent that it forces warm tears from my eyes.

'Oh my God! When did you— What? I can't believe you're all here!'

So, Farah is not working days after all, Eimear is clearly not in Rotterdam for work and Kemi looks far too good to be in bed with the flu! The opening of a champagne bottle adds to the evening's surprise, and by some moving magic, cascading bubbles fill tall glasses held in the hands of our intimate circle. My queries of how and why and when are met with laughter, hugs and kisses before The Girls present me with a turquoise box wrapped with a white ribbon which I have only seen before in Christmas adverts. I open it with unbelieving hands to see a diamond and black onyx gold bracelet. The sparkling thing that Farah is fastening on my wrist makes my words stick in my throat. I look them all in the eye when our glasses clink to cheers.

'Congratulations, Counsel! We're so proud of you!'

Mine are blurry with tears.

'Thank you so much.' My heart is pumping gratitude and wonder and love all around my body.

PUPILLAGE

I am navigating my way through Chambers with uncertainty and anxiety. Grace is my co-pupil. Thank God for Grace, who suggests we meet before we actually start pupillage. I hadn't had the initiative or the foresight to contact her.

'Is the Red Lion pub okay?'

'Sounds great. Look forward to meeting you.'

Grace looks like a pupil who knows what she is doing; better yet, a barrister who's done it. Her blonde hair is tied back neatly in a bun. Her eyes are big and blue – or green. I thought they were blue when we met outside, but under the lighting of the Red Lion's green lamp-shades, they have taken on a green colour. We don't hug or anything like that. We are co-pupils not friends, not yet. Her vocabulary is sophisticated and she talks in seamless sentences. Her eyelashes are unfairly long. In contrast, I am stuttering, rehearsing every sentence in my head before I say it out loud. I don't know why I am so nervous, so afraid to be Stella. And I don't know how to feign interest when she talks about her love for football. I think of telling her about the time my dad took me and Sol to watch Ghana play Nigeria and we chanted, 'We will put *peppeh* in your eyes. You will see. We will score you!' from the stands, accompanied by a full brass band. I think better of it. I am relieved when Grace starts to talk about pies. She loves pies: making them, baking them and eating them. When we establish a shared love of food, I start to find my voice. Grace is as nervous as I am to start pupillage. It doesn't show. I confess that I am too. She wants to make of me her friend not her foe. I had not considered that in my co-pupil I could find a friend. We start pupillage with a research task: the best pub for pie on Fleet Street. Grace spent her gap year working at a pub before travelling to South America to do some 'white saviour-ing', so she's got it covered.

Chambers' tea lady takes our orders at 11am and 3pm. Instead of 'a white tea with no sugar, please', what I really want to say is, 'Can I give you a hand, Natalie?' Most people in Chambers are friendly, especially the junior tenants. They go out of their way to help you and to make you feel comfortable. I work in the common room on the fourth floor. I've identified this as the most relaxed working environment, the place in Chambers where I am least likely to stutter and wear a false smile. Where my brain is most likely to cooperate with the butterflies in my heart. In January, we will start weekly advocacy exercises. In preparation for our Second Six when we will enter the magistrates' court. With briefs in our own names. Representing our own clients. Talking before a real judge. As real barristers. Mercy.

Giselle Barnes is my pupil supervisor. She is perfect. And scary. She is perfectly scary. Rule number one: Starch Your Bands. Potatoes come to mind. I don't know what she means but I'm not going to ask because I should probably know. Relief as she hands me a can of starch spray.

'Spray it on your collars before you iron them. It will make them lovely and crisp and wrinkle resistant. If you fold them like this, they will keep their structure. There is nothing that says I do not take pride in myself or my work more than an unstarched collar. Keep it. I bought one for me and one for you.'

'Thank you, Giselle.' I wonder if my mum could use starch to cook, instead of olive oil.

She places her collar into a purpose-built holder, black with a gold fastening. I make a mental note to buy one.

In preparation for the prosecution of a rape trial, I am going to read the case papers provided by the Crown Prosecution Service and draft the indictment. There are two defendants and four victims, including one with learning disabilities. I am going to give consideration as to whether any special measures are required for the witness or witnesses to give evidence at trial. If so, I am going to draft the appropriate applications. We will discuss the case tomorrow.

I knock on Giselle's door and enter her room. Fresh daffodils sit in a vase on the windowsill. A Jo Malone reed diffuser releases a gentle fragrance into the room: lime, basil and mandarin. I think of salad dressing. There are at least one hundred A4 lever arch files on her shelves with different case names. In each, an arrangement of coloured tabs is carefully placed. They match the coloured highlighters to the left of her desk. A mug of coffee on her right, Cath Kidston, floral. Her room is immaculate.

'Hello, Giselle, sorry to disturb you.'

My voice comes out an octave higher than I want it to whenever I speak to anyone in Chambers, apart from Grace. And I preface too many exchanges with 'sorry'. I am 'sorry' to ask a silly question, or any question. I am 'sorry' when I boil the kettle, and someone comes into the kitchen to get a glass of water. I am 'sorry' when I walk past people exchanging pleasantries in the corridor and make eye contact with them. I am sorry that I don't know who I am in this place.

I ask Giselle if I can borrow her Archbold, the Crown Court practitioner's textbook. Which one? The most recent one, if possible. I do not know the exact date that the Sexual Offences Act 2003 was enacted, but I will find out. Archbold 2014 is on her shelf and I can borrow it, of course, but how is that going to help me when I am drafting an indictment for offences that occurred in the eighties? I had not considered that in much, or any, detail. I feel my face flush with heat. I will find the Sexual Offences Act 1956 in an older version of Archbold. I will find that on a shelf in the corridor, outside the boardroom.

'Sorry, Giselle, and thank you. I'll have a look.'

Giselle asks for my view on the disclosure of a text message that helps Defendant One. I'd like to send a message that says, 'I can't think about that right now because I've seen one magpie three times today and it's not even midday.' Instead of doing actual work, I have spent the morning staring out of a window that looks onto the Royal Courts of Justice, in search of another to mitigate the disaster that awaits me. The promise of doom constricts my voice as I reason, 'I don't think we should provide the text message to the defence because it is harmful to our case.'

I hear the words as they exit my mouth and I want to dig myself an early grave. Giselle asks me to familiarise myself with the disclosure test as soon as possible, her green eyes blinking concern. I *know* it. I just couldn't find it in my brain because there were butterflies in my chest. They flap their wings loudly every time she asks me a question. The sound of her voice sends the butterflies into a frenzy and I can never find the answer which I actually know. *Disclosure is providing the defence with copies of, or access to, all material that is capable of undermining the prosecution case and/or assisting the defence. It is a duty incumbent upon the prosecutor and essential to a fair trial.*

An MG6C? It sounds like a motorway leading to nowhere and I am in the fast lane. Mercy.

'The MG6C is the schedule of non-sensitive unused material.'

*

I seek refuge in the toilet. Grace is doing the same. I am losing any confidence I thought I had. I confuse my lack of knowledge and experience with the ability to learn. It deflates my spirit. Grace has had a tough day too. We look at each other, pie on our faces. I am worried that I am entering an Addisonian Crisis. I am so tired all the time. The muscles in my face hurt from smiling at seniority and my legs ache from trying to keep up with the physical demands of the job. A full day in court, back to Chambers and, finally, home.

'I'd love to. Maybe next time.'

Is the answer I give when anyone in Chambers invites me out for a drink. I am failing to strike the balance between socialising and surviving. My brain hurts from second-guessing every word I say and how I say it. I scrutinise every decision I make, contemporaneously and retrospectively. I just want to sleep. I dry my tears before I head back to Giselle's room for another round of 'Who Doesn't Want to Get Tenancy'.

'I've had a look at your draft indictment – it is very good, well done. Next time, when you are drafting for me, it would be helpful if you can add, in tracked changes, your reference to the underlying evidence so I can check these against the case papers.'

She agrees with my application for special measures in the form of an intermediary for the witness with learning disabilities. It is thorough, yet concise. The application requires two minor amendments before it can be served on the court and the defence.

'Thank you, Giselle. Would you like a cup of tea?'

'No, I'm fine, Stella. Thank you for offering. Why don't you go home? You look exhausted.'

SECOND SIX

Counting down to 'being on my feet' in court is like counting down to Armageddon: a necessary evil, a rite of passage. I am as prepared as I can be, and yet, I will never be prepared enough. I have sleepless nights in the weeks leading up to my first case. My instructions come through at 5.14pm the afternoon before the morning of.

> *Aaron Daniels. Croydon Magistrates' Court.*
> *Possession of a Class B drug with intent to supply. Ketamine. 4kg.*
> *Suspected street dealing.*
> *Previous convictions: Possession of Class B drugs x2. Cannabis.*

Giselle is on standby. She takes me through everything I need to know. Again. From walking through the court door. To the listings board. To the cells – if he's there. If he pleads 'guilty', I know what to do. If he pleads 'not guilty', I know what to do. My plea in mitigation is fit for purpose. I have her mobile number and Blackstone's practitioner's text at the ready. I look at Giselle for reassurance. If she wasn't an Iron Lady, I would swear a wetness to the whites of her eyes.

'You are ready, Stella.'

*

Grace and I celebrate the first day of our Second Six with a pie and a pint before rushing home to catch up on sleep. We survived and I only had to call Giselle four times. We brace ourselves for a physically and mentally demanding six months ahead. Every day represents a different court, a new defendant, a new set of case papers; a new experience. The learning curve is steep and exhausting but exciting – if only I could let myself feel it.

It is hard to surrender to the moment or trust in the knowledge and experience that is building alongside my ability to learn. It is the magpie who determines the success of my cross-examination, closing statement or the judge's mood. I surrender to fate whenever it eyeballs me from wherever it perches, yielding its demented power, foreboding in its solitude. My fatigue mounts as I struggle to mitigate the constant threat: delaying my arrival at court to make sure I lay eyes upon the magpie's mate. Only then can I begin my performance as a competent and self-assured advocate. Delaying evening respite to wait for the next train; there has to be another one around here somewhere.

Rupert Heston-Jones QC has asked Grace to attend a client conference with him. Again. He has asked me to make the tea. Again. I don't notice it at first but Grace does. She flushes with fury on my behalf. Like it's not hard enough, Stella. Like it's not hard enough to be relied upon for the 'hard skills' to justify being instructed at all. To stand nose to nose with overconfident male peers to argue that the sky is blue when they say it is green and to be patronised for the pleasure. Let alone to be a black woman.

And then there is 'Rigor Mortis', whose inflated ego relies on her being the only black woman in Chambers. Who won't give me a break lest there be two of us. Who sends me emails to 'remind' me of the requirement in Chambers that pupils 'demonstrate exceptional ability'. She is not sure that I am tenancy material. She is confident that I 'understand' the meaning of discretion, within the context of a threat, she neglects to add. 'Rigor Mortis', who speaks with such an affected accent that I wonder if she has permanent toothache. So stiff, so hateful.

Jules is Chancery Lane via Billericay, Essex, and the University of Oxford. I needn't worry about not having applied; she lived the horror for me. She is intelligent and selfless and witty. Her one-liners are well timed and well delivered.

'That positive attitude of yours, Jules! I hope it's catching.'

'Don't get me wrong, I made some good chav mates at uni and now I've got you!'

We bond over abscesses at Bar School.

'Stella, why are you walking like a pirate?'

'Jules, why are *you* sitting with one arse cheek in the air?'

Pilonidal abscess, located at the top of the bottom, in between the buttocks. The humiliation. She cares not for the volume of her voice, when she asks, 'Do you get it on your arse often?'

If she ever exposes me like that again in public, our friendship will be over.

Wednesday, 11.24am.

'Is it too early to go to the pub?'

Jules is a Family Law barrister being driven to destruction by her belligerent client. If he doesn't get contact hours with his children at tomorrow's hearing, 'someone is going to get hurt'.

'I'm not sure that's going to help your case. Try not to say it out loud.'

I've finished my Crown Court sentence. It's not too early, we decide. If we get a table, they'll think we're going to have lunch.

'Perfect.'

'On my way.'

'Be there in ten.'

We turn up in trainers. Because there is no one to impress.

DEPARTURES

After thirty-six years of caring for premature babies at St Thomas' Neonatal Intensive Care Unit, my mum is contemplating retirement. She has worked hard and she is tired. Dr Gates cannot imagine the NICU ward without its beloved Senior Ward Sister. She is the longest-serving nurse on the ward. Together with Dr Gates, she has witnessed the evolution of neonatal medicine over the years. The other nurses look to my mum for her knowledge and expertise. She is part of the make-up of the ward, its very fabric. There is not one tube or monitor or sound that she does not know. The ward is her home. My mum remembers the name of every preemie she has ever cared for. I know that there is a special place in her heart for the ones she has lost along the way. The best part of her job is when the babies are strong enough and well enough to go home and when she gets cards and pictures from their parents to show how beautifully they are growing and how much they are thriving.

My mum confirms her last day at the NICU three months before the event, an acceptable notice period for a nurse of her standing to receive the farewell she deserves. Her plan has always been to move back to Ghana. Although money was always tight, she managed to send some home to build her house in Cape Coast over the years, little by little. It is a huge accomplishment, some ten years in the making. She entrusted Uncle Kofi to give life to her vision: a five-bedroom bungalow, beautiful and spacious, each room with an en-suite bathroom, and an outhouse for the help. Bordered by six-foot-high white walls and an electric fence, a black gate opens to reveal the fruits of her labour. She will take her time to do the garden just as she dreamed it these past thirty-six years. A place to call her own.

On a rare day of rest for us both, I watch my mum in the kitchen as she makes omelettes for breakfast. I try to save our bread from the erratic thermostat of the toaster while the kettle boils for tea. She is really looking forward to a slower pace of life, an end to shift work and more time for herself. She will paint in her spare time. It's been such a long time since she painted. Oh, how relaxing it will be. She would like me and Sol to come to the NICU on her last day. It will be nice for us to meet her colleagues and vice versa. They have organised a small reception for her at 3pm on the Thursday. Can I make it? Sure, I will ask the clerks to keep my diary clear for the afternoon. We can go for dinner afterwards. That would be nice.

'Mum ... working in the NICU must have been really hard for you – after losing Coral ...'

I wait for the silence to be filled. It lingers in the air with the smell of our nearly ready breakfast.

'It was. It was really hard, Stella. But God does not give us more than we can handle.'

I avoid eye contact to give her the confidence and space to visit some unexplored place within. To enter the forest of her thoughts, populated with sadness and darkened by regret. From there, we can navigate the tangled branches of her life's hopes and dreams against the reality that she has lived. We can explore the roots of sorrow that were sown after she said the words 'I do'. I am searching for some clearing or brighter place. Why did you stay with him for so long? To find a crossroads from which we can emerge, together. Understanding. A place from where we can see the light.

My mum signals the end of the conversation with the humming of an unmelodic hymn, the words to which she does not know or cannot recall. The music brings an abrupt end to the solemnity of the moment and signals to me the end of some hope that she will open up to me and impart some knowledge about her life from which I can understand mine. It will come, one day, I hope. The promise of the omelette is more exciting than its taste. We eat our breakfast in silence, but for the contact of cutlery against plates, the biting of toast and the sipping of tea.

I meet Sol at Westminster tube station and we walk together across the bridge. A magpie hovers to the left of Victoria Embankment crossing, its blue and green hues shimmering against London's skyline. It drains my mind of colour and hope and introduces a distracting tension into my neck and back muscles as we make our way across the bridge. Sol is unfazed. He doesn't believe in all that crap. I look earnestly, but unsuccessfully, for another one before crossing my eyes to make-believe his mirror image. Before I can make the two magpies appear from one, I bump into the shoulder of a single-minded walker. He is in a hurry to get somewhere at a dangerous pace. I lose my footing on the dropped kerb of the crossing and a black cab beeps his horn for a long time to let me know that he was close enough to hit me. My impact with the tarmac wakes me from my reverie and Sol's hands collect me from my fall. I dust myself down and look back. I don't know who shouted. No one stopped.

'Yeah, I'm fine,' I assure Sol as we wait for the green man to appear again.

We meet Mum at the entrance to the NICU. She is wearing a blue sash with white writing – 'Officially retired!' – across her scrubs. She beams with pride as she presents us to her colleagues. They know our vital stats without the need for a formal introduction.

'You must be Stella, the barrister! You are the spitting image of your mother – a beauty with brains!'

The staff are absolutely charmed by Sol, who engages them in meaningful conversation and commends the incredible work they do. The nurses and doctors conclude that my mum will be very busy in her retirement screening applicants for the position of Mrs Sai II. She must be the proudest mother in the world. A reception has been planned on the fourth floor. The staff take turns to give personal tributes. The kindness of their words forces my mum to realise the impact of her work. She is quietly overwhelmed with emotion. The Medical Director makes a visit to the reception to thank her personally for her service to the Unit and to tell her how sorely she will be missed. She is the pride of the NHS itself. Dr Gates gives the final word of thanks. He presents her with a beautiful bouquet of flowers and a white envelope. If it contains Marks & Spencer vouchers, she will put them to immediate use. This prompts laughter from the panorama of smiling faces.

Mum navigates the NICU in the same way Giselle Barnes navigates a court room, with confidence and authority. The deference of young doctors and nurses alike demonstrates that, among her colleagues, Sister Sai is The Oracle, Commander in Chief of the NICU. Perhaps authority breeds devotion? Perhaps that's why she loves her babies so much? When I hear my mum issue directions to Dr Cofie and Dr Sulleyman, it is like hearing a stranger speak for the first time. Her voice is loud and clear and unhesitating. She uses the imperative and places exclamation marks at the ends of her sentences. She does not ask – she tells. She does not try to make herself small at the NICU, or invisible. Her shoulders are unbent, her back is tall and proud. I think of the tiny babies on the floor below and how much my mum loves them, 'my babies'. She works so hard to protect them from sickness and harm so they can be safe and well and go home. She protects them and loves them and fights for them.

More than she ever protected me.

More than she ever fought for me.

I did not know that my mum could tell a man what to do. I did not know that she could be assertive. I did not know that she could ever be more than what she was – at home. I wonder whether she has always been two different people: Senior Nurse Florence and my mum. I raise a plastic flute of champagne, along with colleagues present, to toast the One and Only: Senior Nurse Florence.

The champagne is bitter and sharp. It tastes of confusion.

Sol and I meet Auntie Baaba at Heathrow to say goodbye to Mum. I survived pupillage because she helped me, too tired to eat let alone cook. I have not paid attention in the kitchen over the years she has laboured. I do not know how to prepare the meals that I was raised on and love, already asleep before waking up to work late into the night. I do not know how I will survive without her. I wave goodbye at the departure gate, but I don't know who it is I am actually waving to.

'Safe flight, Mum. Call us when you land. Love you.'

'Love you more.'

ATROPHY

I am a bird without use of its wings: useless and condemned to an existence of fleeing predators from any and every direction. My survival is dependent on anticipating and weathering such attacks because I cannot escape them. I am not equipped to soar, and yet, I have neither the instinct nor the ability to surrender to that which promises my condemnation. David Attenborough could make a documentary about me. He would explain my life's shortcomings by analogy to a bird who is not forced by her mother to come out of the nest to seek food. Alas, she spends her birdhood in the nest, aware that, at regular intervals, her mother will come and drop food in her mouth. She will have sustenance. She will not die – physically. But will she thrive in that nest place? Will she know how to survive if, and when, she is pushed?

A birdhood without the practice of venturing out onto a branch – branches – will lead to muscle atrophy. Such that the spreading of the bird's wings to ease her fall on descent, if once instinctive, is rendered not so. Flying is now physically impossible. How can a bird whose wings have never known flight do so at the age of maturity? She cannot. Without flailing, for a few seconds, if that, before a deadly drop to earth. If she survives, it is only because her fall is broken by some collection of leaves or softness of mud, orchestrated by a pair of magpies close by. She can only hope for such intervention; a gift from God via nature, but she knows that it is not guaranteed. Thus, to attempt flight is to confront death, on each and every occasion. And she is a bird, not a daredevil.

What, then, for her nest? Can she reside there securely and contentedly, forever and ever, Amen? It is constructed in an unremarkable fashion with sticks and twigs and leaves. From a distance, it appears well made. However, on closer inspection, the discerning birdwatcher will note that it is bound neither by saliva nor mud nor spider's web. Held in place by the delicate physics of its fragile construct, the stability of the nest is not guaranteed. Far from it; it relies on the mercy of the elements. In that knowledge, the bird lives in perpetual fear of moving and breathing and living. To move too suddenly, breathe too deeply or live too freely, is to risk her very existence.

Born with the same promise of those birds who take flight around her, the bird is confined to the dangerous nest she inhabits. She knows not whether to attempt reversal of her atrophy: to build strength in her wings and, in maturity, attempt flight. She knows not how. She knows not whether to accept that both nature and nurture are against her. And that she is condemned to live and to die as a flightless bird.

If I felt pride in watching my mum come alive in the NICU, I am confused in the wake of her departure. That I would go to such lengths to protect someone I do not know. To advocate for someone who could have advocated for herself. To live in such close proximity to a stranger and to pay a price for my devotion. I am unable to reconcile the idea of Nurse Florence, sending her preemies into the world healthy and well and eager to live, with the knowledge that my mum has gifted me a life to mirror her own. I do not care for *omo tuo* and groundnut soup as much as I do for Nurse Florence. When she calls from Ghana, I can think only of betrayal. I let my phone go to voicemail.

I am learning the liberty of being able to choose who I speak to and when. Whose call to answer and whose to reject. It's a simple decision. I speak to Sol lest he turn up unannounced at my flat. Sol speaks to our parents – his parents. I give myself the gift of distance. A foundling, finding feet.

'It doesn't take a lot to send a text, Stella. It would be good to hear from you a bit more.'

Our conversations have become rudimentary for my part and not for want of trying on Sol's. My responses are simple and restricted to confirmation that I am well and working. He does not take my cue for brevity but insists instead on sharing details of his life, namely, cohabitation with Sienna. She has been promoted to Fashion Editor at work. They are going to celebrate with some bubbly tonight before she starts the 5:2 diet on Monday. She is perfect just the way she is, of course. Sol would do the diet too, for moral support, but he's training for a triathlon with the boys. I couldn't care less about Sienna's dietary regime, is what I want to say, or whether she has been promoted to the position of Anna Wintour Wannabe, N16. What I want to say to Sol, what I want to ask, is why have you always been such a passive bystander in my life? So happy to be a silent spectator in the stands of domestic chaos, so wilfully blind? For the first time, I see his inconsistency, his inclination to sacrifice principles for an easy life, his willingness to do anything but 'the right thing'. I wonder about the person Sol is at work – would I recognise him if I saw him there?

I think it's a sickness, 'Multiple Personality Disorder'. I saw a girl on *Oprah* once who had six people in her tiny ten-year-old body, each with its own voice and violence. Her mother was afraid of her. I wonder how many people there are inside Sol and my mum because everything I know, I do not know. No, I can't come over for dinner next week because I'm working, sorry.

To be out of sight is not to be out of mind. Their words and silence, action and inaction, are with me always. I am a foundling, with a family, bound together by conspiracy.

ROOMIES

'I'm never ordering Deliveroo again, Stella, not after yesterday. The driver practically threw the Panang curry in my face as he was running off. Zero fucks given.'

'Time is money, Eim, you know that. You've got to respect his hustle.'

When she has finished seeing the funny side of it, Eimear insists that I move in with her. She has her own place. She's hardly ever there because she's always travelling for work. Sean is committed to North London in a way she struggles to understand and she is not ready to move north of the river. I can water her plants while she's away. And she will cook for me, a tempting prospect now that Eimear has replaced vegetarianism with omnivorism. This will cause Deliveroo much chagrin, but it is time, and she is ready. Eimear is back from a trip to Venezuela. Her auburn hair is highlighted with hints of gold and the sun has brought out the freckles on her face.

'You look sunkissed, Eim.'

'Washed out, you mean. International travel isn't as glamorous as it looks. I'm knackered.'

*

Home is a spacious open plan flat with two double rooms and spot-lights in competition with generous streams of natural light. It is a relief to unpack my belongings and settle into our Herne Hill abode. And a weird type of rebirth to walk through Brockwell Park from this direction and along these streets. To be so close, and yet so far, from the place we lived as a family of four. Suffocating in oppression and ignorant of freedom. The juxtaposition between wealth and poverty no better reflected than on Coldharbour Lane, where our Sunday strolls often take us. To the right, the brutalist Southwyck House Estate. I can only think that it was designed by someone with an aver-sion to natural light. Why else its tiny, prison-like windows? What opportunities for the eight-year-old child raised in a building described as 'the Barrier Block'? Social mobility, an unimaginable concept. Opposite: the Brixton Square housing development. A call to middle-class graduate migrants: gentrified, wealthy and young profes-sionals. Half a million pounds for the same square footage, an entire world apart. I struggle to reconcile the two in theory or reality.

When she is not travelling, Eimear loves to cook. A time to zone out, switch off and create magic. She enjoys weekend trips to the farmers' market and hours in the kitchen. The place where both wine and words flow. Eimear and I agree that Irish and Ghanaian people have much in common. Big families. Religion: christenings, first holy communions, weddings and funerals. Food: I see your potatoes, and I raise you with cassava. Language. Names that English people can't pronounce or won't learn how to. History. Political revolution. English rule. Oppression. Independence. Superstition. People: industrious, resource-ful, friendly, proud. Supermalt meets Guinness. A good party!

Eimear puts on an endearing accent for effect. It is Galway meets Boston, where she spent her primary school years, returning to Connemara, Galway, every summer, to enjoy country life with her cousins. Playing in rocky fields, running across bogs, collecting limpets.

'What's a limpet, Eimear?'

Helping to move cows between fields, climbing hills, picking blackberries.

'Blackberries, do they grow on trees?'

'You can take the girl out of South London but you should probably just leave her there.'

Eimear's voice is permanently hoarse, her laugh mischievous. I try to remember what I spent my childhood doing. My memory is pixelated. I leave it be.

Eimear cooks with love. Meals that require time and effort and the weighing of ingredients by sight. A perfect Sunday roast: chicken, lamb or pork belly with garden-grown herbs and greens. Lasagne, freshly made béchamel sauce. Red wine bolognese, half the bottle, 'for taste'. Carbonara, rich and creamy. For a Ghanaian girl, I am a disappointment in the kitchen. My mum could spend her entire Saturday cooking. I never took much interest but I love to eat. My favourite Ghanaian meal? *Omo tuo* and groundnut soup. You have to eat it with your hands, Eimear.

'Yeah, I can do that.'

Over dinners, so many of them, we exchange stories of Ireland and Ghana. Eimear tells me of Oliver Cromwell's conquest. The confiscation of Irish land. The treatment of the Catholics. The laws passed against them. The bubonic plague. The potato famine. The suffering. I am ignorant. I had no idea how much Irish people had suffered under English rule.

'Who hasn't suffered under English rule?'

Fair point. Why don't we learn this as part of the curriculum? It's our history after all. My education feels improperly biased and lacking. She talks of Michael Collins, the Irish politician and revolutionary. That he was sent to London to negotiate a peace treaty to establish Ireland as a free state. That it was based on an Oath of Allegiance to the Crown. The controversy caused. And the 'freedom to achieve freedom'. She explains that the pain is still very raw for many Irish people.

In return, I speak of Kwame Nkrumah, the Ghanaian political revolutionary. An advocate of Pan-Africanism and developer of infrastructure in Ghana. I explain that Ghana played a leading role in African international relations during decolonisation, as if by my own effort and hand. That we were the first of Britain's African colonies to gain independence on 6 March 1957, Sol's birthday. Before independence, Ghana was called the Gold Coast. On independence, the Gold Coast flag was replaced. With its colours of red, green and yellow, Ghana's flag symbolises bloodshed, agriculture and mineral wealth. Its black star: African freedom.

When Kemi and Farah come over, the laughter levels border on uncontrollable. Eimear shares her concern that there is not enough 'penis traffic' passing through my bedroom. She is concerned that cobwebs are growing in light-deprived orifices. The situation is desperate, she concludes, and needs to be addressed as a matter of urgency. She puts the case so eloquently that I can offer little resistance to the surrender of my phone. The evening is lost to the installation of a dating app.

'"MasterBlaster" is looking for "a sexy sweetheart". "No drama. No baggage. No Geminis!!! White or Asian girls only!!!" What should I do now?'

'Swipe left, Stella! For God's sake, swipe left!'

Eimear's Pisces is a perfect match to my Taurus. Living with her is easy and joy filled. It feels good; it feels like peace. When Sean proposes, and Eimear moves out of our Herne Hill home to be one half of their whole, I am scared to be alone. Because my wings don't work.

'You'll have to come to Connemara one day, Stella!'

'I'd love to.'

MAI

I have a recurrent dream. I am back in Brixton, in the maisonette on Saltoun Road. An adult. I am looking for my *Grease* tape. I cannot find it anywhere. I am looking for it. Frantically. No one will help me. No one can hear me when I ask, 'Have you seen it?' In the kitchen, my mum is busy blending onions and tomatoes. I am shouting. But my voice cannot carry over the sound of the blender. She has turned her back to me. I am crying. I have the sensation that when I open my mouth, no words come out. I am sure I can hear them. But no one else can.

My dad is in the living room. Behind the cabinet with the *Encyclopaedia Britannica.* Killing mice. With his shoe. When he turns around, he has a mouse in his left hand. He is walking towards me. 'Do you know that you are in-so-lent?' I shut the door behind me. And run. My eyes are blinking loudly. Upstairs to the bedroom I share with Sol. He is watching his christening video. Over and over again. He has the remote control in his right hand. A chicken drumstick in his left. He rewinds the video back to the bit where the priest pours holy water over his big black hair. He laughs loudly each time. His hair gets wet. In the video. They are all laughing. Baby Sol. My mum. And my dad. It is the happiest day of their lives. There is no

Grease tape. Not any more. My tears start to fall. Hard and fast. When I remember: I don't live on Saltoun Road any more. I have my own flat in West Norwood.

A beautiful and spacious little flat. It is all mine, charge from mortgage lender aside. A pale blue living room, the colour of calm. Spotlights that decorate the ceilings like stars. Music that Alexa plays at my command. My TV sits on top of an old fruit crate to the right of a bay window which gives the gift of light. Temporary white blinds that I've never got around to replacing, rolled up. I have a fireplace and a mantelpiece. A king-sized bed with white bedding centres my bedroom. The mahogany bed frame matches the mahogany chest of drawers that sits to the left. On the right, a white side table which matches the white wardrobe on the back wall. Simplicity over patterns. French doors give the gift of even more light – and the constant threat of magpies. I look out to my garden. I need to mow the lawn or call the gardener. White walls decorate my hall, kitchen and bathroom. A haven, my haven. I live alone.

My heart rate slows down when I remember my flat. A wave of relief. The butterflies calm their dance. I head for the door. And without a goodbye, I start to run. Addison free. To the bus stop. Past Marks & Spencer and down Brixton high street. I cross the road at the Body Shop in the direction of H&M and—

I wake up.

I always wake up before I make it to the bus stop. Heart racing and sweating. I never make it to my flat, to my haven. I never arrive.

I am going to get a dog because I need something to love. Eimear has Sean, Kemi has Jackson, Farah has her job. I need to care for a living thing and to think of someone or something other than myself. Sometimes, I need a reason to get out of bed on Saturdays and Sundays when I am home alone with no court to get to and no defendant to represent.

I read that dogs can help to reduce stress. Maybe a dog will help me. I study the Rehoming page of the Battersea Dogs & Cats Home website and apply to rehome a rescue dog. I worry, initially, that I won't satisfy their eligibility criteria. They are concerned that the dog would be alone for long periods by herself but I will take her out to play every morning before I go to work. I have already found a dog walker to help me give her a beautiful life. I will work from home as often as I can, and she will have a social life to rival that of any butterfly. On the weekends, I will take her with me everywhere I go, if having her gives me courage to leave the cocoon of home. I will love her within an inch of her life.

I decide on a whippet, a gentle and affectionate dog, a lover of human companionship. When she visits my house for the first time, she shakes with fear at the newness of it all. She is tiny, black and shiny with innocent doe eyes. Her ears are cartoon-like, her features endearing. I hold her to my chest and feel the softness of her fur. Her trembling quietens as I hold her close. I stroke her gently and become calm as she does. I will call her Mai, my puppy love. She is the runt of the litter. Much smaller than her brothers and sisters, who eat her food as well as theirs. She is dinky and fits perfectly in the crook of my arm. I love her as soon as I lay eyes on her.

I prepare for Mai's arrival with a trip to Pets at Home. Eimear insists on coming to direct the operation. We work our way through a list of 'Puppy Must Haves': a bed, toys. A harness and lead. Shampoo and conditioner. Food. A name tag. My surname, not her name. In case she is stolen. By who?! We form a two-person Welcome Committee to celebrate Mai's arrival with champagne and cupcakes, for her benefit and ours. We struggle to contain our excitement. Eimear is adamant that puppies can benefit from skin to skin contact as well as babies. She swaddles Mai in a pink and teal feather boa.

'To replicate her mother's touch.'

It matches her green-fade John Lennon sunglasses and a pink mobile phone prop that appears from nowhere. I photograph the scene to begin documenting Mai's life and ours, together. I draw the line at the suggestion of dog shoes. Mai has a personalised toy box and a tug toy to add to her collection. She circles them with curiosity before she investigates. Chewing and snuggling come instinctively.

Everyone who meets Mai falls in love with her. When I let her off the lead for the first time, she looks at me as if to say, what should I do now? After quiet observation, she learns how to play with other dogs. Her style is wrestling and gentle nibbling, the bigger the dog, the better. She chooses a bull mastiff as her first friend: Little and Large. Mai is enamoured – and energetic. She does not tire of running or playing, ever. Occasionally, she will sit in sweet protest if I need to go somewhere, particularly when I am in a hurry. I carry her because that is the quickest and easiest way. And because she is just a big baby. And I love her. A simple creature: she plays and runs, sleeps and eats. Repeat.

'Naughty, Mai!'

My skirting board is ruined and I wonder, in the first few weeks of life with her, whether I will spend the rest of my days cleaning dog wee from the kitchen floor.

The grass is always wet first thing in the morning. I buy wellies and a raincoat. A selection of matching knitwear for us both, #twinning. When she shivers in the cold, it hurts my heart. Mai grows into the size of her paws and I find tiny white pieces of porcelain around the flat: puppy teeth. Her adult set establish themselves in a cute and crooked fashion. She has a flatulence problem for which she begs pardon. And she is unfazed by lightning. In the park and among our new dog-walking friends, I am known as 'Mai's mum'. She assumes that everybody we meet wants to make a fuss of her and that all dogs want to play. There is magic in her legs and sweetness in her heart. Every time I see Mai run, it takes my breath away.

*

'Stella! Is she smiling?'

A happy girl. It makes me happy to know that I can bring joy to the life of another living being.

I meet Beverley 'Queen of the Park' for our morning walk. She is pushing her granddaughter in a buggy. It takes Bev a while to warm to me. I kill her with kindness until she succumbs. When she does, I discover the entire dog-walking community at Norwood Park welcomes me with open arms. We see each other on our morning and evening walks. Every day. Throughout the seasons. In all weathers. There is a code of care among dog walkers. A forming of unlikely friendships. The joy of watching our dogs play. This community is a happy contrast to the underside of the park, which sits in close proximity to Portland Estate. I meet Bev by the memorial that commemorates the spot where Dwayne Johnson, aged fifteen, was recently stabbed and killed. His short life is remembered with a collection of white and yellow flowers. Solar candles burn through the night lest the fact he lived be forgotten.

Mai licks her lips in anticipation of a treat for which she has done no work, a block of cheese. She inhales it and runs off to play. Bev affectionately calls her granddaughter Tinker Bell. Her real name is Tia. Tia is the product of an unsavoury union between Bev's first-born and a local drug dealer who is the father to three children under the age of three with three different women. She shows me a photograph on her iPhone. I can see through the cracked screen that Leon is no oil painting. Mottled skin peppered with black scars, and a gold-capped front tooth, his prominent features. His chat must be good. I agree with Bev that he is 'an ugly fucker'. Thankfully, Tia looks like Bev's side of the family and nothing like her 'dickhead dad'. Tia has chubby cheeks and her neck is divided into rolls of fat. A gold chain hangs over her grey Adidas tracksuit top. Matching gold bracelets decorate her right and left wrists. She smiles when Rocco and Mai sniff each other's bums.

Bev wears her signature patterned fleece pyjama bottoms and purple shell jacket. Her eyes are sometimes green, sometimes hazel, depending on the light. Her hair is long and curly and brown. She wears it tied back in a bun. When she takes out her hair band, she reminds me of Rapunzel.

'You look so different with it down, Bev!'

Bev chuckles, a smoker's laugh. I agree to pick up some cigarettes for her from duty free on my next holiday and to shut up when I remind her of her pulmonary fibrosis. Bev is faithful and loyal and kind. We understand each other in a way that children who are forced to grow up too quickly do. You will never catch Bev walking underneath a ladder. She's had enough bad luck in her life and she don't want no more, babe. I have told The Girls about her, 'Bev, Queen of the Park'. She tells me that she's got a name for me too.

'Miss Posh Pants.'

'Chancery Lane via Brixton,' I remind her.

Our laughs meet in the early morning air.

'Red sky at night, shepherd's delight. Red sky in the morning, shepherd's warning.'

I tell Bev that English is not my first language and I've never heard that expression before. She calls me a silly cow before seeing me off at the gate.

YOUTH COURT

Facebook

Nuff respect to the school children eating Monster Munch, Space Raiders and Nik Naks for breakfast. I'm not struck by the absence of nutritional value. No. I'm amazed and envious that your bodies keep up with you! How loyal is the frame of a fourteen-year-old? Know that a time will come i.e. late 20s when you can no longer eat what you want and get away with it. When that Dr Pepper will necessarily transform into a skinny soya milk no fun substitute. When you will come to consider caffeine and not Chicken Cottage your best friend. That time for some is now. Disclaimer: I have never eaten from Chicken Cottage. #TfLChronicles #thestruggleisreal 86 likes

Comments:
Sol Sai: Don't hate the player sis! Haha. Those were the days! You free for breakfast tomorrow morning before work?? My treat!!! <3

A barrister. Wow. If they could see me now. Running to Camberwell Magistrates' Court, trolley in tow, dignity behind. I smile as I rush to the security gate and greet the court staff.

'Good morning! How are you?'

'Back again?' Tony helps me with my trolley. 'Take it easy, Miss Sai,' he calls as he hands me my watch, which I forgot to collect from the tray.

I am running late and sweating. My journey from South East to South West London is unexpectedly slow and stressful. Made more so by the magpie that eyeballs me from outside Jay's Newsagents as I wait for my bus. According to Transport for London, it is getting further and further away: three minutes away. Six minutes. Ten. I cannot bring myself to salute the magpie, or enquire about the well-being of his lady wife. I do not doff my hat or flap my arms like wings or caw loudly to mimic his missing mate. Because I am not mad. And I will not give him – a blue and white and green and black bird with a tail as long as his body – the satisfaction.

I need more time than I have left to meet with my client. Court 6. District Judge Walsh. Youth Court. Joy. The waiting area resembles Iceland in Brixton.

'Patrice Sougou?'

I call his name twice before I see him walking towards me. A woman in her early forties walks beside him: his mum. Patrice is fourteen years old and the colour of Cadbury's hot chocolate when you make it with milk. His head hangs slightly as he walks but I can guess his height at about five foot six. His dimples are prominent and frame his face in a sweet symmetry. His hair is neatly cut, his finger-nails, clean. He wears his school uniform and smiles timidly as his dark brown eyes meet mine.

Patrice is accused of joint enterprise robbery. Specifically, that on 13 September 2017, he and Olawale Oyefeso robbed Rufus Marshall of £4.60.

His mother, Jeanette, is at pains to tell me what a good boy Patrice is: the eldest of four children. Helps at home with his siblings (younger sisters and brother aged eleven, nine and six). Good grades at school – never had a detention. Mum works as a carer (nights). Dad is an Uber driver (days). I can tell from her accent that she is from Francophone Africa.

'Senegal. We speak French at home and Mandingo.'

'My family is from Ghana.'

Patrice was born in Senegal. They have lived in London for five years now. I try my best to quieten her anxiety.

Patrice does not speak at first. When he does, there is a *français africain* to his English accent and he swallows the words at the ends of his sentences. Patrice enjoys school. He likes playing football and video games with his friends. He knows Rufus from school. They are in the same form. He lives on Aylesbury Estate in Peckham, in the same block as Olawale. They go to the same school. Patrice and Olawale are very good friends.

Patrice went to McDonald's after school with Rufus, Adam, Ashley and Olawale. They are all in the same year. He didn't have any money and was hungry. Rufus had £10 and said he would lend him some money. Rufus gave him £5 in £1 coins. Patrice bought a Quarter Pounder with cheese and a Coke. Cost £4.60. He gave Rufus 40p change and promised to pay him back. Patrice did not steal. He doesn't know why Rufus would say that. He thought they were friends. No force was used. The only physical contact made between Patrice and Rufus was when Rufus gave him £5 by placing it in his hand. He has never been in trouble with the police. No previous convictions.

I struggle with the fact that the matter has come to trial. For what it is worth, I believe that Patrice is telling the truth. But what I believe, how I feel and what I think do not matter in court. I think he will do well under cross-examination.

'What do you want to be when you grow up, Patrice?'

'A pilot.'

Patrice reminds me of Sol; they have the same dimples.

*

When Patrice and Olawale are convicted, I feel anger rise in me like lava as I stand to address DJ Walsh on sentencing. The District Judge was, he says, 'persuaded' by the account given by Rufus Marshall and finds beyond reasonable doubt that:

> *Patrice had not asked Rufus to lend him money but prised it from his hands with force. He had followed Rufus Marshall, Adam Walters and Ashley Dickens into McDonald's, knowing that he had no money on his person and with this intention in mind. He had acted in concert with Olawale to intimidate Rufus. They had shown aggression and a readiness to use force against their victim whose account was corroborated by reliable witnesses Adam Walters and Ashley Dickens.*
> *Sentencing adjourned for the provision of a pre-sentence report.*
> *Indication: Youth Rehabilitation Order.*

Outside court, my voice cracks as I share with Jeanette and Patrice their devastation. A tear runs down my right cheek. I am being unprofessional. I am embarrassed. I use the sleeve of my suit jacket to wipe my face and try hard to convince Patrice that he has the brightest of futures ahead of him. I explain to him that his conviction will be 'spent' long before he applies to study piloting. That means it will no longer appear on his criminal record.

'I have a criminal record?'

'You won't have it forever, Patrice.'

I know in this moment that his future sits on a knife edge. Boys like Patrice wander in and out of DJ Walsh's court every day. I want to pardon him, for not seeing the promise of Patrice Segou, from Senegal, who does well in school and helps his mum with his younger siblings at home. Patrice Segou, who wants to be a pilot when he grows up. For believing the accounts of the boys whose blue eyes mirror his own. I wonder if DJ Walsh will know his part in defining Patrice's life. I wonder if he cares. I want to hug Jeanette.

*

I can't bring myself to type my attendance note and I can't stop thinking about Patrice. I eat a tub of Häagen-Dazs salted caramel ice cream for dinner; Eimear would weep. My phone beeps before I silence it for bed.

Do you like my new tattoo? It's Bev.

I download the image to see Tinker Bell from *Peter Pan* etched in green ink between blue veins on white skin. Pixie dust surrounds her. I can't make out the body part.

OMG Bev, I love it!!! #GlamMa <3

TAIWO

Facebook

I am engaged in an awkward game of 'knock knee' that I didn't sign up for. Opposite me: a Spread Eagle showing no sign of flight. I am burdened with far reaching knees badly designed for public transport. He is burdened with bold and bad manners. The carriage is full, the day has been long. Spread Eagle is trying to create an obtuse angle where his legs meet at the crotch. It's a party of one and I'm party to the party. Our knees knock once, twice, three times. 'Sorry,' I mutter on each occasion. Spread Eagle stays silent. And now – a mild form of rubbing? I question the boldness of man as I look away.
#TfLChronicles #thestruggleisreal
78 likes

Comments:
*Sol Sai: Sorry for what?! Spread Eagle is a waste man!! Don't worry sis, chivalry lives – ask **Sienna Bannerman**! Haha. Be good to see you soon x*
*Sienna Bannerman: **Sol Sai** Awww bub. Chivalry is alive and well. How lucky am I?!! x Stella, we would LOVE to see you!!! Let's make it happen <3 x*

*

It takes six goes before I understand the source of Taiwo's income.
Date One.

'I'm an oz-o-lah.'

'A what?'

'An oz-o-lah.'

'I'm sorry, a—'

'An oz-o-lah, an oz-o-lah.'

'An-us-solar?'

He manages his frustration with a wide smile. His lips are covered in
Vaseline. I wonder why I swiped right. Unnaturally shiny and coun-
tered in texture by white crust at the corners. He chews his Beef Lo
Mein loudly. The sound effects. I gag.

'A HUSTLER?!' Jesus Christ. Is this guy for real?!

Taiwo is delighted. The white crust cracks and becomes
powder-like. 'Abuja-Code' Level One – completed. Anti-climax is
an understatement. He confuses my understanding for encouragement. Taiwo used to work in IT but realised that he could make a
lot more money working for himself as an 'independent trader'. He
wants to be his own boss. Taiwo spends his days trading unspecified
'commodities' on the stock market. He wants to retire by the time
he is forty. I'm pretty sure Taiwo is pushing forty-seven. He laughs,
a hearty laugh. The laugh of a Nigerian man who enjoys *ogbono*
soup and *suya* kebab. The laugh of a man looking for a wife who
knows how to cook. I am out of the running.

Taiwo has adopted the grooming style of his Muslim friends. A
shaved head and imitation prayer beads hang from his neck. A
lustrous and full-bodied black beard bobs up and down when he
laughs. It shares the same glistening properties as his lips. Nothing
unique about his interpretation of *smart-casual*. A navy blazer meets
blue shirt and jeans. Taiwo is of the no-socks-brown-suede-loafer
brigade. He wears a watch which purports to show the time in
London, New York and Tokyo. It is extravagant at best, ostentatious

at worst. Taiwo has lived in London for six years now. He schooled in Abuja, boarding school. One of five siblings. A twin, the firstborn. That is the meaning of 'Taiwo'.

Have I ever been to Nigeria? No. He can take me. A weekend in Victoria Island. I will love it, he promises. I should ask a question.

'Have you seen Louis Theroux's *Law and Disorder in Lagos*? The bit when the army general shouts, "Shut up, don't be stupid!" at his neon-shirted army brigade?'

I laugh, for the first time. I am laughing alone. Taiwo hasn't seen *Law and Disorder in Lagos* and he hasn't heard of 'Lou-wee Faru'. Do I like Nollywood movies? Negative. I try to understand why Taiwo speaks with an American accent. He has friends in the States, Atlanta. He is going to celebrate his 'fortieth' birthday there but is yet to visit. I wish his offer to take me with him would distract me from scanning work emails on my phone, to which, I inform him, urgent responses are required.

I spend the remainder of our date examining the tension between the fifth and sixth buttons of his shirt. I will the fifth one to pop and for the button to go flying across Modern China. I don't motion for my bag, purse or phone when the bill comes. Not least because I have spent an hour and a half, now permanently lost from my life, analysing Taiwo's ability to speak and swallow at the same time.

'Please, allow me!' His volume is theatrical and unnecessary.

'That's very kind, thank you.'

Taiwo would like to call an Uber for me. He is opening up the app. I am running for my train and away from online dating.

MENTAL HEALTH COURT

Facebook

There is a Trisha come Ricki Lake relationship expert on the 0748 train from Norwood Junction to St Albans City. The 'nuff' things she knows about boys you know! Sadly, she is not familiar with the 'stare to silence' being executed in her direction. This journey can be an education for all, symbiotic like. Your bredrin's boyfriend has anger management issues AND he is definitely cheating. Commuter silence is golden.
#TfLChronicles #thestruggleisreal
69 likes

Comments:
Sol Sai: Cycle sis, you'll never look back. Promise. Call me!!! x

I am at St Albans Magistrates' Court. My client, Mr Adura, is charged with criminal damage; namely, damage to an electricity cable valued at £200, belonging to his neighbour. And using violence to secure entry to her premises, without authority or lawful excuse. He tells me that he did both. Specifically, that on 9 July 2018 at about 12.30pm, he was woken up from his sleep by loud music coming from his neighbour's flat. The music was Eminem – or house music. He cannot recall which. He asked his neighbours to switch the music off. Through the wall. He shouted four times. They ignored him. He could not sleep. He got up to cut the power cable to the flat. He needed the music to stop. All he wanted was peace and quiet. He fell asleep. He woke up again shortly after. He did not see the time. He heard a woman being raped. 'No. Stop. Leave me alone.' She was screaming. From the same flat. He jumped out of bed and knocked on the door. A woman opened it. 'Excuse me, I can hear a rape happening here. Can I come in to check that everything is okay?' The door was on a chain. He could not see inside. He put his arm through the gap. The woman started smashing the door against his arm. She told him to get out of her house and to leave her alone. He put his body weight against the door. To try and stop her. And to check the rape. When he got his arm out, it had marks from where she had slammed the door onto it. He went back to his flat. The woman had stopped being raped by then.

Mr Adura did not understand why he had been arrested. He was detained under the Mental Health Act. My instructing solicitors have provided me with a psychiatric report. It proves essential. Mr Adura has been diagnosed with long-term mental health difficulties. He has been sectioned on two previous occasions and has an established diagnosis of schizophrenia. Mr Adura has been prescribed with antipsychotics. At the time of the alleged offence, he had not taken his medication for three weeks or so.

Mr Adura communicates well. He is well presented and pleasant albeit nervous about the day's proceedings. The matter is listed for trial before a lay bench of magistrates. The CPS prosecutor confirms that she has seen the psychiatric report. She is not prepared to take a view or to send the case back to the reviewing lawyer for reconsideration of the charges. The trial begins. I take Mr Adura through his evidence.

'Have you ever had an auditory hallucination before?'

'Yes.'

'Can you tell the court what an auditory hallucination is?'

'It's when you hear voices in your head.'

'On 9 July 2018, were you having auditory hallucinations?'

'No.'

'How do you know when you are having an auditory hallucination?'

'Someone usually tells me.'

'When?'

'When it's over.'

'Has anyone told you that on 9 July 2018, you were having auditory hallucinations?'

'No.'

'Is it possible that you *were* having auditory hallucinations at the time, and that you didn't know?'

'Yes. Yes, it is possible.'

In my closing speech, I rely on the defence of insanity established in the case of *M'Naghten*.

> *To establish an insanity defence, it has to be proved that, at the time of committing the act, the defendant was labouring under such a 'defect of reason', from a 'disease of the mind', as not to know the nature and quality of the act he was doing, or, if he did know it, he did not know that what he was doing was wrong.*

We cannot be satisfied, so that we are sure, that in cutting his neighbour's power cable, Mr Adura knew that what he was doing was wrong. Nor did he know that in trying to secure entry to his neighbour's premises, there was someone present on the premises who was opposed to the entry. In fact, he believed the opposite to be true, that there was a woman being raped who needed help. Mr Adura's auditory hallucinations caused such a defect of reason from a disease of the mind, namely schizophrenia, that he did not, by criminal standards, know that what he was doing was wrong. In Mr Adura's mind, he was trying, desperately, to prevent a woman from being raped.

The justices are persuaded by my 'cogent legal argument', the psychiatric report and Mr Adura's compelling evidence. On acquittal, Mr Adura thanks me with a sweaty handshake. He will continue to take his medication and speak to his GP if he starts to feel unwell again. He is feeling a lot better now than he did back then. He has settled well into a new hostel where he only has to share a bathroom and kitchen with five other people. He sees the psychiatrist once every two months and speaks to the mental health nurse once a fortnight. Mr Adura thanks me so much for making him not go to prison and he hopes to see me again soon.

I treat myself to a chai latte on my walk back to the train station. A pair of magpies congratulate me outside Pret. I keep them in sight for as long as possible, checking, before I feed my ticket through the machine and walk to the train platform, that they are still there. 'Thank you,' I whisper-say. I am relieved to take this feeling home with me, overnight and into the next day. I type my attendance note on the train home.

CARNIVAL

Kemi played carnival for the first time when she was three years old, kiddies' carnival. Since then, she has played Notting Hill Carnival, Trinidad Carnival and Barbados Crop Over Festival. She has earned international stripes, an addiction to bacchanal and a collection of exquisite costumes. For Kemi, carnival isn't limited to an August bank holiday weekend. It's a way of life, a series of events that establishes and maintains her serotonin levels throughout the year. Carnival is an event to look forward to and plan for and dream of and celebrate.

On the Tuesday that follows the bank holiday weekend, 'carnival tabanca' sets in. Think of the devastation that follows the worst relationship break-up imaginable. For a brief time, Kemi will confuse the morning's refuse collection with the sound of the carnival truck; it's a form of grief. She will indulge it for a week or so, as she rests and recovers from the festivities. In November, SOCA artists will release their songs in preparation and readiness for the Trinidad Carnival in February: the Greatest Show on Earth. Kemi streams them online. By August, she is word perfect. In March, the designs for the Notting Hill Carnival costumes are released. There is no hesitation or indecision when it comes to choosing her costume. The colours and designs – they speak to her. In April, she will ensure that she has a 'body readiness' plan in place. By June, she has identified the pre-carnival parties she needs to attend, the fêtes. By August, she is ready for the magic of bacchanal.

When Kemi tells me that Notting Hill Carnival is 'a once in a lifetime experience', I agree that my life needs this kind of event. I don't commit to preparation with the level of dedication that Kemi suggests – or curb my carbs. In fact, my belly hangeth over. Our costumes are ready in 'C minus three months'. We travel to East London to collect them. I am on the wrong side of the river, I'm sure.

The sight of my costume gives me butterflies. My headdress is the most beautiful arrangement of cobalt, emerald and black feathers splayed like a proud peacock. It is magnificent and regal and bold. My leopardprint bikini is set with ivory shells and brown topaz-like costume jewellery. I wonder who made it. I want to say thank you. It looks like it was made with love.

Carnival Day calls for false eyelashes and lipstick. Kemi looks fiyah. She wears green false lashes to my black and lashings of eyeliner. She blinks deliberately and beautifully, fluttering on command. Her lips are magenta. They pop against the cobalt of our costumes. Her hair is pulled back to hold her headdress. With an expert hand, she applies a face of theatrical make-up to mine. I admire the beauty smiling back at me in the mirror. Addison's Who? My headdress is transformative in a Beyoncé/Sasha Fierce sense. Not to be wasted on the Circle and District Line, no sah! We journey to Notting Hill at 7am to meet our float. Stepping out of the tube station is like birth itself. Floats line the roads as far as my eyes can see. Each boasts an independent and powerful sound system. It synchronises with the beat of my heart.

The front-line costumes of each float are incredible and extrava-gant. Restricted by the weight of the costumes, their wearers' movements are deliberate and impactful. They enjoy the envy of the crowds as they lead their floats. In the midline, I dance moves I don't know I know and sing to songs I hear for the first time. I will find them later: Machel Montano, Destra Garcia, Kerwin Du Bois. Kemi is in her element. She knows every single word to every single song. She displays moves that I commit to learning, mentally. Free from my habitual shyness, I dance bumper to bumper with men whose names, ages and vehicle registration numbers I do not know. Addison's What? Women with rolls of fat in form, location and size I have never seen the likes of parade in their bikini sets without a care in the world. They smile with their eyes as well as their cheeks. I feel free when I see them. The Gays impress with flamboyance and choreography. They are happy and proud. They are loving it; we all are. There is no judgement, only joy. Come as you are.

I drink rum, a lot of rum, from the 'unlimited' drinks float and put off using the public toilets for as long as I can. The confined space, the shared use, the stench – I can't. When I mistake spilled rum running down my leg for wee, I give in. I make a promise to myself to hold back on the alcohol.

The barriers that line the route separate the 'haves' from the 'have nots'. Once you have been *in* the Notting Hill Carnival, you can't simply *go to* the Notting Hill Carnival. Those who know, know. We take pictures with other masqueraders, with people along the route and with Farah and Eimear, who meet us at Westbourne Grove. Our joy at seeing each other another reason to 'jump and wave'. Farah and Eimear mirror our dance moves in civilian summer clothing as Kemi and I scramble over the barriers. We fall into their embrace.

'You guys look A-MAY-ZING!' Farah cries, promising to join us next year.

Eimear cannot get over how incredible we look, or how delicious the jerk chicken and curry goat is from that stall, right over there. From my carnival rucksack, I pull out two tiny colour blocks in the shape of squares: one red, the other green. I hand the red one to Farah and the green one to Eimear. After a collection of inquisitive utterings, they open the protective polythene and the folded squares to reveal the tricolours of the Egyptian and Irish flags. They cause delight and joyful waving. Farah asks a passer-by to take our picture. That he is beautiful is a happy coincidence. Our smiles reflect the same thought: four friends, four flags, feting for posterity – and for Mr Fit.

We've got dance moves for days, The Girls and I. We've show-cased them on dancefloors in Brixton; at the foot of the Eiffel Tower in self-congratulations post A-Levels. We've partied in Mykonos to celebrate being twenty-one, hedonism on a budget. Eimear 'I'm an expert traveller' Kelly, the reason we almost missed our flight. Her silver Air Miles status counted for nothing when she forgot her passport at the British Airways check-in desk. Passport reunited with owner and panic over, we ran to the departure gate suffocating with laughter. We won't let her live it down.

We dance together in the street, energised by the sunshine and the bass lines of the passing floats. Kemi and I kiss The Girls goodbye in search of our float. We will see them again at Kensal Road. They wave us goodbye with their flags and sweet smiles.

I will watch the news afterwards and hear about the knives, the anti-social behaviour and the arrests. I will read about the complaints from local residents. Their concern about the increase in violence year on year. But for now, all I see are the friendly officers who line the route. In good humour, they oblige revellers who insist on dancing with them and taking pictures. Make room for PC Ashley Banjo, clearly an undercover raver. He body pops at the Rampage set and wins the respect of the crowd. The video will go viral.

I am so happy to be here, living this experience. My Ghanaian pocket flag meets Kemi's Nigerian flag in the air as we jump and wave to celebrate the magic of carnival. We dance into the early hours of Tuesday morning and fête until our feet tell us that it is time to go home. Reluctantly, we concede. But first, one last whine!

Facebook

Farah posts our picture. Tagged: Stella, Kemi, Eimear.
#NottinghillCarnival2018 #TheGirls
263 likes

Comments:
Sol Sai: You guys look awesome!!! Can't believe I didn't see you 🙁 *Tried to call but couldn't get through. Hope you've taken tomorrow off work!!* 😊

'Wait until we go to Dimanche Gras!' Kemi promises an unimaginable experience in Trinidad.

'I literally can't wait.' My voice is hoarse. With happiness and rum.

A FOUNDLING FINDING FEET

COLM

Colm is six foot two. I can wear heels. A professional with blue eyes and brown hair, City based.

He is handsome and Irish. I swipe right. My assessment is brief. I take it as a positive sign that in our first night exchanging messages, we consider topics that I never heard my parents discuss in their entire marriage: politics and ambition, for starters. What then for the main course and dessert? He has good chat. Me? I confess that I am 'honorary Irish'. We agree to meet.

Date One. It is December and cold. He arrives late but unflustered.

'I thought I'd make a really good impression by arriving on time,' he says. 'Sorry about that, terrible traffic! Please, let me get you a drink.'

I am wearing a mixed print dress with a cold shoulder. It sits just above the knee. He is dressed in brown shoes – with socks – dark jeans and a white shirt. I don't feel over or underdressed. His eyes twinkle when he smiles and I thaw as he wins me over with charm and humour. He talks enough but not too much. Colm is the child of divorced parents. He is close to both. One of three children, the middle child. He is from Waterford in the south-east. Have I been?

'Not yet.'

What kind of honorary Irish am I? He is comfortable with eye contact and unfazed by silence. His last relationship ended about a year before he acknowledged it. They were together for four years and lived together for two. His greatest sadness is that he was ready to start a family but she wasn't. I take joy from this part of his sorrow, encouraged that he has given thought to family life. We discuss the challenges of finding a work/life balance. I find his ambition attractive.

His eyes move from his pint glass to my eyes, twice, before he says, 'You are beautiful, Stella.'

I look between my glass and my ankle boots.

'Thank you.' I smile. I am shy. I wonder if he can sense it.

I am a lightweight and three glasses of Malbec in. Would I like to go back to his place? It's not far from here. I hesitate and hear Sol's voice ringing in my ears, 'Stella, if you want a guy to take you seriously, you *never* go home with him on the first date.'

'I promise I will put you in an Uber at the end of the night.'

'The early hours of the morning, you mean?' It's quarter to one.

Our cold hands find companions in each other. I don't want the evening to end.

'Yes.'

'Yes?'

'Yes, I'll come back to yours.'

We take a cab to his apartment in the Isle of Dogs. It boasts amazing views of Canary Wharf. A skyline of corporate fairy lights signposts the sterile scene. I wonder if anyone ever turns them off to save electricity? A week's worth of pale blue, pink and white shirts hang in his coat cupboard, recently dry cleaned. He moves them to the wardrobe in his bedroom. A navy blue duvet cover with geometric patterns distracts from the emptiness of the room. His bed is recently made. Colm's life is facilitated by a cleaner-cum-housekeeper-cum-lifesaver. He navigates his kitchen with the *savoir faire* of a person who doesn't cook but knows how to pour a drink. A collection of whisky and brandy bottles sit on top of a drinks cabinet. He is on the phone as I emerge from the loo and points the camera in my direction.

'Paddy, I've met an absolute beauty. This is Stella. Isn't she stunning?'

He is grinning from ear to ear.

'It's my cousin Paddy, in Waterford!'

'Hi, Stella, can't wait to meet you!'

I smile and wave. 'Hi, Paddy.' I shy away from the camera. 'Colm!'

'What type of music do you like?'

'Anything with a beat. I love to dance.'

Colm ends his call with Paddy abruptly and without warning. I guess brotherly familiarity. He pours two large glasses of red wine before channelling Stevie Wonder's 'Isn't She Lovely' through speakers; a deliberate choice, I hope. I surrender to his rock 'n' roll moves. Limbs loose, a bottle of wine later, we dance in the living room, Colm spinning me round until I am delirious with happiness or close to throwing up, or both. At 2.52am, I am ready for bed, my bed. He calls an Uber to take me home as promised. A kiss goodbye to wish me sweet dreams.

'See you soon.'

I have heard from him every day since we met. And, rightly or wrongly, I have pictured myself meeting Paddy in person and the rest of Colm's family. I have imagined myself living in Waterford and going for walks along the coast, hand in hand. Our second date is a prequel to a Black-Tie Event for us both. Colm is off to an Annual Dinner for the Association of Civil Engineers. Venue: somewhere swanky, Park Lane. I am going to the Annual Fraud Lawyers' Association Dinner. Venue: somewhere equally fancy, Mayfair. It is the only night we can both do this week. I am encouraged by the effort he has made to see me and I imagine shopping for engagement rings in Hatton Garden. I am wearing a high-neck dress, à la Meghan Markle, in black. My hair is pinned up in a modern beehive, exaggerated volume and texture run throughout. My earrings are gold, metal, floral and dangling. My black eyeliner is carefully applied. I receive 'wows' from the clerks' room and friends in Chambers. I am far enough from my daily court attire, or 'no relationship prospects' self, to feel a million dollars. I like the person I see in the mirror. I want to be her every day. Colm? He looks like James Bond himself, a picture of tailored testosterone. He is on time. I hear him draw breath as he lays eyes on me.

'You look absolutely stunning!'

'Thank you! You look so handsome.'

'We may be slightly overdressed for this pub. What do you think?'

'Perhaps,' I smile.

We stick out like a sore, but perfectly manicured, thumb.

Over a glass of wine, we learn a little more about each other. Colm tells me that his interest in engineering was inspired by time spent at his father's architecture firm as a child. His dad is his best friend and Colm would be lost without him. He has benefited from nepotism but he didn't get a free ride; he has worked hard. His dad came from humble beginnings and reminds him how fortunate he is – not that Colm needs reminding; he knows. When he was twenty-seven, Colm was offered an incredible opportunity in London and accepted a role that he was probably underqualified for. The kind of thing a woman would never do, I think but don't say.

My mind turns to Sol when I hear Colm speak about his dad. The admiration and reverie in his tone both familiar and distant, a parent who can do no wrong. I wonder whether Sol's interest in tech was inspired by time spent at KPS Autos as a child? His ambition, a desire to emulate what he had seen? Sol is so deliberately selective, it wouldn't surprise me to learn that he has transformed the mechanics of changing a tyre into an algorithm for happiness and success. Sol hasn't benefited from nepotism, but he has benefited from a loving and devoted and gentle father. The gulf between us is extreme. It was established in infancy and has deepened with time.

I can tell that Colm downplays his professional success. His modesty enhances the sweetness of his kiss. I don't know how to pout or flirt. I hope my blinking comes across as endearing and not symptomatic of an eye problem. Colm thinks I downplay my professional accomplishments too. He expresses admiration for my ability to advocate on behalf of others. Isn't it hard to represent someone who you know is guilty? Well, I don't know that someone is guilty unless they confess their guilt to me. My role is not to determine their guilt. I take instructions from my client and advise them on the strength of the evidence against them. The question of guilt is ultimately determined by the jury as the tribunal of fact. And everyone is entitled to legal representation. That is how I approach my work. Colm is intrigued and attentive. He doesn't believe me when I tell him that I am shy. Someone who argues in front of a judge and jury for a living couldn't possibly be shy.

'It's hard to believe, I know.'

In his spare time, Colm goes back to Waterford to see his family. He shares a love of rugby with his dad and they often travel to watch Ireland play. I impress him with my knowledge of Gaelic football and hurling. He likes to relax because his job is full on and he is always on the go. Me? I like to relax, run and see friends in my spare time. I have a dog. We go for long walks on the weekends. Similarly, I really value chill time. Where do I see myself in five years?

'Well, what I want for myself now is very different to what I wanted for myself when I was first called to the Bar. I would like to have a family one day. I think as a woman you can have it all, but not necessarily at the same time—'

We are interrupted by an Irish woman attending her office Christmas party. She interposes herself in the small space between us without invitation or announcement. Christmas Party Lady is wearing a pair of reindeer earrings. They flash red light at Rudolph's nose. Silver tinsel decorates her neck like a scarf and a green sequinned dress completes her festive look. In my head, I call her Mairead. Mairead is filled with the spirit of Christmas, the spirit of mulled wine, and the spirit of hot buttered rum. Her accent confirms her Northern Irish roots. I love it.

'Can I just say, of all the people in this pub tonight – and I've walked past them all – of everyone here tonight, you two are the most beautiful and the most glamorous! What a beauty! Is she your wife?' She is theatrical and dramatic and loud. She does not wait for an answer.

'Oh, are you here on a date?'

Or an opportunity to confirm or deny—

'You'll have to marry her! She is beautiful. Beautiful!' Red wine swirls in her glass as she gestures grandly. It reaches dangerous heights. I am concerned for Colm's white shirt.

Mairead spills her wine as she zigzag-walks away, glee filled. Colm's grin finds mine and we order one more glass to toast Mairead's enthusiasm for our meeting. It is a perfect end to the Black-Tie Prequel when Colm says, 'We should go for a Sunday roast this weekend if you're free?'

'I am and I would love to.'

'Bring Mai, I'd love to meet her. We can go for a walk after?'

I have found Mai a dad and become the mother she deserves.

We share a black cab to our black-tie dinners. He opens the door for me and holds out his hand to help me navigate the seat with my floor-length dress. He reassures me of the good in this world when he asks the driver to drop me off first. Chivalry lives, beyond the world as I have known it.

*

I book the Northcote in Clapham Junction for 1.30pm on Sunday.
Colm can't wait.

It's my turn to be late. Train delays, sorry. Be there in fifteen!
I send a message as I power-walk to the pub. I don't think I can
manage lateness with the same calm as Colm. I don't want to turn up
looking flustered or sweating. I think nothing of it when he does not
reply immediately. Two ticks, blue. When I arrive at 1.47pm, I
assume he is already there.

'Hi. I have a reservation for two people in the name of Stella.'

'Follow me.'

I am seated at a table for two. My guest is yet to arrive. Would I
like something to drink?

'I'll wait, thank you.'

I wait for another fifteen minutes before I call. No answer. Another
message:

Hi Colm, here now. Can I get you something to drink? Two ticks, blue.

Another fifteen minutes. I call again. It rings through. My mouth is
dry. I should have asked for tap water.

I replay the Black-Tie Prequel in my head, just to be sure. He did say
I looked 'stunning', didn't he? I check with the waitress when she
passes my table – for the fourth time – that it is Sunday. Everyone in
the pub is eating a chicken or lamb or pork roast with potatoes, gravy,
two veg and someone who loves them, or likes them. I check my
WhatsApp messages, just in case I imagined it. I wait for an hour
before I leave. I hope he has not had an accident. What if he died on
his way to meet me? What if he was killed? A cloud follows me as I
walk back to the station with Mai on a loose lead. My feet are heavy
as I place them one in front of the other. One. *Thud.* Two. *Thud.* It is
not good to go from feeling like you have met a nice person, a man
you can trust and see yourself falling in love with, to realising that he
has tricked you and he is not the person you thought he was. It makes

you feel like you don't know what your name is or where you live and why. A pigeon's wing narrowly misses my ear and I hurt my neck dodging it. People look at me when I scream.

I am looking for magpies. Two of them. I promise that if one appears, I will doff my hat and flap my arms like wings and caw loudly to mimic its missing mate. I check my phone on the minute every minute after I leave the Northcote. As the train pulls out of the platform at Clapham Junction. And on the walk from West Norwood station to my empty flat. My eyelids are heavy, my vision, confused. I open the doors to my garden and look. At the sky. Between the trees. On the telephone wires. And fences. 'Where are you?' I send my voice into the air so they will hear me. If I plead with them, they might have mercy on me. The two magpies that I need to see.

He messages at 11.18pm. His name on my phone screen is like lightning in my eyes, 'Colm'.

Sorry about today hangover from hell!

I cannot sleep for exhaustion and overactivity of the thinking part of my brain and the feeling part of my heart. On Monday morning, my mouth is fixed with the taste of a sickly thing like liquorice. By Tuesday, I feel lava rising from my legs to my stomach to my chest. On Wednesday, the butterflies are angry and beating their wings wildly in my chest. By Thursday, I know that I am 'unlovable'. Did I do something wrong? On Friday, I stop checking my phone and put it on silent. He messages a week later. Something about being really busy with work. Probably not the best time to start dating. I don't respond because I don't know what to say. He is a man, I know. Indifferent and irresponsible. Liable to hurt, humiliate and destroy. Me? I am both woman and girl, adult and child.

Farah tells me not to cry and not to worry. I don't need someone like that in my life. Better I know now than two months down the line. Of course I am lovable. I am the most lovable person she knows. I deserve more. We breathe together to calm my tears: in for four, hold for four, exhale for six. Again.

Farah wants me to try yoga. She thinks it will be really good for me. There are so many different types. She does a mix of ashtanga and vinyasa. It is muscle strengthening and toning, and great for meditation too. How do you meditate? Well, you exclude other thoughts by focusing on your breath. Your mind will wander but that's okay. When you notice, you bring your thought back to your breath. And eventually, you get to a place of calm where that's the only thing you are thinking about and focused on. 'Stella, I think you would really enjoy it.'

I feel better. Just listening to her.

'Yoga on Sunday?'

'Okay. Sounds good.'

I want to see her do a headstand.

SHAKING

I have a recurrent dream. I am back at Sudbourne. It is my History A Level exam. I head to class. I am the last person to arrive. Mrs Wardell is there: red nails, blue leather skirt, black cashmere cardigan, signature heels. She smiles, a quiet smile. A smile which says: You've got this, Stella, I believe in you. I have prepared you for this. You have the knowledge. You know the answers. You are ready. I see Giselle and Grace. They smile at me with serenity. I fumble frantically through my bag. It is today! My History A Level exam is today! I did not know. I have not prepared. I am not ready. My skin starts to itch as my chest fills with a flutter of butterflies. The exam starts at 9am. I have five minutes to learn everything we have covered in the last two years: the Cold War, the Poor Laws, Mussolini. There is not enough time and I do not know the answers.

I am going to fail my History exam. I feel the devastation of opening my results envelope to reveal: English (A), Classics (A), History (**F**). The 'F' is prominent and offensive in bold lettering. I have failed in my exams and in my life. Self-flagellation and self-deprecation take hold and overwhelm. As I wake. I am awake.

Facebook

This morning's commute takes me through the valley of the shadow of death as I witness a commuter by the name of Lucifer finger his nasal cavity as if digging for gold, explore the product of the excavation and handle the carriage poles while sniffing violently. The offending hand now rests by my shoulder as the train driver directs that we squeeze in to try and get as many people on as possible. No thank you, sir.
#TfLChronicles #thestruggleisreal
89 likes

Comments:
Sol Sai: Haven't been able to reach you this week. Hope you've seen my missed calls? Can you call me please?

I shake throughout my trial. Assault occasioning Actual Bodily Harm. Croydon Crown Court. I am prosecuting a defendant who has obvious anger management issues, a habit of swearing from the dock and a clear dislike of Serco security staff. A successful conviction. Overwhelming evidence. Nothing remarkable. By the time the jury has returned its verdict of 'guilty', I have been shaking for four days. On the inside. I wake up that way. Shaking. Something is dancing a paso doble inside my chest, an angry performance in which I am being led. It shakes violently. My heart. It is going to burst. Or my skin will rupture under the pressure building inside.

My case opening rests, double spaced in size 12 Times New Roman font, on the lectern in front of me. The letters play a game of hide and seek before my eyes; now you see us, now you don't. By the time I look from the jury back to my notes, the letters have moved around the page: word scrabble. A cruel game played by inanimate objects to trick the mind of the trembling. I lean on the point of my right heel and steady myself with the flats of my palms against the lectern to ground myself. I pour some water from the jug in front of me to soften the coarseness of my voice. My hand shakes and the water soaks my opening notes. I don't trust the letters any more. Or the words. Or even the sentences. I pause to ask the court clerk for a tissue. My eyes look to the jury without permission as the question leaves my mouth. 'Please may I trouble you for a Kleenex?' Jurors 5 and 6 look at each other and smirk. Juror 10 looks at his watch. I can't look behind counsel's row. If I do, the defendant will look me in the eye and laugh at me from the dock, a magpie perched on his head. My heel balances delicately on the soft ground. It is too delicate. It could give way at any moment. It cannot ground me. It cannot bear the weight of my body. I grip the lectern tighter for support. When I readjust, there is a mark of sweat. Handprints. It can be used as evidence against me. Evidence of insanity.

When he is convicted, the defendant condemns my spirit to hell and swears that I will know the vengeance of his brethren. Do I know what it means to 'swim with the fishes'? He curses the day I was born and advises me to sleep with one eye open. Look at his face and remember it because we will meet again—

The judge instructs the defendant to be taken down to the cells immediately. He is in no hurry to go.

When I miss my train home by two minutes, I exorcise oxygen from my lungs and tears from my eyes. On Platform 4, a magpie sits on a tree branch behind the tracks. With its grotesque voice, it calls my name: 'Stella, you and me, we are one. One for Sorrow. One and the same.' The rain falls with my tears. They meet on my cheeks in mournful company, a confluence. I am agitated but they are not. I am still but I am not.

'Good morning, Mr Magpie, how are Mrs Magpie and all the other little magpies?'

I loathe myself for asking.

'I really honour you for choosing to share your story with me today.'

I know it won't work within forty seconds of our first session. I choose Claire Benson because her eyebrows are perfection.

However, she has neither the experience nor the expertise to 'fix me'. I need help and my therapist wants to 'honour' me. Mercy. What brings me here today? Apart from a deep-seated desire to be honoured? This is an opportunity, I tell myself, and take a deep breath.

I am so scared of magpies. I see them on my morning walks with Mai and they determine whether my day is doomed or whether I can survive it. My mind agitates and my heart starts to race. I think of all the things that could go wrong in my life. When something bad happens, I feel relief. I can tick it off and stop waiting. Sometimes, I ask the air a question and wait to see how many magpies will come. I only ever see one magpie. I am always looking for two.

Claire asks if I enjoy my job. I wonder if it is possible to enjoy a job that forces you to wake up at 6am and spend your day running between a train station and a custody suite, hauling a trolley behind you, within and outside London. Perhaps there is an appeal about losing money, once you have deducted your train fare from your fee for attending court, that I am yet to discover. A joy in arriving at 9am to meet with your client, only for him to turn up after 2pm, with little regard for his personal appearance, freedom or your time.

'Can you get to Reading Crown Court for a sentence at 2pm, Miss?'

'From Cambridge Crown Court?'

I don't know, James, it's 12.40pm, and I'm still in court. Are you sending a helicopter?

'It is challenging at times but I can't imagine doing anything else.'

I spend the rest of the session looking between my chipped nail varnish and Claire's perfect eyebrows. Microbladed or pencilled? I really want to ask. They are the same shade of brown, her eyebrows and her hair.

MESCAL

We are on first name terms with the waiters and rewarded for years of patronage with strawberry daiquiris on arrival. Virgin for Farah, who doesn't drink alcohol. On the house, olé!

'The usual to start, ladies?'

'If it ain't broke, Desio . . .' Kemi is practising GCSE Spanish with alarming efficiency. The roll of her 'r's' this early in the evening encourages easy laughter from her supporting cast. Farah peruses the menu with the concentration of someone who doesn't know its contents off by heart. She wonders if she should try something different today?

'The usual please, Desio.'

I speed up the process so we can hear Farah's news, an act of mercy for everyone. Before she updates us, a ritual:

'Can you please tell us "The Tampon Story" just one more time?'

We plead with her to indulge us.

'Stella, I can't. I've got PTSD and I'm really trying to forget about it!'

Farah shudders at the memory of removing a tampon from her patient four days after insertion and on her first day in A&E. She

192

laments the fact that she is repeating the story so soon before eating. Guacamole, sour cream and salsa are exchanged across the table as we surrender to laughter.

'We've all done it, Farah.'

'I haven't!'

'Guys, toxic shock syndrome is not a joke! The smell was just – I can't.'

Platters bearing tastes of happiness and memories of friendship are placed around the table. Nachos and fajitas. Taco salad and chicken wings. Quesadillas and onion rings, coming right away!

'Another round, ladies?'

Our chorus of 'yes' serves as a reminder to Desio to keep the cocktails coming.

Alicia Keys' 'Girl on Fire' is the anthem to The Girls' lives. They are so extraordinary and accomplished. Eimear is too busy doing voyage calculations and fixing charters to plan a wedding. Sean wants to move back to Ireland to be closer to his parents. What about hers? The art of compromise. Eimear could be persuaded. Corporate life is draining. She craves something more – simple, less capitalist. She wants to ride horses, grow her own food and live near the sea. Farah is a real-life cardiothoracic surgeon-cum-superhuman. Dr Cristina Yang, eat your heart out. She dizzies us with talk of transaortic valve replacements and angioplasties. A workaholic and a perfectionist, both. The very thing that gets her out of bed in the morning keeps her awake at night. Did she do everything she could possibly do for her patient? Could she have done more? Farah doesn't rest, she reviews: every decision, every scan, every incision. She is tired and needs a break. Kemi? Kemi is firefighting, constantly. In fact, Kemi spends so much of her time firefighting, she often confuses Downing Street for a London Fire Brigade department, Catford branch. An expenses scandal? What, another one? Kemi is still struggling with

Brexit shell shock more than two years on. She wonders if, and how, she will ever recover. She feels disillusioned. She would love to have a baby but timing is everything. She has worked so hard to get to where she is. To step aside and entrust another soul with the role she has developed over the past seven years is something she battles with. Plus, she needs to lose the 12lbs she's gained from stress eating before she lets Jackson anywhere near her.

'Stella, tell us your news!'

My turn. I don't know. I have permanent imposter syndrome. I can't seem to shake it. I feel that everyone around me knows what they are doing, in life and love, apart from me. I have this permanent fear that I'm going to be exposed as a fraud and it makes me feel so fragile, you know. Sometimes, when I'm in court, I catch myself and I'm trembling. I don't think that's normal. The girls listen to me with concern on their faces. Farah thinks it sounds like I'm experiencing anxiety. I work so hard and my job is both demanding and stressful, it's completely understandable. A lot of people struggle with anxiety, I'm not alone. I haven't spoken to my GP about it. The Girls think that it would be a good idea if I did because there are so many things you can do to help with anxiety. I am 'smashing it' – life, in every way, and they are so proud of me.

My love life? It's non-existent. Do you know where the hottest guys are? HMP Brixton. I'm serious. I've seen them there. I don't know, I think I'm just more comfortable relying on myself, you know? If I let myself down, it's on me. I'll hold myself accountable and do better next time. I don't know if you can expect that from another person, can you? Maybe relationships aren't for me. Swiping left and right certainly isn't. Do you think I'm having a 'tertiary' life crisis? Is that a thing?

Desio is approaching bearing a tray of mescal shots and a shot of an alternative for Farah. She hopes it's apple juice, otherwise the colour is more than disturbing. The mescal is from the gentleman on that table. It is unsolicited, but timely, and welcomed. We toast to life and to each other. I am nominated as special envoy to express collective thanks.

'Isn't a synchronised thumbs up enough?'

He holds out his hand to meet mine as I approach his table.

'Hi, I'm Christian. Nice to meet you. I hope you're enjoying the mescal? You guys look like you know how to have fun!'

'Christian, you're an enabler! Thank you so much. Nice to meet you too.'

My objection is performative and short-lived. I agree to give him my number before my mescal-inspired walk takes me back to The Girls.

THAILAND

Facebook

If we have shared a train carriage for 30 minutes on a Monday morning and at the end of that journey I can recount details of your weekend, including quantities of alcohol consumed and accounts of sexual triumph with accuracy, something has gone terribly wrong.
#TfLChronicles #thestruggleisreal
74 likes

Sol has stopped trying to maintain a relationship with me in person and/or on social media. A case of unrequited sibling effort that would tire the most determined soul. It is not his fault, it is mine. I have not met him at the junction where siblings should meet. It is too difficult to reconcile his 'big brother' status in my mind. As an adult, Sol goes to great lengths to oversee my well-being: *Just checking in to make sure you're okay. Have you eaten, want to grab lunch? Hope you're not working too hard, Stella!* It is not his fault, but at the same time, it is. Where was his concern when I was a child and needed it? There is an elephant in the room and it is obstructive. I don't blame him when he stops trying on a daily and then weekly basis to reach out.

Save for a WhatsApp message marked 'URGENT' and followed by a phone call to let me know that his dad – our dad – whatever, is really sick, Sol and I have had little contact. Sol is flying to Ghana ASAP to see him.

It's bad, Stella, he's in hospital. Do you want me to book your ticket?

I know that Sol's question is rhetorical, and that the correct answer is 'yes', but my fingers reject the proposal with the complicity of my mind.

I can't go, Sol. I've just started a trial.

Meanwhile, my mum has discovered the capabilities of group messaging on WhatsApp. I cannot imagine that Matthew, Mark, Luke or John contemplated, when writing their Gospels, that they would reach unintended audiences in this way. Her messages are consistent in their biblical themes and endings. *Stella, I hope you are well by God's grace. When are you coming to Ghana? Your omo tuo and ground-nut soup is waiting for you. Have a blessed day. Love you.*

I read somewhere that anxiety is an inability to live in the present. I spend the months before my birthday thinking a single thought: if I go away, I will not have to acknowledge my thirty years, much less celebrate them. Farah is going to a yoga retreat in Krabi, Thailand, for two weeks. I am going with her. It's not so much a question as a direction. We both need the break. I have just watched *Eat Pray Love*, I am inspired.

'Sounds great, Farah. Let's do it.'

It's my first time in Asia. I have never seen *The Beach* with Leonardo DiCaprio and I didn't take a 'gap yah'. We arrive in Bangkok airport via Doha, where Farah declares my enthusiasm for the women's toilets extreme. The smell is surprisingly inviting, oud and musk, Farah's smell. I am fascinated by the women whose eyes catch mine in the reflection of the mirrors. Their bejewelled hands and designer shoes, a sign of otherwise hidden wealth. I envy a hand steady enough to apply such exquisite eye make-up. Farah exchanges respectful pleasantries with an older woman in Arabic as I make a note to self never to wear leggings and trainers to travel again.

We arrive at Krabi airport after twenty-four hours of travelling. We are relieved to see that the retreat is off the beaten track. Positioned high in the hills, it is open and airy. The backdrop to the yoga studio is the forest, green and vast and breathtaking. We receive a warm welcome from Tasanee, the owner of the yoga studio. She is Thai. Her spirit is warm and calm; it transfers in her hug.

'Farah, Stella? We have been expecting you! Welcome. Welcome. How was your flight?'

It is teachers' training week for local people who want to qualify as yoga instructors or learn more about the discipline. She does not expect many tourists this week. Relief, we have avoided the '18–25 gap year massive'. We need sleep before we can think of Warrior 1, 2 or 3. Our room is simple and rustic: grey walls and stone floors. My bed sits low on the ground. It is everything I need. I sleep deeply and soundly after my first Thai massage.

7am the next day. Guru Naveen sits at the front of the studio in a silent seated pose. His eyes closed, his back towards the forest, facing the class. I take a practice mat and two blocks from a neat pile at the back of the class and consider Guru Naveen's pose. My eyes wait for his to open. I am ready for practice, if not jet lagged. Guru Naveen is young and handsome. He wears a bindi on his forehead and white linen *kurta* pyjamas with brown prayer beads around his neck. His long hair is tied back in a ponytail.

Jal Neti. 'If you can brush your teeth, you can cleanse your nose.' Guru Naveen demonstrates the practice of pouring lukewarm water through one nostril as part of nasal cleansing. The water flows out of the other nostril. He explains the health benefits as he directs, 'Your turn.' I would be laughing, loudly, if I were not trying to stop myself from inhaling water as I pour it in one nostril and watch it come out of the other.

'*Jal Neti* helps us breathe the life-giving oxygen.'
One nostril is the sun, the other is the moon.

We hire a scooter after class and I conclude that Farah is best to ride it; her motor skills will be put to good use. I glance to my left and right to see toddlers and babies on the backs of bikes, their riders helmet-less. I dig deep for the courage of the three-year-old boy on the moped in front of us. He sits in front of his father. His newborn sibling is strapped to the back of his mother – with a piece of cloth. When the traffic lights turn green, they speed off in the direction of danger.

The beach is as warm as a bath and the water is the kind of turquoise you see on postcards or in dreams. It is heaven and para-dise, both. We stop for a Thai massage on the way back to evening yoga. The women are small but strong. Their touch is intuitive and hypnotising. Farah and I are lost to laughter when my masseuse lifts me off the massage table from behind – by my armpits – in a swift upward motion. *Crack crack crack* along my back. She is tiny, I am not. When I start to unfold with poorly suppressed laughter, Farah's discretion disappears completely. The nimble masseuse is laughing too when she tells me, 'Finish.' It is the best £5 I have ever spent.

Guru Naveen likes us to 'smile' during practice. I am smiling when I see two butterflies during evening class. They are beautiful. One is black with white spots, the other is orange and black. They are dancing. I fall on my thumb during asana. I am distracted by the Butterfly Dance. It hurts but it is a funny pain that makes me laugh. 'Pranaa is the life-giving oxygen,' becomes our mantra. Guru Naveen swears by it. Whenever he says it, Farah and I make eye contact from our mats and smile. After class, we see Guru Naveen eat a Snickers bar and confess our disappointment in his fallibility. We want to believe in his reverence but now we are unsure. Guru Naveen calls Farah 'Farah-Ji'. It sticks.

*

I wake up on my birthday and I know that I am where I am supposed to be. We go to the beach for morning meditation, a less perilous journey. We consider the application of Buddhist principles to life, which is so often a struggle with the self, an internal war between moving forwards and slipping backwards. We look towards the calm water and close our eyes. It is hard to tell how much time passes in that moment but there is something about the stillness of the water that helps me focus my mind on the inside part of me, my breath. I achieve a synchronicity of mind, body and breath that I have never experienced before: a birthday gift of meditation.

Farah considers how different her life could have been had she been born and raised in Saudi. Her Sudanese-Egyptian expat life affording her opportunities denied to local girls of the same age living outside the walls of her international compound. How different her life would have been had she been born to a father who did not want as much for his daughter as he did for his sons. A father who was not prepared to make personal sacrifices to guarantee it. How lucky she has been. She thinks about it often, an alternative existence: not to know a full education or profession. Her fate determined at birth by her gender. Destined to marry and raise a family. To be identified only as woman, wife, mother. I think of what else my life could have been too, without particularising. I don't want the beauty and peace of the moment to conflate with painful and suppressed memories.

I have researched ethical elephant sanctuaries in Krabi with care. I choose one which promises sanctuary for tired elephants who have been used for logging, entertainment and tourism. They are rescued and returned to their natural habitat, or so the website promises. I swiped right on a man posing with a sedated tiger once. Compelled to educate him on the cruelty of wildlife tourism, the unnecessary suffering inflicted on wild animals for human gratification. He confessed that he 'couldn't pass up the opportunity to take a photo with such a magnificent creature'. Ego in pants – deleted.

Panit is our guide at the sanctuary. He gives us blue Chinese-style overshirts to wear for the afternoon. It is hot and we don't understand why we have to add layers. I think Panit wants to make sure that he doesn't lose us. 'Suits me,' Farah declares, as she models her blue shirt. Panit clarifies that Farah is not Chinese, before sharing with us his unsolicited thoughts on visitors from China.

'They come, so many of them, and they steal.'

Farah and I question with our eyes whether we have heard Panit's hushed tones correctly. There are fourteen Chinese tourists in our group and an Irish couple, from Dublin. The Irish man shares that he is not keen on Thai food, but it's okay because there is a McDonald's around the corner from their hotel and a café that does a full English breakfast. Because that's what you come to Thailand for? Sure. We start the day with discreet laughter.

The elephants are beautiful. All female and each with her own handler. We feed them bananas. They are insatiable. We walk them to the stream and bathe them in mud. If we weren't returning elephants to their 'natural habitat', we would be at Infernos in Clapham at a foam-and-mud party. The guide explains that the mud baths keep the elephants cool. I wonder how the elephants feel about their daily activities being transformed into a tourist spectacle three times a day.

At dinner our eyes outstretch our bellies. From the Jungle Kitchen menu, we query whether there are any items we have not ordered. We go home via the Night Market – and McDonald's in honour of the man from Dublin. We eat French fries and declare shame for our souls.

At 6.30 the following morning, we rise to climb 1,237 steps to Tiger's Cave. I think of the ascent as a synonym for my life. It is really tough and my legs tremble as muscle fatigue sets in. Periodically, I pause to catch my breath. I am encouraged by people on the way up and down and by Farah. When I reach the top, I am overwhelmed by the view.

It is stunning; a panoramic view of Krabi. I am still shaking as my legs rest. A combination of the height, the lack of protection and the exposure. The Buddha at the top of Tiger's Cave is gold, glorious and ginormous. I wonder if human hands really placed him there, or whether divine intervention played a part. On the way down, we see a sign: '*If monkey wants water bottle, let him it.*' We put our bottles in our backpacks and continue our descent.

We decide to try our hands at king prawn fried rice, Thai green curry and beef massaman curry at a Thai cooking class. It is rewarding to enjoy the fruits of our labour at lunchtime but the Thai green curry is too spicy for my 'pretend' Ghanaian palate. I leave it to Farah and enjoy the beef massaman curry instead. I eat it all, like Goldilocks. That is why I have to ask Farah to pull over en route to dinner some six hours later. Someone is doing a Chinese burn on my intestines and there's a sound coming from my stomach like the last gurgles of water before it disappears down the drain. Unable to stand straight, I stagger off the moped and call on God for a miracle.

'I've got the shits!' I cry to Farah as I hobble-run to the nearest café.

My voice breaks as my insides implode and I long for the sanctuary of my own toilet. Pray urgency.

The café affords me neither the privacy nor the sound-proofing qualities that my dignity requires. I emerge an altered person: dehydrated, dazed and undone. When she tells the story, and tell it she will, Farah will explain that the expression on my face could only be described as 'shock'.

'*Khop kun ka.*' I don't know if I should thank the waitress or apologise to her.

Farah cannot stop herself. She cannot speak because she cannot breathe. She cannot breathe because she is overcome. By uncontrollable laughter. When she tries to speak, it starts again. The howling, the spluttering, the laughter.

'Don't worry, Stella. Better out than in! We'll pick up some Imodium and activated charcoal tablets from the pharmacy on the way back. That should help.'

I share my greatest fear with Farah in the form of a whispered secret.

'What if I – I'm really scared that – I'll shit myself on the seat of the moped.'

At this point, I lose Farah to a vibrating force. Her shoulders move up and down in front of me as I cling to her waist with a weakened grip. The movement of Farah's shoulders indicates, over the noise-cancelling effect of the wind, that the laughter has resumed. I clench my butt cheeks with desperation and determination, until I reach the safety and proximity of my hotel room.

A tsunami in my arse, Farah. Mercy.

BLACK MAN, BLACK WOMAN

When Christian invites me on a date, The Girls will not hear my excuses. I concede. I have no good reason to say no. I emerge from our Mexican Quartet as a solo performer when we meet for the first time in a dimly lit bar in Tower Bridge. Christian is mixed race, an English mother and Kenyan father. At thirty-nine years old, he is nine years older than me, a mature man. His eyes are beautiful and brown and almond shaped. The lighting, as if by design, highlights his cheekbones and the profile of his nose.

'You smell gorgeous.'

'Thank you, it's nice to see you again.'

His beard gently grazes my skin as he kisses me on the cheek. At six foot four, his physique is gently imposing. A slim, softly spoken giant. He is intelligent and gentlemanly.

Christian lives in Islington, North London, but grew up in Brentwood.

'An Essex boy?' I would never have guessed.

There is no need for me to visit Brentwood if I have not already been. There is nothing there for me. He goes back occasionally to visit his dad but doesn't stay for too long if he can help it. He has a sister in Australia. He's not sure that a black man has any business in Australia, but he has promised to visit next year. He recently lost his mum to cancer. They were going to go together. His parents divorced when he was about eight years old.

Christian works in finance but was recently made redundant. A numbers man. He played the guitar once upon a time and football but he hasn't picked up a guitar in years, or run the full length of a pitch, come to think of it.

'What about you?'

My family is from Ghana. My parents have retired there, separately – they're divorced – that is enough information for now. I have an older brother, Sol. He works in tech. I'm a barrister, born and raised in South London, as if that alters the fact in some attractive way. His ex-girlfriend lived in Camberwell. He knows South London fairly well, wouldn't get lost there. We disagree about which side of the river is best.

'The thing about North London is everything is in walking distance. Once you're there, it's all on your doorstep.'

'What currency do you use in Islington?'

I like it when he laughs. He has perfect teeth and a beautiful smile. I am relaxed in his company and want to know him more. We take turns to buy drinks.

Can I cook? I'm embarrassed to say no. Well, not really. I don't starve but I don't like to chop onions either. Christian laughs. He loves to cook. Have I been to Ghana? Yes, but not since I was a child. I would love to go again. Do I like spicy food? I'm embarrassed to say no again. I've just never built up a tolerance to it. Am I sure I'm Ghanaian? I don't even know. Christian loves spicy food. He cooks with chillies and scotch bonnet. He thinks my taste buds can adapt.

'Have you been to Kenya?'

'A couple of times, yes. I would love to spend some more time there. It has the most beautiful landscapes I've ever seen and everyone knows that East Africa trumps West.'

'You want North London *and* East Africa?'

I like it when we laugh together.

We walk along the river and admire the skyline.

'What's your favourite bridge in London, Stella?'

We take turns to navigate London's bridges in conversation: Chelsea, Waterloo, Blackfriars, Southwark, Westminster—

He leans against the black rails that separate us from the water and pulls me towards him, with gentle strength. His kiss is sweet and soft. His energy, enigmatic and inviting. Star sign? Virgo.

'You don't believe in all that, do you?'

'I don't read my weekly horoscope, no. But if you asked me to describe myself, I would say I'm a typical Taurus.'

'What's a typical Taurus like then?'

'You'll have to do some research, Christian.'

'Okay, I will.'

We meet in Borough for our second date and enjoy samples of cheese, bread and charcuterie as we wander through the market. We share a love of all things truffle and visit stalls offering samples: truffle oil, truffle honey, truffle crisps. We share a truffle-infused kiss near the market's exit, and promise to come back for more. Over a drink – Malbec for me, Estrella for him – we discuss childhood experiences in more detail. I dance around the subject of family. We both do. He follows my lead, I think.

I'm really lucky; I don't think I've experienced much overt racism. I guess the language used to describe black women irks me. We can never be accepted as 'assertive', we have to be 'aggressive'. That's tiring. On the other hand, I've probably benefited from attempts to diversify the Bar and I am grateful for it but it can come at a price. I don't want people to think that the only reason I got a scholarship to study the Bar Vocational Course is because I'm black, you know? I do think that being 'different' in a profession that is dominated by white middle-class, middle-aged men can offer opportunities to showcase your talent in a unique way. Intrigue in difference doesn't have to be a bad thing; it can be offensive or inoffensive. If it's born out of inoffensive curiosity, a hunger for knowledge and the broadening of horizons, you can engage with it and let it work in your favour, you know? My primary and secondary schools were so culturally diverse that racial difference was celebrated. That's what I grew up with so that's what I'm used to. Until I went to university, where I was the only black girl in a hall of two hundred people. I definitely found that tough.

Christian's experience is completely different. His mum was an accountant and worked hard to move his family to a nice area of Brentwood. His dad didn't work. Essex was tough in those days. Christian was one of three or four black kids in his school, including his sister. There might have been five Asian kids in total. He was very aware of being tall and black and different. As a young adult, it wasn't uncommon for Christian to go to the pub with his friends to watch a football game and hear them make racist jokes in his presence. It's a sobering moment when you realise that the people you thought were your friends are casual racists. Comfortable enough to make monkey noises or use the 'N' word around you to express their dislike of a black player from the opposite team. You're all right, Christian, you're only half. He recalls that, in the early eighties, the term 'half-caste' was accepted and explores, in pedagogical form, the history and use of the word. He stiffens as he speaks.

Christian identifies as mixed race and black and English and Kenyan. I identify as Black British or British Ghanaian, not English. I am a Londoner, a South Londoner. Being a South Londoner is its own identity, separate and distinct from being a North Londoner. Ha. We talk about the use of the words 'black' and 'coloured'. I can lead on this subject. I tell him about my very first temping job, working at a marketing agency in Clapham, aged sixteen.

Within the first twenty minutes of my arrival, the director enters the accounts office where I am trying with newbie nerves to settle. He has with him a boxer dog. His introduction is brief and direct.

'Hi. I'm Viv. You're not scared of dogs, are you?'

'No. Not really.' I lied.

'Because most blacks are. Terrified.'

And with that, Viv heads upstairs with Bess the boxer, pleased with my answer: an exception to the rule. The room has gone quiet. Gail is the Head of Accounts and HR. She was doing a great job of settling me in – before Viv arrived. Now, she appears mortified and in search of words which escape her.

'I am so sorry. I don't know why he said that. He is the least racist person you will ever meet. I mean, his wife is black. A beautiful black lady. Beautiful. Lovely long neck. Beautiful long neck. So elegant.'

Gail moves her hands up and down the length of her neck to demonstrate just how long Viv's wife's beautiful neck is as I start to wonder if Viv is, in fact, married to a giraffe.

'A beautiful African lady. From Trinidad.'

I am laughing on the inside. Poor Gail, she is flushing with embarrassment. But I have confidence, if Gail can do accounts, she can familiarise herself with the continent of Africa and the islands of the Caribbean. I am grateful when she suggests a cup of tea before we talk through the morning's tasks.

I think about the dogs I watched from a distance as a child during my visit to Ghana, quietly intrigued, but too scared to approach. Ewurasi's dog, Otto, a yard dog. Allowed in the house? Never. Do Something made it his business to shoo Otto away if he was ever curious enough to come within a three-metre radius of me. 'Go-way-you. Foolish dog.' Ekow's warning ringing loudly in my ears: 'If he licks you, you'll get rabies. I swear!'

'Ekow, don't be so silly. Do you hear?'

Auntie Maame's reassurance was of limited effect. I wouldn't touch Otto, and I wish Ewurasi wouldn't either.

*

Over the next six weeks, Viv stops for a chat every time he walks past my desk. I am charmed by his dog, stroking her gently whenever she is near. He has three children in their thirties from a previous marriage and a seventeen-year-old son with his wife. I learn that while she is indeed from Trinidad and incredibly beautiful, Viv's wife is not a giraffe. Viv loves Trinidad and is going to retire in Tobago. He shows me pictures of his family with pride. His son is mixed race, a handsome boy called Jivaan.

In contrast, when an investigating officer on one of my cases refers to charging 'the coloured fella', I let him know, without hesitation, 'Nobody really uses that term anymore.' For somebody who has spent over thirty years of his professional career saying 'Suspect: IC3 male' into his walkie talkie, he ought to know better and I'm concerned that he doesn't. Mark blushes when I correct him. My intention is not to embarrass. I tell myself that if I had been older, I would have gently corrected Gail. But I *am* older when my instructing solicitor tells me that her Australian boyfriend is 'always trying to act black'. In fact, I am twenty-eight years old but I don't challenge her. It will always bother me. The fact that I never asked, 'What exactly do you mean, "trying to act black"?'

My phone vibrates as I share my experiences with Christian. It's Kemi.

Can't stop listening to Beyoncé's Homecoming album!!!

Kemi is the Champion of the Black Woman. It does not surprise her to learn that the attractive blonde-haired, blue-eyed associate is invited to new client meetings time and time again. While the black associate, arguably more capable, is confined to the back office. Is her natural hair, neatly styled in twists, 'corporate' enough for this environment? She struggles to get her 'break' and works longer hours to prove her worth. Kemi is the Advocate of the darkest-skinned black woman, overlooked by the Other and her own kind. The first to question why black footballers and rappers and actors appear to unanimously reject black women. It's not an opposition to mixed-race relationships but it's not a coincidence. It's a legitimate question: why are we not good enough? Why are we so undesired? Why would we only be 'more attractive' if we had lighter skin, or straighter hair?

Kemi is the Condemner of Colourism within black society. And do not get her started on the 'fetishism' of black women.

'Do you know that black women receive more left-swipes on dating apps than any other racial demographic? Black women and Asian men?'

I don't know but I'm not surprised to hear it.

'Don't lust after me because I am black.'

'And don't undress me with oversexualised eyes. I am not a pros-titut-a, grazie very much.'

Italy is intense. We have both experienced it.

'I love black women.' Yes, but why?

Kemi's delivery cannot but cause laughter. She will call a spade a spade. And guess what, she will not be responsible for 'educating' ignorant people on the subject of racism. Have you heard of Google? Use it. She will probably-definitely give you 'side eye' if you use an expression like 'caramel complexion'.

Kemi and I agree that being a black Londoner, second generation African or Caribbean, is a unique experience and a blessing. Imagine if our parents had migrated to Spain instead? We are not blind to the condition of black people when we travel to Europe. We note it, naturally. The African street sellers in Paris lining the Seine and the Champs-Élysées. Outside the Musée d'Orsay. Bagging up Eiffel Tower trinkets on sight or sound of a police officer and running for their *liberté, égalité, fraternité.* The conflict between a sympathetic smile and avoiding eye contact that we struggle with internally. I don't want or need to buy that trinket but I feel so bad for you and the position you are in. I wonder what you were before you migrated here. I want more for you and I know you want more for yourself. We want to see people who look like us, who dress like us, who have jobs like us. We want to see local black people who can afford to take weekend city breaks like us. We smile at the 'Others', the non-blacks who just can't figure us out. Who are we? What do we do for a living? And how can we afford to share this exquisite rooftop view with them, drinking cocktails and champagne at sunset?

'That's why I like Lisbon. I feel like I see the equivalent of me there.'

'Yeah. Me too.'

Perhaps I am too quick to say that I haven't experienced racism. Whatever my experience, I know that as an educated black Londoner, I am lucky.

I pick up my phone to respond to Kemi.

OMG I've watched the Netflix doc three times!!! Love it!!!

I agree to organise another date.

'I'm thinking something cultured?'

He likes the sound of it.

We meet outside the Tate Modern for our date. It is 6pm and the weather is respectfully mild. Christian is punctual and effortlessly cool in a cotton pink shirt and jeans. He is surprised when we walk past and not into the gallery. The sun catches his face as he searches mine for clues and I feel something inside me dance with joy. The South Bank is a hive of activity and provides a romantic backdrop to our early evening walk. We settle at a bar with outdoor seating and pause to take in our surroundings and each other. I study the patterns of his irises in between sips of wine. When our knees touch under the table, he doesn't move, nor do I.

En route to our destination, we walk past a mobile bungee jump and admire a thrill seeker reaching for the sky.

'No chance!'

'Not after that wine!'

We stop outside Shakespeare's Globe theatre.

My smile reflects his as he leans in to take a selfie of us. Above, a sign says, 'A Midsummer Night's Dream'. It is lit by purple and blue and green lights.

CHRISTIAN

When we are not together, he calls me every day and messages. When we are not together, I know that it will not be more than two days before I see him again. He likes dogs; he loves Mai. His hello kiss is always soft and welcoming. It feels like home.

Christian loves to cook. His kitchen in Islington is well stocked and stores spices that I have never even heard of. He grows fresh herbs in his garden: coriander, basil, oregano, mint and thyme. They are well watered and cared for. He is happiest when he is cooking. He is experimental and considerate of my food intolerances. Over time, we learn that when I say 'I don't eat' something, what I actually mean is: I have never tried it, but I don't think I would like it. Or the last time I tried it I was a child, and I don't think I liked it. Or I don't like the way it looks. He has gradually introduced the offending foods into my diet and I have discovered that mustard is not so 'disgusting'; cabbage isn't 'the most boring vegetable ever'; and chilli can be tolerated in small quantities, *very* small quantities.

Curry is his signature dish and I know that I am in for a treat when he opens the front door and the smell wraps itself around my nostrils.

I call him Maharaja when he is creating a culinary masterpiece. He laughs. He is going to teach me how to make a curry from scratch. It's not as complicated as I think.

'They couldn't make it better on Brick Lane, Christian.'

To me, his food is always divine. He is a harsher critic. If he thinks that something he has made is not up to scratch, he will become sullen and self-flagellating: 'It's not my best.' 'It should have stayed in longer.' 'It's not as tender as I wanted it.' No matter what he says, it always tastes great to me. He teaches me the word 'umami'. I use my new word every day.

'Christian, this is so umami!'

He laughs. I love to watch him when he cooks. We play music and dance in between chopping and stirring and kissing. The first time he asks me to help by chopping an onion, I freeze. I am ashamed to admit it but I have never actually chopped an onion before. Onions make my eyes water – and I don't like to handle raw meat. No is not an option. What kind of Ghanaian girl am I? I don't even know. He shows me how.

He navigates my kitchen with confidence and ease. And over time, the ingredients in my cupboard grow to mirror his. Before long, my interest is piqued. I surprise him with pancakes for breakfast on a Saturday morning. Sweet with sugar and lemon; savoury with ham, cheese and tomatoes. He loves my 'Ghanaian omelette'. It is absolutely umami.

'What makes it Ghanaian then?'

'Well, I'm Ghanaian and I made it!'

I am becoming a bona fide sous chef.

We prefer a homemade roast to a pub roast because our collaborative effort produces delicious results at a fraction of the price. Pork belly, with crackling, is our favourite and we are partial to a generously seasoned chicken wing. He removes the bones from each wing before handing it to me. It makes them easier to eat. That is so sweet,

Chrissy. He doesn't cook with much chilli these days. He doesn't want it to be too spicy for me. There is always yogurt on standby. In case my mouth catches fire and we need to make my curry milder. We enjoy lazy Sundays and each other.

It feels really nice when we bump into Christian's best friend, Bobby, and his girlfriend, Zara, on an afternoon walk with Mai. After introductions, Christian suggests that we go for a drink. I feel like a meaningful part of his life.

'I can't wait for Croatia! Have you bought your ticket? It will be great to have a girlfriend for company. You can see what it's like when they get together!'

I can't bring myself to tell Zara, over a glass of sparkling wine, that Christian hasn't mentioned his holiday plans to me let alone invited me to go with him. Maybe it's too soon? Or perhaps he has bought my ticket and he is going to surprise me? It's hard to concentrate after Zara mentions Croatia.

'I can't wait either,' I agree. I top up my glass from the bottle and try my best to ignore the knot in the bottom of my stomach.

'Nothing's confirmed, babe,' Christian reassures me, with mild irritation. 'Bobby suggested it, but nothing is finalised. We've not even discussed dates.'

Zara is excitable and the only reason Christian tolerates her is because she's Bobby's girlfriend. If he goes to Croatia, then of course I am coming with him. The fact that he hasn't mentioned it to me is not a reflection of the way he feels about us.

'Shall we invite Kemi and Jackson to come too?'

'To come to where?'

'To Croatia? It will be so much fun! I think you, Jackson and Bobby will get on really well, what do you think?'

'I think that makes no sense. I don't know Kemi or Jackson. They're your friends, not mine, and it's not your holiday to be inviting people on.'

I'm sorry I suggested it, I didn't think it through. I don't want him to think that I don't know his likes and dislikes, because I do. I feel stupid for speaking without thinking.

He cooks, I wash up, that's our deal. When the sun is shining, we sit outside in the garden, on the wooden pallet furniture he made a few summers ago. Two benches that can seat four to six people and a table in between. His garden is decorated with an array of colourful flowers and plants: geranium, rhododendron, lavender and more. I love sitting outside with him and eating our lunch with the smell of jasmine around us.

Christian's living room is home to around eight carefully potted green plants, both large and small. He is proud of them and cares for them lovingly. He waters them daily, tends to their leaves and moves them around to ensure they get the best light. In the corner, there is a guitar, the one he used to play. He takes it out at my request and dusts it down. When he strums Bob Marley's 'Redemption Song', my ears recognise it as the most beautiful song they have ever heard. Maybe that can be 'our song'.

At my flat, Christian helps me to transform my garden space.

'It's got so much potential, you just have to put some time and energy into it.'

He fills the holes in the grass that Mai created with soil and sows grass seed on top. I blame the foxes, like every proud mother would. Together, we track the sun spots of the garden and decide where is best to plant new flowers. He shows me how to train my climbing rose; it will flower beautifully in the summer, he thinks. We treat ourselves to barbecue dinners in the evenings and enjoy the solar lights when they come on. Whoever is up first makes the tea. Christian doesn't have a sweet tooth, but he does like a teaspoon of sugar in his tea – and me, he likes me, a lot. As my garden fills with flowers and my cupboards fill with food, so too does my heart begin to fill with love.

*

When I meet Christian, something special happens inside me. My blinking becomes slow and gentle like the waves of a calm sea and the butterflies that normally live inside my chest, frantic and agitated, are still and quiet. They are well fed and happy. The sun is shining inside me. My heart is full.

The special thing that happens inside me when I meet Christian makes me long for my mum. I wish for her that she had known this feeling with my dad. I feel cheated for her that she didn't. I want to tell her how nice it is and how good it feels. Perhaps she would have known it had she married one of the doctors at 37 Military Hospital. I am sorry that Papa persuaded her to leave Ghana and opportunity for London and my dad. Did they even have a song? Ever since I met her, I have longed for Nurse Florence to be my mum. Nurse Florence filled me with wonder and awe. She used the imperative when she spoke and commanded respect. Nurse Florence would have stood up to my dad. She wouldn't have let him terrorise her life and mine. I wonder if she knows that he is sick in hospital. I wonder if she cares. Should I?

I feel guilt wash over me in waves and reach for my phone. I need to tell my mum how sorry I am. I want to tell her that I have met someone, a man called Christian, and that he is amazing. He is nothing like Dad. I want to tell her how happy he has made me; happier than I have ever been. I want to tell her about love and what it feels like. My thumb hovers over the green dial between fear and bravery. It terminates the call before a connection can be made. I seek the comfort of my laptop and the security of its keypad. It is easier to write it than to say it. Sol says she checks her emails regularly.

Hi Mum,

Thank you for the pics. The garden looks beautiful. I'm sure the flowers bring a smile to your face every day. Auntie Maame's birthday lunch looked like a lot of fun. How many people came in the end? It was nice of you to host it although it looks like you ordered enough food to feed the five thousand! I know I promised to try and come to Ghana next month, but I think I am going to have to postpone my trip. Work is just so busy right now and my diary is full of back-to-back trials for the foreseeable. It's a good thing, it means I have a busy practice. I know you were looking forward to seeing me. Next year, I promise.

Love,

Stella x

PS Retirement in Ghana clearly suits you, your skin is glowing!

It is easier to write the words that my fingers want to type than those that my heart wants to say. I attach a picture of my garden in the afternoon sun and press send.

The special thing that happens inside me when I meet Christian makes me wonder what guilt and anger and happiness make when you put them together and mix them up.

LOVE

I am rummaging through my bag outside Angel tube station, looking for my Oyster card, when it happens. It is Sunday evening and the dark clouds have given way to gentle showers. Christian picks up my fallen keys from the floor as I find my Oyster card in my pocket. The hazards of changing coats and bags, a woman's prerogative of the first-world variety. Christian's hand lingers in mine with the keys and he brings his right hand to join his dominant left, holding my one hand in his both. We are an obstacle to North London's Sunday evening tube users. Hovering, inconveniently, at the entrance to the station, oblivious to the blockage we are causing.

'You're a stranger to a hard day's work, aren't you?' His hands are so soft. 'Don't go.' He smiles as he talks.

I search his eyes to understand whether he is asking a question or making a statement.

'I can't stay tonight because I'm in court tomorrow but you can come to mine if you want?'

'Move in with me, Stella. I want you to move in with me. You and Mai. What do you think?'

What do I think? I think that God is merciful and good and kind. I think that He prepared me for this moment. That if I hadn't known desperation and sadness for so much of my life, I wouldn't know the feeling of true joy and the beauty of this moment. I know what it is to have sunlight inside you, to shine from the inside out. I know how it feels for the butterflies that live in your chest to be banished to some faraway land. I know what it is to walk with a pair of magpies-cum-angels, one on each shoulder. Two for joy. Two for joy. He is wonderful and gorgeous and kind. And he is mine. I think I will rent out my flat and move in with my boyfriend. I like the way it sounds. That's when it happens. That's when I know that I am lovable, loved and in love.

I arrive in Barnsbury, Islington, just after 2pm on a Saturday afternoon in June. Christian helps me unload my suitcase and boxes and hopes and dreams into his now familiar house. Mai is not to be forgotten. She greets him with habitual happiness and dances a canine dance of joy that looks like dressage. The joy is reciprocated. Christian kisses Mai on the forehead and smothers her in love. He takes her lead as we head inside.

'Mmm, something smells good.'

'I hope you're hungry, sweets!'

We smile in symmetry.

He holds me sweetly as we lay down to sleep, drawing me close and wrapping his arms around my body. Our first night in our new chapter. I don't tell Christian about the butterflies in my chest, the ones that flapped their wings wildly. I don't tell him about David Attenborough or my atrophied wings, because I have developed muscles and I have learned how to fly. He is proof; we are. It feels good to know, after thirty years, that good things can happen to me.

MEETING IN THE MIDDLE

Bernard Park is a lovely park, eight minutes away, where Mai makes new friends and plays. Christian and Mai are cultivating a close relationship and deep love. Mai adores Christian because his hand span covers her entire belly and because he creates exciting treasure hunts for her around the house and garden with treats. They sleep together and eat together, Christian and Mai, Mai and Christian. During the week, we take turns to walk her. On weekends, we go for walks together, like a family.

The Girls miss me now that I am north of the river. Who even are you, Stella? And when can we meet Christian properly? I miss them, of course I do. But I am happy and there are no greater advocates for my happiness than The Girls. I have longed for this moment. To be one half of a whole. To wake up with a person I love and to share my life with him. To live together, cook together and plan our future together. They have longed for it for me. They miss me but they could not be happier for me.

Christian is tolerant of my bad habits: working late in the evening, every evening, and tossing and turning in bed at night. His daytime

TV favourites are BBC news, sports and cooking programmes. I think he should apply to *MasterChef* because he is so talented in the kitchen. He enjoys playing games on his Xbox during the day and does not like to be interrupted by me mid-game. It is 'selfish' of me to think that as soon as I take a break from work, or finish for the day, he is just going to be 'available'. He could benefit from some structure to his day. A job would provide that but he is taking his time to find the right role and that is important. There is no point rushing into the wrong thing. At about 6pm, Christian and I need to discuss dinner plans. Otherwise, I will get home from Chambers at about 7pm, exhausted and hungry, and if the first thing that comes out of my mouth is 'What's for dinner?' that can sound 'demanding' and 'entitled'. I'm sorry. I didn't mean for it to sound that way. Christian doesn't mind cooking and eating late. He can eat dinner at about 9 or 10pm. I find it harder, especially if my Addison's is playing up, but that doesn't mean I can't just wait. He is the one cooking, after all.

Christian is a procrastinator. He talks about it jokingly but he is serious. A master at putting things off; it's actually a skill. It means he lives in the present and doesn't worry about things that haven't happened yet – or things that have, things he can't change. I should try it sometime. I'm getting better at that but it takes practice. He endears himself to me when he expresses anxiety about getting a job. Procrastination has delayed this by some eighteen months. I try to imagine him as a Wolf of Wall Street and his many rebirths. Goldman Sachs Christian. Christian the Guitarist. Unemployed Christian. It is not my business to ask him about the results of his job search on a daily or weekly basis. He is financially savvy and comfortable and, putting it bluntly, his finances are not my concern. I'm sorry. I wasn't trying to pry. He pays his bills and I respect that. Neither of us is motivated by money. I am motivated by happiness and peace. I think he is motivated by a desire to be free from the control of any person or thing.

*

He doesn't like talking about past relationships. He doesn't see the point.

'How does that add value to the present or future?'

My mum would agree. I can think of a few ways, but I don't say them.

As soon as I get home from Chambers, I take a shower. There is something important about it, the act of washing away a stressful day and welcoming the evening. Around the same time, Christian opens his first can of San Miguel. It's his way of winding down and relaxing, our 'his and hers' downtime. Over the course of the evening, Christian drinks four to six 500ml cans of beer. He drinks because he wants to, not because he has to; there's a difference. He will open a bottle of wine, for me. I don't drink white, or at all most evenings, especially if I have to work late or have an early start in the morning, but it's there if I want it. Not tonight but thank you for thinking of me. Christian ends up drinking between three quarters and the entire bottle, alternating between wine and beer. He's not drunk. He knows how to handle his drink, he's a grown man. Who am I, the Beer Police? I head to bed at about 11pm.

Christian normally comes to bed between two and three in the morning. After he has finished watching TV, playing games on his Xbox and drinking. He tries to be as quiet as possible when he comes upstairs. He is incredibly thoughtful in that sense. He will use the light on his phone and not the light on the side table or the main light to get ready for bed. He doesn't want to wake me. I will wake, naturally, but I can fall back to sleep. Don't worry, it's fine. He will kiss me when he gets into bed. A precursor to sex. If I don't look at the time, I feel less tired when my alarm clock goes off in the morning and I have to get up for work; it's a psychological thing. I want him to go to sleep happy and to have sweet dreams.

Mai sleeps in her bed in our room but she will invariably climb onto the bed every morning. When he wakes up, Christian will invariably decide that we shouldn't allow her on the bed. He says that every morning, while cuddling Mai within an inch of her life. I leave them in a tender embrace as I head off for court or Chambers.

I am working from home and the morning has escaped me the way it does when I have so much work to do and not enough time. I have left my breakfast bowl in the sink. I will wash it when I take a break. I'll be done in half an hour. Christian would rather I washed it now. It's a bowl, for goodness sake. How long is it going to take to wash up? It's not exactly the kind of thing you need to soak, is it? Christian is not as angry about the fact that I have left the bowl unwashed in the sink, as he is about my 'attitude'. Is he supposed to wait until I take my break before he can use his kitchen? I need to wash up so he can make lunch.

'I am going to, I promise. I've just got to send this Advice off quickly. Can you give me fifteen minutes?'

He cannot make lunch if there is no space to cook. Can I think of someone other than myself? What is he supposed to do? Christian speaks in a tone that I don't recognise and at a volume that is new. His face takes on an alien expression as he addresses the issue of dirty dishes. His gaze does not break as it holds mine, his eyelashes do not blink. I mark my place in my papers and make my way to the kitchen sink. His eyes follow me. I make a mental note never to leave dishes in the sink ever again.

Now, after every meal, and as soon as the last piece of cutlery is laid to rest on its plate, I stand to clear the table. I wash the plates, the cutlery and the cooking utensils. I do not leave them in the sink to decorate it or to let them soak. It is only fair after he has spent so much time and effort cooking for us both. If, for any reason, I am too tired to wash the dishes straight away, because I've had a really long day or because my Addison's is playing up, I tell him that I will wash them first thing in the morning. So he is not surprised if he goes to the kitchen before he goes to bed and finds dirty dishes in the sink. I don't want him to get that angry again, not over dirty dishes.

We don't argue about serious things. But our arguments can be serious.

'If you take my charger when my phone is charging, can you put it back on charge when you've finished using it!'

It's not a question and it's not something I did on purpose. I checked his phone before I unplugged it. It was on eighty-seven per cent battery, mine was on fourteen per cent. I am annoyed at myself for leaving my charger in Chambers. I meant to put his phone back on charge but I got distracted by a work call.

'I didn't not put it back on purpose. I forgot, sorry.'

His anger is loud. His reaction, disproportionate. I think I made a mistake when I said, 'It's not a big deal.'

'Why do you have to have a response to that? Can't you just say sorry? You are clearly in the wrong.'

When he storms upstairs to our bedroom, I follow him. That is a mistake. When Christian is angry, he does not want to be followed. He does not want to speak to me or even see me. I should not push him to try and engage in conversation because that is not what he wants. What he wants is to be left alone.

'Get out of my face.'

He shuts the door in mine.

Sometimes, when he is not angry any more, we try to understand how we managed to get to such a terrible place so quickly. Christian says that living with another person is not easy. He knows he can be moody but my actions are antagonistic and do not help the situation. Overall, he thinks we get on eighty-five per cent of the time and that I am amazing. He is happy that we are living together. He couldn't ask for anything more. He has a temper and when he is angry, he needs to be left alone. I need to give him that space and not follow him around the house when he has asked for time to himself. He doesn't want to say or do anything in anger. It's really important that I respect that and give him space to cool down. I try to take it on board. I am happy we are together too but I think we need to work on our communication.

I try to explain what I meant in Dirty-dishes-gate and Charger-gate. I am very aware that I am in his house and that he probably has established ways of doing things. I don't want to interfere with that. I would never deliberately set out to upset or irritate him. It's really important for me to resolve conflict as soon as possible. I hate the feeling of knowing that he is angry or upset with me, especially when we are in the same house. I only followed him upstairs to make peace. I thought that would make the situation better. I did not want to make it worse. I would never want that.

We are working hard to meet in the middle. When I take a break from work and want to speak to Christian, I check that he is not in the middle of his Xbox game before I start to speak. If he is, I wait for the game to be over first. I know the game is over when it makes a jingle sound. Sometimes, I forget to wait and talk to him without looking up or checking first. When he ignores my question, I know that he is still playing the game and that he has not been listening to me. I pause and wait and try again. It is hard to talk to him with these rules. He promises that he will make an effort not to play in the evenings or on weekends. I really want him to meet my friends. He will, soon. He promises.

In the middle of the night, I am convinced, as I stir, that I cannot breathe. Perhaps I am running to the bus stop from Nursery Road, trying but failing to get to my haven. Or arriving at Sudbourne to find that my History A Level exam starts in five minutes and I am unprepared. Perhaps there is an F grade among my A Level results and it is the end of the world. Or maybe I am falling in a bus off a bridge.

'I can't breathe. I can't breathe!'

He holds me close and tells me, 'You're okay. You're okay, I'm here.'

I fall back to sleep in his arms, safe and still and breathing.

PICKING FLOWERS

KNOCKING

Dearly beloved, we are gathered here today to join this man and this woman in holy matrimony.

Here.

Electric gates open slowly to Sienna Bannerman's family home in Trasacco Valley, Accra. The grounds are breathtaking: a swimming pool. A fleet of cars. A perfectly manicured lawn. We are welcomed with glasses of chilled champagne by well-briefed ushers in *batakari*.

'Hello, please. You are welcome.' A welcome reception before the ceremony begins.

We.

My mum, Auntie Maame and Auntie Baaba. Ghana's answer to Destiny's Child. Coordinated within an inch of their lives in *kente* and lace *kaba*, beautifully sewn. Soundtrack: 'Independent Women'. In green lace, my mum assumes the inimitable role of Beyoncé. Auntie Maame and Auntie Baaba complete the trio in complimentary blue. From my WhatsApp'd measurements, Ewurasi has had sewn for me a beautiful lace cloth. Off the shoulder. Cinched waste.

She has chosen a one-shoulder number for herself, for the sake of her breasts, the buoyancy of which her two children have robbed her. We wear matching green lace and gold *geles* on our heads for extra glam.

'It's all about the *gele*!' Ewurasi assures me.

I am fortified to have Christian by my side. He embraces his African roots in a tailored shirt and trousers. Green to match my cloth and trimmed at the collar and wrists in *kente*. Ewurasi is beside herself with excitement. When are Christian and I getting married? What colour will the Maid of Honour wear? Can he pay the bride price?

'*Ayefro dondo!*'

I pinch her to make her lower her voice.

'Ewurasi, he can hear you! And the only wedding bells ringing are Sol's!'

'Okay, okay, but let's discuss locations later.' She's thinking a destination wedding.

'I've missed you so much!'

'Me too-ooo, me too!'

We are laughing and hugging and kissing at the joy of being reunited.

Christian is being mobbed by Auntie Maame, Auntie Baaba and my mum. Overcome by his aesthetics and the fact of my good fortune in finding him: *Akwaaba!* You are welcome! So handsome. Fine Boy. Our cloth suits you nicely. It's a sign. You are one of us. Kenya? We will go with you, God willing. Within minutes of meeting him, he is elevated to the status of deity. You are welcome, you are welcome, you are welcome.

My mum's eyes tell me that she is heartened to see me with Christian. To know that I have found my person and my peace. Her smile tells me that her prayers for me have been answered. She is thankful to God that we have met and that ours is a union of love. She understands without need for words that Christian makes me happy.

'That's why he's here. I wanted you to meet him.'

In her role of Mother of the Groom, my mum is the happiest I have ever seen her.

Gathered.

Finlay is wearing a tailored tuxedo: a white jacket with black trousers and a black bow tie. The lapels of his jacket are made from *kente*. Modern with a traditional twist. He personifies sophistication and masculine charm. Finlay has the gait of a man who has never questioned his appeal to the opposite sex. He wears black suede shoes, sockless. And sunglasses by Tom Ford. I hear Alessandro before I see him. In the middle of an excited crowd. His Ghanaian-Italian accent is distinct and intriguing. Alessandro greets his friends in the way Ghanaian men do; their fingers click when they shake hands. He gesticulates in an animated fashion when he talks. When I hear him speak Pidgin, I know that Ghana is his home. Bea is confident and glamorous. She navigates the Bannermans' manicured lawn on the tiptoes of red-soled heels. A fitted dress. Neon orange. Strapless. She commands attention and is comfortable with the gaze of a crowd. Her ears are decorated with diamonds, of significant carats, four on each side. Her smile is beautiful and brilliant white. It belongs on the cover of a magazine. I know them all. From their pictures and my dreams.

Mr and Mrs Bannerman wear the smile of proud parents who know that their only daughter has found her forever love in a kind and loving and wonderful man. They are dressed in matching *kente* in the dominant colour of blue. His and hers. The tan lines on Mrs Bannerman's shoulders and chest, a testament to the years she has spent by her husband's side in Ghana. A faithful wife. A peaceful marriage. An example of love. They walk together across the lawn and greet their guests, one at a time. They save their warmest welcome for Sol's family.

Uncle Papafio has arrived, in his eleventh month of pregnancy. He positions himself besides the door from which the canape-wielding waitresses emerge. A Star beer in hand. He greets me enthusiastically before interrupting his interrogation of my marital status with the consumption of a spring roll. I greet my aunties and uncles, maternal and paternal, before we take our seats. We are plenty in number.

Holy matrimony.

We are here for the business of 'knocking': for the Sai family to introduce their son to the Bannerman family. And to make them formally aware that Sienna and Sol are 'intending to date'. It is irrelevant that Sol and Sienna have lived together for the past two years and enjoyed a committed relationship for six. A minor detail. A nod to tradition. A Ghanaian custom preceding marriage. Traditionally performed among family members but to a larger audience for the inclusion of Sol and Sienna's international guests.

I am watching the sunlight dance across the swimming pool and sun loungers when Finlay approaches from behind. Sol would like me to come inside briefly. Can I spare a few minutes? He holds out his arm so I can link mine in his to navigate the grass and gravel pathway into the Bannerman palace that they call home. To see Sol standing at the top of the spiral staircase is to know a new feeling in my heart. He is wearing *kente* of white and gold in large checked squares carefully draped over his left shoulder. His right arm, evidence of his commitment to CrossFit. Sol wears white shorts, *chokoto*. And a neatly trimmed beard. In *oheneba* slippers, he has transformed into somebody's real-life prince. My brother, Sol. The feeling – it is pride. I am so proud of him. To hear him speak is to feel our roles reversed for the first time in my life. I have not seen Dad yet or Uncle Nii Ade but they are probably here by now. The first words Sol speaks come out in a high-pitched whisper, as if his voice is breaking, all over again. We aren't going to start the 'knocking' without them, don't worry. Sol clarifies that Auntie Coumba will not be attending, from which I gather his previous reference to 'problems' between her and Dad have not been resolved. I am grateful for the update because I have no desire for my mum and I to lay eyes on her for the first time at my brother's wedding. Sol looks down onto the landing agitated with concern. I understand that he needs me today.

'It looks incredible outside, Sol. I'm so excited for you.' I squeeze his hand before returning to the reception, passing Italian marble floors, suspended chandeliers and gold brushed coffee tables on my way.

We have gathered. For Sol and Sienna. All one hundred and eighty of us.

Beloved.

Christian performs the role of consort in a way that helps me walk with a straight back and confident gait. His presence encourages intrusive questions regarding my body clock and fertility from guests, as well as relatives whose acquaintance I have just made. When will my own wedding be? I jest discretion. Christian assures not before long. After today he cannot wait to marry into the Sai family. He is good at this stuff. A social butterfly given wings by Star beer and champagne. The ushers keep him in generous supply.

Do you take this woman to be your wife, to live together in holy matrimony?

We are seated under a large marquee. Uncle Nii Ade was the obvious choice for the Sai family orator. Senior, comical, serious – when necessary. Uncle Papafio vied for the position but lacked the 'sophistication' to perform such a role, my mum concluded. After a brief introduction and thanks for hosting us in their beautiful home, Uncle Nii Ade addresses the Bannerman family orator.

'We were passing your house today when we saw a beautiful flower in your front garden. We want to pluck the flower, but as well-intentioned people do, we have come to ask for your permission first.'

The Bannerman family are represented by a female orator. Pint-sized in proportion but not to be underestimated, Mrs Tagoe. Her voice is theatrical, her manner, entertaining.

'We have so many beautiful flowers in this garden.' She gestures grandly. 'Please, help us. Which one are you talking about?'

Sienna is identified in her absence. A reminder that 'knocking' is a custom for the two families. Because of this introduction, the Bannerman family should not be surprised or alarmed if they see their daughter with our son. The orators speak on behalf of their respective families. The 'we' and 'our' are used collectively.

'Our daughter is royalty, *deshie.*'

The seated guests are drawn into laughter by the interaction. Sienna is beloved and precious to her family. She will not be given away lightly.

'In that case, they are well matched. Our son is well educated. He is strong and tall and handsome. He is from good stock.'

I look around at our delegation, our stock. We are seated on the left-hand side of the wide aisle where Uncle Nii Ade and Mrs Tagoe are demonstrating, with flair, the art of oratory. I know that Sol is joy filled to see us all here. We have done him proud. Especially his dad, who is seated on the right, closest to the aisle. A space created with urgency for him by the ushers on his arrival. Sol's dad is here but mine is not. Because. The man seated in the wheelchair, his head hanging from his neck. Dressed in a two-piece Dutch wax print and slip-resistant orthopaedic shoes. Is. Not. My Dad.

To live together in holy matrimony, to love her, to honour her, to comfort her—
I wonder if Sol knew during the first days of their meeting at La Cucina, the Black Star Hotel or the polo club that Sienna would be the love of his life. I wonder where he learned to love and to honour

and to comfort her. He cannot have learned from my dad because my dad doesn't know those things. And you can't teach someone something you don't know. When Sol smiles, it could trick you into thinking that he grew up like Finlay. With a father who loved his mother so much that he asked her to leave her family and career as a civil servant and move cross the Atlantic Ocean with him. A father who knew that when he came of age, he would have to take over the family business, in metal and steel import. But who could not do so without the woman he loved by his side. A mother who loved his father enough to follow. A mother who built a happy and comfortable family home by her husband's side in Ghana. A mother who adapted to Ghanaian culture with ease and enthusiasm. A father whose love for his wife increased when he witnessed her give birth to his two children. A son followed by a daughter, both adored. A father who comforted his wife through the grief of losing her parents. Realising that she had sacrificed time with them to be with him. Loving her more for her selfless sacrifice.

I wonder what it is to be Sienna. To have always known what it is to be loved and honoured and comforted. To know how to fly because her mother taught her. I look between my mum and Christian and congratulate myself for jumping off the branch without being taught. For learning how to fly despite my example. For teaching myself.

And to keep her in sickness and in health, forsaking all others, for as long as you both shall live?
A luncheon represents in artificial time the period between the 'knocking' ceremony and the formal 'engagement' for the benefit of their international guests. Sienna remains hidden from view. The diligent ushers show us to our tables under the cover of a separate marquee and via a 'no expense spared' buffet of salmon and chicken and lobster and fried rice and jollof rice and plantain and *kenkey* and fried fish and *shito* and stew. Heated by stainless steel chafing dishes, oil burners and the mid-morning sun. Extravagant. Perhaps if I eat

something, I can silence the moving gravel in the pit of my stomach and look my dad in the eye. Or at least say hello. Uncle Nii Ade wheels him from the front row of guests to the table – my table. He cannot walk unaided. Not since the stroke.

I can introduce Christian to my mum but not to This Man. I hear the sound of falling silverware and look up without thinking. My dad has been defeated by the coordination required between left and right hand to eat. Uncle Nii Ade has disappeared momentarily. To where, I don't know. I stand from my seat, involuntarily, as Finlay steps forward to help with the mess.

'Don't worry, I've got it. Thanks.'

My heart is racing in my chest as I approach The Man Who Is Not My Dad.

'Hi – Dad – how are you?'

I will the moment to pass. For God's sake, where is Uncle Nii Ade? Where is Auntie Coumba? The gravel in my stomach becomes heavier as I watch him try to speak. The right side of his face will not cooperate. His left eye creases at the corner. And the left side of his lip perks up. As if – as if – he is trying to smile.

'F-f-f-fine—'

His left arm reaches to touch mine in sorry consolation for his inability to speak. His fingers are bulbous and stiff. His hands, rough and cracked. I shudder at this man's touch. He might actually not be my dad. Because. The pigment of this man's skin is greyish brown not coffee brown. And he is older than my dad's sixty-one years. By some ten years or so. An imposter.

To see the stillness of the right side of his body is to witness the sky turn from blue to green. To question whether I have always confused day for night, the sun for the moon. The powerful right hand of my father, which could grab me by the collar and slam me against the wardrobe in an unannounced WWF match. Lies limp and dormant next to his body. The hand that rained punches on my head as a child. Cannot so much as swat a mosquito. The hand that pushed my mum down the stairs when she was pregnant with me – I will him to say the word 'in-so-lent', to hear that he can. But I know he cannot. The mouth that bellowed throughout Saltoun Road and caused butterflies to flap their wings violently in my chest. Now struggles to speak. To see him dribble Supermalt down his chin makes my heart pound with fury and confusion. I wish he had worn *kente* and *chokoto*. I do not know this feeling. And I do not know this man.

THE ENGAGEMENT

I give you this ring as a token and pledge of our constant faith and abiding love.

We are seated, again, and it is time for us to make our intentions known. Uncle Nii Ade presents the case on behalf of the Sai family. His learned friend, Mrs Tagoe, appears on behalf of the Bannermans. Fast forward in real time.

'We came to your house some time ago to do some "knocking". Our young people have now met, and they have decided to spend their lives together. We come today because our son would like to formally ask for your daughter's hand in marriage.'

Mrs Tagoe is going for Oscar gold; she feigns amnesia.

'You talk of our daughter. We have so many beautiful flowers in this house. Please, which one are you talking about?'

'Your beautiful flower is well perfumed and has overpowered us. We want to have this flower in our lives. She is like a mirror: very good to look at. Even the way she walks, it is beautiful to us.'

The laughter of the guests forces childhood memories of my dad in his role of Master of Ceremonies at countless Ghanaian functions.

He was always making people laugh, a contagious laughter. I cannot reconcile that memory with the image of the man slumped over in his wheelchair. Unable to clap with the rest of the guests. Because the right side of his body is defiant. And paralysed. I am more scared of him in his wheelchair than I ever was when he was my dad.

Uncle Nii Ade is marketing Sol with enthusiasm. 'His face is there, look at it. He is handsome, isn't he? Look how tall he is. He is muscular. He has a good physique.'

Sol is asked to stand up and turn around so we can see just how handsome and tall he is. He performs, dutifully. His guests are tickled by the 360-degree show. Sol is invited to sit at the head of the aisle, facing his guests. He looks in our direction and smiles. He looks at his dad and winks. He loves his dad so very much.

Now enter from stage right the Fake Brides. Think Cinderella's sisters, the Ghanaian ones. Three women, with faces covered, are called upon to walk the length of the aisle. Mrs Tagoe wants to be sure that Sol can identify his 'special flower'. Uncle Nii Ade responds on his behalf. Number one is nice but the flower we have come to pick is 'really special'. Number two has a fine physique but our flower is 'slender'. Number three is also nice but 'too short'. Our flower is 'tall and elegant'. They are sent back from whence they came. We have not come here for a daisy or a tulip. We have come for a beautiful rose. Mrs Tagoe understands.

Time to barter. Mrs Tagoe now knows which flower my uncle is talking about but the flower has some brothers and cousins – male – who have looked after her very well over the years. They have kept her safe and chased away many admirers. They have guarded her chastity, fiercely, as loving brothers do. Finlay is laughing in the knowledge of what is to come. Before her brothers and cousins can let her go, they need to be compensated for their efforts, paid off: *akontasikan*. Sol returns Finlay's laughter. He is prepared and hands Uncle Nii Ade six white envelopes with cash contents to pay off Finlay and Sienna's male cousins so they will let her go from their house to his. Finlay opens his envelope and gives a thumbs up after looking inside. It is only now the flower can appear. We wait with excitement to lay eyes on her for the first time since our arrival.

Sienna beams from ear to ear as she walks down the aisle. She looks exquisite in white and gold *kente* that matches Sol's. His and hers. Fitted. Off the shoulder. Fishtail. She wears a set of coral beads around her hair and three layers around her neck. Sol is smiling like a schoolboy. It makes me happy to see him like this. I like that Coral is with us today in some way, shape, form. It makes me feel complete. Sienna takes her seat next to Sol. The future Mrs Sai.

If, once upon a time, there was a custom that required the groom's family to pay the wife's dowry, that custom could not be followed by my family. Not after the sacrifice that my mum gave of her happiness and her life in her godforsaken marriage. Not after the full-time nursing care that Sol provides for his sick father at his bungalow in Tema. Not after everything that has happened in our fraud of a family. Sol has organised and paid for the gifts, carefully and lovingly chosen by my mum.

The Bannermans are not a family to use the engagement of their daughter as an opportunity to acquire wealth. In any event, they are not in want. Uncle Nii Ade presents the dowry and gifts to Sienna and her family on behalf of the Sai family. We gift Sienna six pieces of cloth to dress her for the major occasions in her life. White cloth for the birth of her first baby. She will wear it at his traditional naming ceremony, seven days after birth: the outdooring. *Kente* cloth for a special occasion and four Dutch wax prints. A going-out wardrobe. We gift her *oheneba* slippers to wear with her cloth. And, because she cannot wear cloth alone, we have bought her jewellery: pearls, gold and costume jewellery sets to decorate her neck, wrists and ears. We gift her toiletries and perfume and any-and-everything else she could possibly want or need. To start married life as Mrs Sai the Third – in our lifetime.

As we are taking your daughter from your house, we have bought her a suitcase to pack her gifts. We present it with a bow. Uncle Nii Ade presents Mr and Mrs Bannerman with envelopes of money, a gesture of thanks, for raising a wonderful daughter for our wonderful son. No one is to labour under the impression that Sienna is being 'bought'; she is not. In the exchange there is the knowledge that if their daughter is mistreated, she will be taken back by her family by whom she is loved and cherished.

Mrs Tagoe addresses Sienna.

'Do you know this man?'

She does.

'Are you sure?'

'Yes.'

Mrs Tagoe is thorough if nothing else.

'These people have come to ask for your hand in marriage. They have bought all these gifts. Do you want to accept what they have bought?'

She does. She is sure she does.

'We accept what you have said.' Mrs Tagoe's performance concludes with authority, and finality.

Libation, to finish. Uncle Nii Ade presents Mr Bannerman with a bottle of schnapps, aka Gordon's gin, and calls upon Sol and Sienna's forefathers to bless their union and matrimony.

'Those who are dead and gone should come, eh.' He pours.

Their spirits should come and be among us as our daughter and son enter this new chapter of their lives. He pours. They should guide them through whatever challenges they may face together as husband and wife. He pours. And bestow upon them the joy and blessing of children. He pours. The Bannerman and Sai family are now one. He pours.

They wear their wedding rings. For Ghanaian purposes, Sol and Sienna are now married, husband and wife. After his conversation with the spirit world, Uncle Nii Ade presents them with a Bible. It is engraved with their names and the date of their union: *Saturday, 29 June 2019.*

What God Has Put Together Let No Man Put Asunder.

THE BEGINNING

My mum was nineteen years old. She was training to be a nurse at the School of Nursing and Midwifery at the University of Ghana in East Legon. My mum's English name is Florence, her Ghanaian name is Maanu, which means she is the second girl in her family. Ghanaians often have two names: a Ghanaian name and an English name. Your Ghanaian name can be the day of the week you were born on or the order you were born in your family. My Ghanaian name is Adadzewa. It means 'woman of steel' or 'iron lady'. Ewurabena is my day name; it tells you that I was born on a Tuesday. My mum was lucky that my dad let her call me Adadzewa after my godmother, Auntie Baaba. Sol and my dad have the same Ghanaian name, Nii Ayi. When he was younger, my dad used to call Sol 'junior' or 'son'. He never had any nicknames for me.

Before I was born, my mum was happy. She lived in Ghana and wore nice clothes and make-up like blue eyeshadow and wine-coloured lipstick. Her hair was thick and long, and she wore it in an afro with a side parting. She wore high heels even though she was already tall and slim. And when she walked, you could hear her coming. As she got closer, you could smell her too. My mum's perfume smelled like flowers. Her back was straight like a ballerina's. She was stylish and elegant, and she attracted a lot of attention. So many men wanted to marry her.

When my mum became a nurse, she worked at 37 Military Hospital in Accra, on the paediatric ward. She didn't look after premature babies until she came to London and had to retrain as a nurse so she could work for the NHS. 37 Military Hospital was the thirty-seventh military hospital built in West Africa when the British ruled the Gold Coast. My mum has always been great with children. The children on her ward adored her; she was their favourite nurse. The other nurses thought that my mum was the most glamorous nurse in the whole hospital. When she changed out of her uniform to go home, everyone admired her. They liked her style and her lipstick. My mum changed her earrings every day.

I think my dad was happy when he was a boy. I think he played with his brother and sisters and probably made them laugh a lot. My dad was just eleven years old when he went to boarding school. I imagine he missed his mum and dad because he only saw them at Easter time, Christmas and during the summer holidays. Everyone says that my dad's mum loved him most out of all her children. That he was her favourite and that he was spoilt. When my dad was a boy, I don't think he knew about WWF wrestling. I think he was funny and kind.

Papa was my dad's dad. He was the chief of a place called Adangbe in Ghana. That made him a very powerful and rich man in Accra. That is where my dad is from. He is Ga. My mum is Fante, from Cape Coast. In Ghana there are many tribes and different languages. Some people speak three or four or five different Ghanaian languages, like my mum. Cape Coast is near the sea.

If you come from Cape Coast, your surname is likely to sound quite Western. That's because of slavery; it is part of the legacy. That's why my mum's surname is Dadson. If she says her name to anyone in Ghana, they will know that she is from Cape Coast and that she is Fante. My surname is Sai, that is a Ga name.

Papa was my dad's dad. He was tall and had dark skin like coffee with no milk. He was bow-legged and long-limbed but that didn't distract from the fact that he was handsome. Papa liked it when people spoke 'proper' English. If they did not, he would correct them so they knew the right way to speak. At the market, when the woman selling vegetables asked Papa how many 'to-man-toes' he wanted to buy, Papa told her, 'It's to-*ma*-toes, not to-*man*-toes.'

Papa loved his children and wanted them to be well behaved, hard-working and do good things. He loved his grandchildren even more. Papa also loved sweets. He loved them so much that if he had a bag of toffee or biscuits, and his own child asked for one, he would look at him and say, 'No way!' Papa was funny and liked telling jokes. When he started to walk with a cane, his grandchildren saluted him when they saw him coming, like he was a captain. Everyone laughed.

Papa was the Director-General of Ghana Broadcasting Corporation, Ghana's equivalent to the BBC. There is a picture of Papa shaking hands with the first President of Ghana, and another of him in a boardroom with more white men than black. That's how important he was. Papa drove a white Mercedes and had lots of gold jewellery. You could only have those things in Ghana if you were really rich; that's how rich Papa was.

Nana was my dad's mum. She was very quiet and never shouted. Nana let Papa do all the talking when they went out. She preferred it that way. When she was young, Nana worked as a teacher. Papa didn't mind. My dad had a nanny called Efua Simpa. She looked after him during the day when Nana and Papa were at work. Efua Simpa was really hard-working and very respectful. When Nana came home from work, she didn't have to worry about dinner because Efua Simpa had always prepared something to eat and the house was always spotless. Nana would be lost without her. Papa was going to pay for Efua Simpa to learn a trade, so she would have job security and employment options when she finished nannying. My dad always cried after breakfast when it was time for Nana and Papa to go to work. Nana knew that he was impatient to join his big brother Nii Ade at school. Nana told my dad not to cry and that when he was older, Papa would drop him and Nii Ade off to school together, only one more year.

One day when Auntie Karley was going to town, she stopped by Papa and Nana's house to drop off *kenkey* and fried fish. There was something strange about the house that day because Auntie Karley could hear screaming from outside the side gate. Auntie Karley had heard on the news that there had been an increase in daytime robberies in the area. Armed men robbing people at traffic lights, pointing guns in their faces. Those same men, burgling homes in broad daylight. Where had these people come from? Was anybody safe? That didn't stop her walking towards the house, quickly and quietly. Auntie Karley walked across the courtyard and towards the window to the right of the main door. She would look inside before she entered. She was soaked in the blood of Jesus, and the Holy Spirit was with her. Auntie Karley was not afraid.

The terrible thing that Auntie Karley saw through the window made something bad happen to her knees. Efua Simpa had tied my dad to his stool by his legs. His hands were tied behind his back. It was a small stool for children made from wood with soft round edges to match a rectangular table that Papa had bought. A table with two chairs: one for my dad and one for Uncle Nii Ade so they could pretend to have important meetings like Papa. My dad's face was wet with fresh tears and dry with old ones. He was naked. And shrieked loudly as Efua Simpa raised a cane above her head and thrashed it down on his. God have mercy. A cry that came from another world. Where children of God seek mercy and tortured souls search for peace. My dad shrieked so painfully that Auntie Karley waited for the windows in the house to shatter into a thousand pieces. His body trembled in the chair as pain flashed through his body like electricity. My dad's three-year-old body convulsed in pain. Auntie Karley didn't know if he was having a fit or if he had left this world for another. He threw his body, tied against the chair, hard onto the floor. It landed next to his urine-soaked pants with a loud thud. My three-year-old dad didn't know if he was alive or dead.

Auntie Karley's heart was beating in her mouth as she ran to the front door. *Kenkey* and fried fish falling behind her. She stormed the back room that Efua Simpa had made into her torture chamber and scooped my dad up with his chair. She wrapped him in her arms, a shroud of safety. Without letting go of him, she released the strips of cloth that Efua Simpa had used to tie my dad to the chair. The knots were tight, so tight. His limbs hung limply when they were free. The pupils of his eyes as wide as their irises. Auntie Karley looked Efua Simpa in her eyes. The cane was still in her hand, raised. Efua Simpa was shocked into stillness and silence. Her mouth opening and closing like a gasping fish.

Auntie Karley was not the one speaking when those powerful Ga words fell from her tongue like fire. It was the Holy Spirit speaking for her. Efua Simpa danced on the flames. Auntie Karley wanted her to know the meaning of brimstone and fire. She should collect her things and go back to the snake pit that she shared with the devil because she was wicked. Efua Simpa was a witch.

When the house was quiet and peaceful again, like it was with Papa and Nana and Nii Ade, Auntie Karley gave my dad a bath filled with Epsom salts and dressed him gently in his pyjamas. His skin was raised in welts where the cane had thrashed him. And he shivered when she poured the warm water over his body. When she tried to feed him mealie porridge, my dad refused to eat. Auntie Karley rocked him gently in her arms and sang 'The Lord Is My Shepherd' softly, like a lullaby. When Nana walked through the door, Auntie

Karley was singing with her eyes closed and my dad was fast asleep against her chest.

Nana could not go back to work after Auntie Karley told her the terrible thing she saw that day.

Papa and Dada were old friends. One day, Papa visited Dada at the big white house at Cape Coast University, where he saw my mum. She was twenty years old. My mum was wearing her favourite blue dress with make-up and high heels. She looked like a model. Papa said that my mum was 'the picture of elegance' and that he would marry her to one of his sons. To show my mum that he was serious, he would send gifts to 37 Military Hospital for her, like *bofrot* and *kele wele*. *Bofrot* is a Ghanaian doughnut. It is jamless but sweet and delicious. *Kele wele* is spicy plantain, cubed and fried. My mum pretended that she was embarrassed when the lady from general reception brought the gifts to the paediatric ward and the other nurses said, 'Eiiiiiiii, Sister Flo!' But she was actually happy to be surprised with so many gifts.

Papa wouldn't stop sending my mum gifts so she would marry his second son, Emmanuel. He looked handsome in the pictures that Papa showed her. The day before my mum turned twenty-two, she saw Papa in his white Mercedes near the hospital. She loved the flowers and chocolates that he sent her yesterday. And the perfume he delivered the week before was very generous. My mum told Papa that she had discussed the proposal with her parents and she had agreed to marry Emmanuel. Papa was delighted. Emmanuel lived and worked in London. He would pick my mum up from the airport when she landed, and he would make a wonderful life for them. My mum was very excited. She had always wanted to go to London. She would work as a nurse and live in a nice house. Emmanuel would be an engineer or an accountant, she thought. He would take great care of her, and they would make a wonderful life together.

THE COLOUR RED

I was fortified to have Christian by my side in Ghana. To hear him assure my mum that we shall soon follow in the footsteps of Sol and Sienna and return to Ghana for our very own East meets West Africa Knocking Ceremony. And that he cannot wait to marry into the Sai family. I am fortified to know that we are back home, continuing our life together without the distraction of my dad's stroke. I didn't not mention it on purpose. I thought I did say he was sick. Can we please not talk about it any more? I try to empty my mind of the image of my dad in his wheelchair, which repeats in my mind at will. And surrender to the love of the one I lie with.

Our children will be beautiful: his eyes, his lips, my smile. He will be an amazing dad. Hands on. A teacher of practical things. A fount of knowledge. A patient helper of homework. A maker of wholesome meals. I go to bed thinking of the names we will call our children. I don't want a big wedding, not at thirty. A registry office would be perfect.

Saturday evening. I am the designated onion chopper. Christian is doing something more complicated. A béchamel sauce for moussaka.

'Christian, why didn't you live with your mum when you were younger?'

I need to know why he stopped me from eating a strawberry yesterday. Why he held my right hand with his left, so tightly. To remove the strawberry from my hand before it reached my mouth. Even though I had bought them for us. Even though there were plenty left. I need to know why he got so angry when I said, 'It's one strawberry, Chrissy.' And why he told me that I had ruined the pavlova he was going to make – just like I ruin everything. Before he stormed out of the kitchen and ignored me for the rest of the evening. His eyes rage filled. His breathing, red. I need to know that no one ever strapped him to a chair and sent flashes of electricity through his three-year-old body. I need to know more about the person he was before I met him.

'What?'

'It's something you've never really talked about.'

'We've just come back from Ghana and *that* is what you want to talk about?'

'I just want you to know that you can talk to me if you want to. You do know that, don't you?'

'I'm not going to talk about that and you're not going to make me.'

'I don't want to "make" you do anything, Christian. I want you to share things with me because you want to.'

'That's a bit hypocritical, isn't it? You've made it pretty clear that you don't want to talk about your dad but you want me to talk about my family. What is it, one rule for you, another rule for everyone else?'

He doesn't wait for an answer.

'That's how it starts. Then there will be another question and another question after that and then you'll ruin the whole evening by saying something fucking stupid – why don't we just fast forward and get it over with? Because Stella always has something to say, doesn't she? Go on, what are you waiting for?'

*

His response scares me. The defensiveness and secrecy of it. It makes me need to know the answer even more. So I don't have to fill in the gaps. I am undignified and undone by suspicion and my imagination.

I am not the only one with a wall.
Christian has one too.
An impenetrable wall.
His temper surrounds it.
I am blinking hard and fast.
When the shaking starts.
He is starting to roar.
The colour red.

Christian rages and combusts. I have to leave him alone. I want to tell him that it doesn't matter. We don't have to talk about it if he doesn't want to. It doesn't have to turn into another argument. But when Christian is roaring, he goes to another place. Something changes in his eyes. They glaze over, glacier like. And his voice bellows from somewhere deep inside. I cannot reach him when he goes there. There is nothing I can say or do to bring him back. In his own time, he can return. But if I say or do the wrong thing. He will detonate.

I almost always say The Wrong Thing.

'Fuck off and get out of my fucking face!'

He stands over me and shouts words that a person who loves you should never say to you. I cannot hear properly because he is standing over me and he is six foot four. The volume is too loud. I didn't think the butterflies would return but they are back. From that faraway land to which they fled. They are beating their wings loudly in my chest. The ants have returned too. They are full of glucose and sucrose and crawling wildly inside my head. Christian grabs my things. And throws them down the stairs.

It is time for me to go.

'Get out!'

I forgot about the beast inside me. It has been asleep for such a long time, but it is stirring. Because. The last time anyone stood over me. And shouted. I had hot water and palm oil and spinach in my hair.

I am standing next to one of his plants. When the shaking starts to spread. From the bottom of my feet upwards. Vesuvius rising. This time, I know that I am shaking on the inside and the outside. There is a glass of water on the table. I pick it up and throw it. Over the soft black curls that grow from his low-cut hair. The curls I love so much. The beast inside me throws it. A plant is within reach of my leg. I kick it. The beast does. Soil scatters across the wooden floor along with my hopes and dreams. The plant lies on its side, suffocating. My eyes meet his for less than a second. Before he hurls a glass of red wine over me. It splatters on the wall. And the stairs. And my hair.

When Christian stands over me. I am standing next to the stairs. He is roaring at me and charging. Like a tiger that has escaped from the zoo. His roar is the colour red. I look at him. Because I need to know if he is going to come back from that place. Or if he is going to stay there. I need to know if I can reach him. If he will come back to me. Because I am looking at him. I am not looking at me. I miss my footing. At the top of the stairs. And slow fast slow. I fall. Down seven hard wooden steps. As I fall, I see in my peripheral vision that he is trying to catch me. His hands outstretched. His expression, one of horror. But I am falling. And he cannot reach me. He cannot stop me. He cannot save me. Or us. It is too late.

I am eight years old when I sit at the bottom of the stairs in Barnsbury, Islington, with red wine in my hair. Or, I am my mum, I don't know which. Powerful and powerless, both. He cannot come near me because I will not let him. He is no longer bellowing; I am. He is crying. He is horrified. He is desperate to know that I am okay.

Please can he help me up. Please can he make sure that I am not hurt. Please can I come and sit down. Please can he make me a cup of tea. Please don't cry.

Mai is cowering under the table in the living room. I am cowering at the bottom of the stairs. When I can, I stand up and assemble my things, half strewn across the stairs. I get my dog. I pack my car and I sit in it. Christian tries to help me into the car and with my bags.

'Don't touch me!'

When I try to speak, it comes out like a scream.

'Don't touch my things!'

They are on the floor because he threw them there. He tries to convince me to come back inside. He does not think I should drive in this state. He is tearful. He is Christian again. Me? I don't know who I am. You should not try to comfort someone you do not love and cannot honour. I switch the engine on and drive back to South London. I am cold. I am shaking.

I don't tell The Girls about the stairs. They will not be okay with that. The thought of him standing over me in anger. They will not be okay with the fact that he shouts at me. Or that he threw my belongings down the stairs. If they know he slams the door in my face when he is angry. They will be distracted if I tell them those things. They will not hear me when I tell them that he takes the bones out of chicken wings for me or that he makes our curries mild so I can eat them. That he always buys yogurt in case I need to cool mine down. They will not know how my garden would look without him. That I would have no outdoor seating or that my climbing rose wouldn't have flowered. The foods I would never have tried if he hadn't introduced them to me. They will not think about how beautiful our children will be. Or how safe he can make me feel in his arms.

*

When we speak his voice is soft and sad. He has never argued like that with anyone before in his life. His greatest fear is that I think he pushed me down the stairs because he would never do anything like that. Would he? I try to explain that if he had not been standing over me the way he was, it is less likely that I would have fallen. He struggles to accept that premise because if I hadn't pushed and pushed and pushed him to talk about something he didn't want to talk about – if I had not followed him when he needed space, we would have avoided confrontation altogether.

I am sorry for pushing him to the point of anger. I am sorry I didn't give him space.

I am sorry.

THE MAGPIE

I am reading an email over and over and over again in Chambers. The letters are dancing in front of my eyes. That's how I know I am going mad. I have drafted and saved an Advice somewhere. The one that speaks to the further evidence required in support of the prosecution case, the application for witness anonymity that must be served ASAP, but it has moved. I know that I have early onset dementia because I can't remember a lot of things, especially things that are important for my job. Case law. Client details. My name.

It is moving. From my feet to my knees. From my stomach to my chest. A tremor in my body. It gets stronger as it climbs. When it reaches my brain it is fire and ice. Someone has poured liquid ice over my brain. And it is dancing like a flame. The shaking makes it difficult for me to think. About one thing at a time. Or anything, actually. My whole body is shaking.

'Morning, Stella. Would you like a cup of tea?'

My eyes are spilling tears down my cheeks. They are falling hard and fast. Wild tears. Fire tears. I stand up from my desk. But I cannot find my words. Maybe they are in the same place as my Advice.

Hiding from me. Tricking me. I wonder if my train is still on the platform. The hand is on nineteen past the nine on the clock. Maybe I can catch it. My train. If I run. I hope the magpie has called his friend. I hope. They are waiting for me. On the platform.

My lungs have stopped working and I think I am going to die. I don't want to die in a Hobbs suit. It is suffocating and heavy as lead. It is black. Like death. My brain is black too. I need to wear something soft. My dressing gown is oxygen. To sleep. So warm around me. Swaddling like baby Jesus. Angel Gabriel, watch over me. I am falling into the abyss. It is the ether. Suffocating and black. My skin. Maybe the wise men will come.

In my bed. It is too bright. Curtains closed. No magpies. I need to be still. When I wake, my jaw is clenched. And my eyes are squeezed shut like fury. My forehead is scrunched up along the wrinkle lines. I think that is why it feels like someone is drilling in my head. When I turn it from left to right the pain follows. And a tear. There is no reason to get out of bed. I could not even if I wanted to because my legs have turned to lead. There are tablets on my bedside table. Nurofen something. I take two and close my eyes. I reach for Mai. To ground myself. She is faithful and constant. I drift into sleep.

I dream. We are scuba diving in calm and crystal blue waters. Thailand. He guides me through the water. With the confidence of an expert scuba diver. I am a novice. He points out, one at a time, the wonders of the sea. Breathtaking coral. A school of fish, yellow tang. Bioluminescent plankton. The colours are so vivid. The landscape, magical. We navigate the darkness of the deep water with the light in his left hand. Until we reach its deepest point. It is marked with a sign on the seabed that says 'A Midsummer Night's Dream', in purple and blue and green lights. We are home. He unzips his wetsuit and slips his feet out of his flippers. I follow his lead. The water is so warm, like a bath. Carefully, he removes his snorkel and lets it sink to the seabed. He gestures for me to remove mine. I hesitate.

'I'm scared.'

'Don't be.'

'I won't be able to breathe.'

'You will. I promise. I'll help you.' He speaks clearly through the water.

He fixes his eyes on mine and gently removes my snorkel. He breathes air into my lungs with his kiss. I fix my eyes on his. And he holds me as we rise to the surface of the water. Four arms, four legs, like an octopus with two heads. Together, we rise. To the surface of the water. Breathing. Together.

WHEN LOVE BECKONS

I look for *The Prophet* by Kahlil Gibran, which Farah gave me last
year. A collection of poetic essays. I can consult it on any area where
I feel I could benefit from clarity and guidance, like the Gideon's
Bible we got at school. I read the chapter 'On Love'.

When love beckons to you, follow him,
Though his ways are hard and steep.
And when his wings enfold you yield to him,
Though the sword hidden among his pinions may wound you.
And when he speaks to you believe in him,
Though his voice may shatter your dreams as the north wind lays waste the
garden.

For even as love crowns you so shall he crucify you. Even as he is for your
growth so is he for your pruning.
Even as he ascends to your height and caresses your tenderest branches that
you quiver in the sun,
So shall he descend to your roots and shake them in their clinging to the earth.

*

The reason I collect Mai's things, pack my car and drive back to Islington is because I love him. We argue on average once a week, which means we get on eighty-five per cent of the time; those are good numbers. Our issue is narrow and easily identified: communication. If we can resolve it, everything else will fall into place. We have shaken ourselves into a new reality, literally. After Stair-Gate, we promise each other that we will never return to that place. It's a numbers game.

His arms enfold me in a loving embrace and his kiss heals me. Our eyes exchange a message of commitment to us, to each other, to our 'knocking'. He has chosen me, his flower. The one he wants to pick. From all the beautiful flowers in the garden, in the world. He is handsome and tall and from good stock. We are here because we have chosen to be together. I am here because he has made me feel whole.

'I made you a beef-brisket curry.'

'It smells really nice, thank you.'

When we sit down to eat, I am disappointed that my appetite is not what it should be. He has been cooking all afternoon and is upset that I won't eat properly. He thought it was my favourite. I pour a glass of water as he opens his third can of San Miguel. I don't know what my life would be like without his cooking. His smell. His touch. His love. The way he kisses and holds me. The way he makes me feel safe in his arms. I want to live as one half of his whole. I want to be complete. I force another mouthful.

'I love you, Stella.'

'I love you too.'

Nobody knows that when Christian gets angry, it is like lightning and thunder and hailstones.

Nobody but me.

BROKEN WINGS

There was no warning from a magpie.
No signal or sign.
No chance to prepare.
Or to brace for impact.
Before I saw The Man Who Used to Be My Dad.
In a wheelchair.
Or Christian roared the colour red.
And I fell down the stairs.
Or he pushed me.
Before I became eight years old and my mother.
In the blink of an eye.
Swift descent.

I am on the left side of my bed in South London. His side. Facing the
French doors that look out onto the garden. I need to water the grass.

There is no magpie roaming free.
There is nothing.

*

I have not eaten properly in eight days. Not since I left North London for South; his home for mine. Again. Not since he threw the remote control at my head with such force that I saw bright stars and a galaxy behind my eyes. Since I presented poached eggs instead of 'sunny side up' for breakfast and he called me 'a stupid bitch'. If I didn't want to make it properly, I shouldn't have made it at all. He cooks for me every single day, and does he complain? No. He is fed up of waiting on me hand and foot. It's a fucking egg, not rocket science. And I'm supposed to be a barrister? What a joke. It doesn't matter that I offered to make it again or that I said 'sorry'. Nothing matters any more.

My taste buds are dead, so it doesn't matter if I eat or don't eat. I don't care about food or cooking, not like I did when we cooked and ate together. When I think about food, I think about him. I am not hungry. I cannot eat. I drink coffee and manage a slice of toast and a boiled egg every day. For eight days. I check my phone for a message. I try to work. Or signs of his activity. Is he online? I need to concentrate. I need to work.

I am mid-trial. Murder. Central Criminal Court. Led by Queen's Counsel. There is a broken-hearted mother in the third row of the public gallery. She comes every day to watch her son sit in the dock flanked by Serco security officers. To listen to the heinous things he has allegedly done to another human being. Denied bail. And in time his liberty for some twenty-five years. A young adult, unrealised potential, a wasted life. There is another mother in the front row. She sits broken-hearted and listens to the merciless way her son was robbed of his life, violently and prematurely. To hear how he spent his final minutes in this life before he passed to the next. She comes to court every day. While her son lies six feet underground in Mitcham cemetery. A young adult, unrealised potential, a wasted life. They grieve. Six feet apart in the public gallery. For the sons they have loved and lost. For their lives irrevocably altered. For the pain that has made its forever home in their broken hearts.

We rise for lunch. A call from Sol to let me know that Dad is in hospital, again. They suspect another stroke. A mild one. He is stable for now. Sol will keep me posted.

I don't know what a mild stroke is. Or whether it will affect the left side of his body in the same way it has affected the right. I don't know anything anymore.

PEACE

Home.
I am looking for the place where there is stillness
and quiet. Where there is quiet
apart from the sound of peace.
I am walking towards the darkness.
It is the only place I will find light.
I am looking for the place of death.

I thought about throwing myself out of a moving car once. On the South Circular. But I was too scared. To open the door. And hit the tarmac. With my head. To meet my Maker. Hollow-headed. Brains splattered behind me. Another time. Running after court. Changed into Lycra. Anthony Hamilton in my ears, 'Pass Me Over'. Inspiration. I wanted to jump. Off Waterloo Bridge. I imagined myself doing it. The thought of hitting the water made me feel free. The protection of my mother's amniotic sac. Before the stairs. Before the birth. Before the trauma. I wanted to sink. To the bottom. Never to rise again. I don't think I was ready to die. Not then. I just wanted to be able to put one foot in front of the other. Without thinking about it. To not have to struggle. For the pain to stop. I couldn't live with the pain any more. I can't live with the pain any more. Not for another second. I just wanted to improve the quality of my life. I can't improve the quality of my life. It felt like death. I felt like I was dying. I feel like I am dying. My whole life has felt like that. My life will always be like this. Nothing good has ever happened to me. Nothing good will ever happen to me. And I was tired. Of living like that. I am tired. Of living like this. I just needed it to stop. I need it to stop.

The packaging cracks as the first tablet pierces its seal. It sounds like freedom. I start to feel better when I swallow. I am on my way to the light. I cannot see it yet but I know it is there. My maiden voyage. From my bedroom and mausoleum. A constellation of silver tablet seals forms on my bedroom floor. I am on my way. The more I swallow, the closer I get. It feels like peace.

Farah is on her way. I called her when the butterflies started beating their wings in my chest and I started shaking like Vesuvius. Again. My lungs suffocating in water. Liquid ice, dancing, like a flame on my brain. Again. The synapses, short-circuiting. Again. Farah says she is coming over in an Uber right now when I say, 'I think I'm dying.'

'If I don't answer the door. You can come through the side entrance. I will leave my bedroom door open for you. I will be at home. I am going home. Take care of Mai for me. Thank you for being such an amazing friend. I love you.'

I am in and out of sleep. Between today and tomorrow. The darkness and the light. I am in between this world and the next. My eyelids are heavy and happy. When I open them, Farah is kneeling by my bed. There are tears in her eyes.

'Farah. You're here. I'm tired, Farah.'

'I know you are, Stella. I know you are.'
She holds my hand. It feels like love.
'Stay with me.'

When I open my eyes again. Kemi is holding my hand.
'Kemi. You came.'
'Hi, beautiful. Hang in there, okay?'
'Kemi. Does it look like I've been burgled? My flat. The dishes—'
'It looks like an angel lives here. I'm going to sort it all out for you, just you wait and see.'

She smiles. A smile of love.

I am not alone. I close my eyes.

I am in and out of consciousness. When I am conscious, I am in the ambulance. Farah is calling my name in between serious conversations with the paramedics. My blood pressure is low. When I am unconscious, everything is black, like peace not death.

Obstruction. They want to keep me in the castle shackled and chained. To stop my crossover to the peace place. The master prefers choking to whipping. He is forcing a tube into my nose because he does not want me to breathe. When I get to the freedom place. He is threading it like pain down my oesophagus into my stomach. He wants to get my stomach. I want to get to the sea.

Farah writes down everything the on-call psychiatrist says about referrals and medication. There are options, so many options available to me. He diagnoses depression and anxiety. The depression is multi-faceted and complex. Farah says the on-call psychiatrist is very competent and handsome.

*

When I leave hospital, Farah teaches me to say something over and over again, like a mantra:

'There are options. There is hope.'

I am lost and scared. I don't know anything about anything.

Farah takes me and Mai back to her home, where she cares for me like the child I have become, unable to care for myself. She walks Mai, feeds her and cuddles her for me. She tells me when it's time to take my medication and time to eat. I don't have to get up to eat. I can eat wherever I feel comfortable but I do have to eat something. I am in and out of sleep. She calls doctors, collects prescriptions and liaises with Kemi and Eimear. They want to know what's going on. They want to be kept informed. My phone is off. It has been for days.

'Farah, can you wipe my butt, please?'

She looks at me, ready to mobilise. I try and make my face smile.

'Stella! You know I would— Right, an episode of you can do it.'

I switch on my phone. A message from Sol.

Stella, I am thinking about you every second of every day. Farah says you aren't quite up to visitors yet. But I am waiting by the phone for your call as soon as you feel ready to talk. You are the most intelligent, amazing and beautiful soul I know. I love you so much. We all do. Please tell me what I can do to help.

I switch my phone off and close my eyes to sleep.

CONNEMARA

Hell 'checkmates' purgatory and makes a mockery of me.

I am in Lettermore, Connemara, County Galway, on the west coast of Ireland.
I know I am here because there is a plane.
Eimear says there is a plane.
I just have to get on it.
She will be waiting for me.
The airport is called Shannon.
Eimear knows about ships. And planes.
That is why I am here. Alive.

In Connemara. I don't have to do anything that I don't want to do. I just have to eat and sleep and stay alive. To stay alive, you basically have to not want to die. I bet you think it's easy for me because I've been through a lot and I've made it this far. Because I wear a suit from Hobbs and go to court. Because I make submissions to the judge and closing speeches to the jury. Because I cross-examine witnesses and say the sky is blue. It's not easy for me. Nothing is.

*

When day is night and night is day, I have to start from the beginning. That means I have to learn how to do everything again, from scratch. I have to learn how to get out of bed in the morning. Sometimes, I don't know how. Because my eyes don't like my ears, my heart doesn't like my lungs and my hands and feet don't like any other part of my body. The biggest enemy is my brain. It doesn't like anyone or anything. And it doesn't want to work. The worst thing I can do is open the curtains. Because there could be a magpie. Waiting for me outside. It could even kill me.

I have to make my legs and my feet move in front of me. Not backwards. I have to put my right foot in front of my left foot lots of times until I get somewhere, like the bathroom. That is walking. If I can get there, the worst thing I can do is look at the person in the mirror because I don't know that person. The person in the mirror is a dead person. With no pupils. That's why she thinks the sky is green. In the bathroom, I have to use my hand, the one I used to write with, to pick up my toothbrush. When there is toothpaste on it, I have to make it go into my mouth and move it up and down. Until I can exhale and say, 'God help me.' Then I have to use my hand to turn on the tap so the water knows it has to come out. I have to run the tap until the water doesn't feel like ice any more. That is a good time to blink. Then I have to move the water from the tap to my face to make it wet. When I have done all those things, I am really tired, like Addison's times ten. I used to use my hand to write Advices because my brain used to be able to do lots of things. It doesn't work any more.

I have to get back to the dark room and swallow the full moons that make me sleep. Until day is night and night is day. Again. And then, I have to start from the beginning. Eimear says, when I start to feel better – and I will feel better very soon, I just need to give my medication a chance to kick in – I can have something to eat. That means I am going to have to make food go into my mouth and my teeth are going to have to go up and down lots of times so I can swallow it. And my body can get some nutrients. Because I'm losing too much weight. Eimear says I need my strength and that I will feel better when I am able to eat something. Maybe I can try tomorrow. It's going to be really hard. All I have to do today is sip some water. Eimear holds the glass to my lips. Because it is too heavy for me.

In the beginning, when day is night and night is day, butterflies race to my chest cavity whenever they want. They are agitated and fast. My heart is racing. And I am shaking from the inside out. My skin is bleeding water. It soaks my clothes. I am sweating. My lungs are suffocating. In water, I think. Gasping for air. I cannot breathe. Liquid ice is dancing. Like a flame. On my brain. Someone has poured it. The synapses. Are short-circuiting. Again. Again. Again.

I am walking through Brixton. In the middle of a war. Around me. Masked boys and men. In black balaclavas and black combat uniform. They are carrying knives and machine guns. They are killing each other. Without mercy. The bulletproof windows of KFC have shattered. I am on Coldharbour Lane. Dodging bullets. And watching men fall. I have to find my family. I try to make myself as inconspicuous as possible. But it is hard. I am not dressed like them. I cannot call for my mum. Or Sol. My dad. I cannot make a sound. If only I can get to Morleys. I can get them to a place of safety. They will be waiting for me. In my mum's Toyota. Silver. Between Morleys and the Body Shop.

It is too dangerous to take the high street. I navigate the back streets. Where the market used to be. The tripe. The offal. The snails. It has been replaced. By 'Brixton Village'. I do not know this place. Wahaca? Champagne & Fromage? Burnt Toast? I do not know this place. The smell I used to hate has gone. I want a beef pattie from First Choice Bakers. And a can of Lilt. The totally tropical taste. But I have to find my family. There is a commotion. Behind me. I look over my shoulder. The night is black. But for gunfire, bloodshed and the whites of my eyes. There are men. Chasing me with knives. They have seen me.

*

'I'm dying. I'm dying! Christian. I'm dying!'

'You're not dying. You're having a panic attack. It's okay. You're okay. Just breathe.'

'I need you, Christian. Don't leave. Please don't leave me.'

'It's okay, Stella. You're okay. I'm here.'

We breathe together.
Slowly.
In. And. Out.

'Don't try to talk. Just focus on your breathing for now. In and out. That's all you need to do. In and out. That's it. I'm right here. I'm not going anywhere. You're okay. I'm right here with you. I love you. You are so loved. In and out.'

'Eimear?'

When I can breathe by myself, I sleep. For a long time.
The day doesn't matter because every day is the same. Every day is today.

I dream of the Magpie. He doesn't want to leave me alone. He just wants to follow me. Everywhere I go. He is there. He doesn't even care that I hate him. Or that he has ruined my life.

In the beginning when day is night and night is day, I open the window. When I see him, my words come out like a scream. 'GOOD MORNING, MR MAGPIE, HOW ARE MRS MAGPIE AND ALL THE OTHER LITTLE MAGPIES?' When Eimear comes to save me, I am blinking to make my eyes see two of him. And flapping my wings. And cawing loudly. To mimic his missing friend.

THE POEM AND THE PAST

SUNSHINE

I hover at the doorstep when the sun appears.
Eimear is outside cutting a shrub for firewood.
'A forsythia. Lunch will be ready soon. Chicken fajitas, how does that sound?'
There is a wall around the garden. It is made from stones of granite.
They are layered, one on top of the other, like Tetris.
'Are they stuck together?'
'No. I don't think so.'
'If you remove one, will the whole thing crumble?'
Like the fragments of my heart.

The granite glistens in the sunshine.
I am outside.

Two donkeys eat their way through the grass.
'I call the baby one Chewie, after Chewbacca from *Star Wars*. We can feed them carrots before dinner. Would you like to do that with me?'
I haven't seen *Star Wars*. I would like that.

*

There are lots of hydrangeas. Like the ones Christian helped me
plant in my garden.
Eimear points out a rose bush. Its petals are bright coral.
Like my sister. She never came to say hello.
I've never seen a coral rose before.

I give Chewie three large carrots. Eimear feeds Chewie's mum.
'Hold your hand out flat so he doesn't catch you with his teeth.'
Chewie's fur is coarse but soothing to touch. His teeth make light
work of the carrots. I wait for him to finish one before giving him
another. He flares his nostrils to say thank you.

We head inside for dinner: fajitas with extra guacamole and sour
cream. In a blue vase on the kitchen table is a bunch of flowers fresh
from the garden. Eimear says she picked them just for me.

In the beginning, every day is the same. I wake up from the horror of
the night soaked in sweat, jaw clenched and eyes shut tight before
opening. I have to remember who I am, where I am and why I am here.
I am Stella. My panic attacks are constant and tornado-like. I call Farah
most mornings with a grief that I can only describe as black. She talks
me down with patience, empathy and love. I just need to wait for my
medication to kick in. I am not a burden. I am going to get through this.
I am not well. She is so sorry that I am going through this. She can only
imagine how tough it is. I have been through so much but I am so
strong, and I have so much love and support around me. It's not always
going to feel like this. She promises. She loves me and The Girls love
me. We will get through this together. I am not alone.
    I know that I can call Farah or Kemi or Eimear from the other
room, to purge me of my morning grief. I rotate so that I am not too
much of a burden to any one of them. Eimear has porridge warming
for me on the stove, every morning. She has a dog, Ginger. And a
beautiful life in Galway.

'It's about as far away from shipping as you can get but I love it here, Stella.'

Ginger's a clever collie, an outside dog. The perfect antidote for missing Mai.

'Ginger's not allowed in the house? What, not even on your bed?'

Eimear jokes that she's going to report herself, and the rest of Ireland, to the RSPCA. She shows me Ginger's outhouse. It is filled with hay and turf.

'She's warm and cosy, see?'

We pick blackberries from the bushes around the house. I'm going to help Eimear to make jam. I've never made jam before.

Eimear wants to take me fishing. Her uncle takes us out on his boat. He has grown up on the sea. There is something heavenly about a panorama of water. Something that calls me back to life. It is so peaceful. The water, still and calm. I watch Eimear and Tomás lower their lines into the water. I want to try.

'You'll know when you catch something. You'll feel a pull on the line. You can't mistake it.'

I quieten my other senses to concentrate on the feel of the line, the wire between my fingers. I listen to my hands: mindfulness. I feel a tug. I think I have caught something but I am too scared to look. Tomás reels in my line. He laughs at the way I mispronounce his name, 'Tom-as'. Five mackerel! Wet and shiny flip-flopping for air. My intrigue meets hysteria as he unhooks them to add to the catch.

'Not near me, Tomás, I'm scared!'

Eimear and I are cry-laughing at my histrionics. I catch twelve mackerel to Eimear's four. My first time fishing! I promise Eimear that I will teach her how to fish – when she learns how to cook. Mackerel for dinner?

I wake up relieved. I didn't dream that awful dream. My pyjamas are dry. The morning passes without its habitual panic attack. And I don't have to think so much – about getting out of bed and brushing my teeth and having a shower. I can put my right foot in front of my left – without having to plan the steps. I think my medication is starting to work. I take Ginger for a walk by myself. I think I can, I want to. We climb twenty-five minutes up Lettercallow Hill or mountain, depending on serotonin levels. Ginger leads the way. At the top, we sit down, proud of our achievement. There is a magpie at the foot of the hill. I can make it out in the distance. I stroke Ginger. She rolls onto her back and presents her belly, more please. The wind is blowing, and the clouds are scattered. The waves ripple on the water below. The sun is trying to break through. I can see the Aran Islands. I sit for a while longer and breathe four-four-six before we head back down, Ginger and I. Another magpie sits on a fulcrum. Does one for sorrow, twice, make two for joy?

Eimear takes me cold-water swimming in the sea. The beach is beautiful. White sand and clear blue waters. The sun keeps us warm as we strip down to our bathing suits and look out to the horizon. Eimear tells me about the surrounding islands, mountains and rocks. We assess the clouds to see if rain is likely. It is not. The weather is perfect.

'It's not cold-water swimming, Stella, it's just swimming!'

'How cold is the water, Eimear?'

'About fourteen or fifteen degrees.'

I look at her, a look of terror. I have heard about the health benefits of cold-water swimming, but seriously, I don't know if I can do this.

'We should have bought goose fat, Eimear. Isn't that supposed to protect you from hypothermia?'

She is laughing. 'It's so good for you. I love it. Going in is the hardest bit. Just breathe through it. You're so good at controlled breathing.'

We wade into the water. Slowly. I am hyperventilating and forcing deep breaths. I wonder if this is something a Ghanaian girl should really be doing. I psych myself up to go under. A motivational monologue with plenty of encouragement from Eimear. In and out. In and out. In and – under! The cold water sends a shock of electricity through my body and popping candy all over my wet skin. The soldiers in my brain stand to attention. My body wants to dance and to jump and to say, 'Well done, Stella! You did it!'

Eimear is in her element.

'Isn't it great?'

She swims out with her snorkel.

'I did it, Eimear! I can't believe I did it!'

HOME

West Norwood. Kemi has sent me a Fela Kuti biography called *This Bitch of a Life*, and a framed photograph of the two of us at her wedding. Jackson wishes she looked at him in the same adoring way. A card to remind me that she is tremendously proud of me. There is going to be a 'Stella' room in her new house. If I don't come with Mai, I needn't come at all. We can resume our 'book club' whenever I am ready. She plucked a massive hair from her neck this morning. What kind of life is this? She loves me so much and she can't wait to see me soon. I put the framed photo up on the mantelpiece.

When the doorbell rings, my heart jumps. I don't feel ready for visitors, not today. I will it to be Kemi at the door, or the postman. I shuffle to the door in my slippers and open it to see Sol's face. My eyes adjust to the autumn sunshine, a halo framing my brother's silhouette on the doorstep. Sol demonstrates a new facial twitch in the short time it takes to say 'hi'. His lips smile but straighten quickly, repeat. His eyes blink in uneven time.

I break away from a brief hug, gently peeling his left arm away with my right.

'Hey, come in.'

*

A package from my mum, hand-delivered by Sol, with flowers and a box of Belgian chocolates. In addition to gifts, and sadness in his eyes, Sol brings with him something else. He doesn't really know where to. He's not great with words. He never has been. Not like me. Maybe that's why it's been so hard for him to talk about it. In the past. He's been thinking about me so much. Since this happened. He knows it will be hard for me to believe. But he has tried to revisit stuff in his head. To remember what it was like when we were kids. He knows that he can never understand what I've been through.

My eyes start to sting as Sol chokes on his words.

He knows there was shouting. And banging. And screaming. And crying. He remembers the time I came back from the hospital with Mum and my arm was in a cast. He heard Mum tell Auntie Baaba that I had fallen in the playground. But he knew I didn't fall because I was fine in Dad's car after school. And after, when everything was quiet again, when he decided it was safe to come out of the bathroom. When he unlocked the door and tiptoed out, and he heard the front door shut, he looked out of the window and he saw me. Holding my left hand, with my right. He knew something bad had happened. He wanted to ask me if I was okay, but something inside stopped him.

Sol's gaze refuses to meet mine.

He knows I've always thought of him as a 'daddy's boy'. He loves Dad. He doesn't know how to stop loving him. It's always been so easy between them. Do I think it's because he's a boy? He doesn't know why. What else could it be? Sol is more like Mum than I think. Have I noticed how they both avoid difficult situations? Mum gives it to God, doesn't she? Any difficult situation. Coral, Dad – your . . . overdose. Sol locks it in a box and buries it. Somewhere deep down.

He's buried it so deep. He doesn't even know where it is. And the key? He's thrown away the key. He's too scared to open the box. He doesn't know what he will find there.

Sol sobs like a seven-year-old boy. I have never seen him cry before. I'm scared to look at his tears.

Have I ever thought about what it would have been like if Mum and Dad actually loved each other? If we had been a 'proper' family? Did I see Sienna's parents at the wedding? They're not acting. That shit is real. They are like that all the time. Holding hands, laughing, loving their kids. It's so beautiful, Stella. The Bannermans welcomed him with open arms. It's like being in a real family. We should have had that. The way Uncle B is with Sienna – so loving and protective. A proper 'daddy's girl'. He adores her. You should have had that, Stella. I wish Dad had given you that. Sienna wants to start trying for a baby, but Sol is terrified. What if something happens to him – catches up with him? What if he doesn't know how to be a good dad? What if he – becomes Dad?

He's thirty-two years old and he's scared. So scared.

He's never spoken to Dad about me. Not like that. Is he a coward? And now it's too late. Because look at him. Sol is scared that he'll never get the chance to ask Dad the questions I need the answers to. Isn't that the least he can do for me, as a brother? He has let me down his entire life. He owes me that and more. And now he has let the chance pass him by. After the second stroke, the doctors don't know if Dad will be able to speak again, not properly anyway.

Sol is breaking. His head in his hands. My hand reaches over to rest on his shoulder.

*

282

He is so sorry I did what I did. The idea of me being so desperate and sad just breaks his heart. He was so scared when Kemi called to tell him. He cannot imagine life without me. I can never do what I did again. Never ever ever. I am the bravest person he knows. He feels so guilty for not being the brother I deserve. He could have done better. Could he? He should have done better. He has never told me this, but he finds it hard to say the words, 'I love you'. He really struggles with it – but he wants me to know that he does – love me. So much. He couldn't have dreamed of a kinder, braver or more deserving sister. He doesn't deserve a sister like me.

Sol looks at me for the first time, pain etched all over his familiar face, his eyes drowning in tears. He is overcome by the destabilising effect of trying to confront his trauma. For the first time in his life.

He just remembers the feeling of being scared. All the time. Loud noises making him jump – on the inside. Investing so much energy into trying to conceal his fear. Do I remember when we went to Ghana and Ebow and Ekow taught us how to play the *djembe* drums? He remembers coming back to London and really wanting to learn how to play the drums after that. Dad promised to buy him a drum kit if he maintained interest. When he started at Jacobson, it was one of the first things he signed up to: drum lessons. But at the first smash of the crash cymbal, something started to hurt in his chest and his heart rate accelerated to an agitated and uneven rhythm. He made an excuse to leave the lesson after twenty minutes. Told the teacher he thought he was going to be sick. He went to the toilets and cried, trying not to suffocate under the betrayal of his breath. The drum kit – it was so much louder than he had expected. The anticipation of being a bona fide drummer, replaced by a concentrated fear – of doors slamming. Me and Mum being pushed. Shoved or thrown. The only thing he knew to do was run – and hide.

*

My heart hurts for my brother and his unarticulated pain. His words root me to the place I need to be. The anger I have harboured against him for so many years is displaced and I am confused. I know that after his visit I will reflect on the times I have willed Sol to speak up for me, to stand up against our dad, to show that he cares. And now, this.

The words I struggle to say to Sol come to me, freely and willingly. 'I love you too, Sol.'

I need help. We both do.

The seamstress has finished sewing my '*Fathia Fata Nkrumah*' *kente* cloth in the dominant colour of pink. It is beautiful, so beautiful. And I have wanted it for so long. I have nowhere to wear it to yet, but I will, one day. I like it so much, the colours.

There is a new *kente* cloth called '*Obama*'. Have I heard of it? It's like nothing I've ever seen before. Think pop art in *kente*. They wove it in Obama's honour. Imagine having a *kente* cloth designed especially for you. How special is that? Sol is going to buy me some the next time he goes to Ghana. We can wear it for Mum's birthday. He was thinking we could organise a party in Ghana at the Black Star Hotel? Auntie Baaba and Auntie Maame will help. He's got it covered. What do I think?

'I think that sounds nice.'

I wait until Sol has left, his tears dried, his composure restored, to open the envelope inside the package from my mum. 'Stella' in her beautiful hand. Inside, a handwritten note:

My Darling Adadzewa,

But I call to God,
and the Lord saves me.

Evening, morning and noon
I cry out in distress,
and He hears my voice.
Cast your cares on the Lord
and He will sustain you;
He will never let the righteous fall.

Psalm 55: 16, 17, 22

You are a 'woman of steel'; an 'iron lady'.
You are so much stronger than I ever was.
Love, Mum x

I send a WhatsApp message: *Thank you for my beautiful Fathia Fata Nkrumah kente. I love it so much. I am okay. I am feeling stronger every day. I love you. x*

When I call Giselle, she is so pleased to hear my voice and to know that I am emerging from the eye of the storm. There is always light at the end of the tunnel. She wants me to come over for a cup of tea when I feel up to it. Don't worry about work for now or at all. You are your most important thing. Focus on yourself. Feel better. Get better. You are already doing it. One day at a time. The sound of her voice doesn't send my butterflies into a frenzy any more. I seek it, for guidance. After she is your pupil supervisor, Giselle can be your friend. She can tell you things like, your work will be waiting for you, don't worry. It is no reason to run before you can walk. Take your time, Stella.

Eight-year-old Stella would never have thought of judges. If she had, she would not have thought of them as real people. Autocratic civilians at best, walking wigs at worst. Stella, aged thirty, walks up Her Honour Judge Barnes's driveway in Battersea with Mai. There is a new car in the collection. It's very shiny and very flash. Giselle offers a warm welcome and tea of the fresh leaf variety from her garden – or some Fortnum & Mason options, highly recommended.

'Do you have PG tips, Giselle?'

I settle on Earl Grey. And watch as she unloads the dishwasher with unnatural efficiency.

'I don't like to think of you doing domestic labour. Don't you have someone to do that for you?'

She laughs as she presents me with homemade banana loaf, generously sliced. A quarter of the cake lands on my plate. Am I still planning to repaint my living room? Have I settled on a colour yet? She has a Farrow & Ball colour chart in her office. I should remind her to give it to me before I leave. Giselle is a frustrated interior designer, sponsored by Farrow & Ball. Who knew that buying paint testers could be an actual hobby? A photograph of Giselle on the day she was sworn in as a judge sits on a shelf in her office. She is holding her five-year-old daughter. They are nose kissing, like Eskimos. She thinks an olive tree will go well in my garden.

'Nice car, Giselle.'

She insists it is not hers. She doesn't drive. She does have a scooter, though. She scooted into town this morning.

'Please tell me you don't scoot to court?' The foundation of my world prepares to collapse.

'Now, Stella. A judge scooting to court – can you imagine that?'

'Do I have to?'

We laugh over tea and cake and paint colours. I think I'm going to go with blue, it's so calming. Giselle recommends Hague Blue; I can't go wrong with Hague Blue.

DR SANAA BAHT

Dr Sanaa's room is small and cosy. She sits in a green chair that faces the door. I sit opposite her in a pink chair that faces hers. Both chairs are soft and made from velvet. There is a table to my left with a box of Kleenex tissues. To the right of her chair is a window with a view of nothing in particular. A table sits underneath the window. It is covered with papers and files. A mobile phone is half-hidden underneath a set of keys. The carpet in her office is blue. Blue is my favourite colour.

Dr Sanaa Baht is a clinical psychologist. She works with people who suffer from depression and anxiety and work-related stress. Dr Sanaa is particularly interested in helping women. She offers appointments over Skype as well as in person. I have never had this kind of therapy before. Will I be able to see her face if we speak on Skype? Yes, of course. Okay, because I don't think I would do very well if I couldn't see her face. She wants to know that we can work well together. That she can work well with me as well as me with her. She uses Cognitive Behavioural Therapy. I have tried this before. At the Student Counselling Service at university. I didn't get on too well with it. I think it was the therapist. She barely looked me in the eye during our session. She was preoccupied with note taking. I didn't go back. Dr Sanaa also uses Compassion Focused Therapy. I have never heard of that before.

What do I want to achieve from our sessions? I want to improve the quality of my life. My childhood was – complicated. I struggle with anxiety and low moods. I have depression. It can be debilitating. I want to learn how to better manage these episodes. They are now a regular feature in my life. I want to be able to cope. And I want to have hope. To know that there is something better for me. That this is not it, my life. I want to know that it can get better than this. Together, we will work through these challenges and difficulties and understand how they are affecting my life, my relationships and my work.

I pay to speak to Dr Sanaa. In the beginning, our appointments are once a week. I feel guilty about spending money on myself in this way but Kemi says I am worth it. She also reminds me how much I spend on my nails every month. I am investing in my well-being and that is priceless. Dr Sanaa is intelligent and experienced and under-standing. She has a kind smile and my spirit takes to her immediately.

The great thing about Skype appointments is that I don't have to worry about travelling to see Dr Sanaa, so it saves me valuable time. I like to start my weekend with a Saturday morning session. It helps me find balance after the working week and to start the weekend in a positive way. I speak to Dr Sanaa in my cowprint dressing gown with a cup of tea close to hand and a box of tissues, just in case. Dr Sanaa reminds me of Farah's mum. I know that, underneath her hijab, she is a beautiful secret.

SUPERSTITIONS

Dr Sanaa knows the poem about magpies. She knows that the first time I ever saw a magpie, I fainted. I was diagnosed with Addison's disease shortly after. She knows that, once, I saw one magpie every day for three days, and that's when I started forgetting things in Chambers and shaking in court. She knows that if I see one magpie in the morning on my way to court, I know that something is going to go wrong. If I am prosecuting, the words to my case opening might start to dance around the page. If I'm defending, I'll probably be convicted, things like that. Dr Sanaa knows that I often miss my train in the evenings because I have to wait on the platform until I have seen two.

Dr Sanaa knows that Henry Foskitt waved his willy in my face because the magpie outside my window in halls wouldn't move. She knows that there are no magpies in Ghana, New York or Thailand. And that I never see one when I am with The Girls. Dr Sanaa knows it doesn't happen often, but sometimes I see two magpies. That's when I can relax my shoulders and breathe normally. I saw two magpies when I got called to the Bar and when I moved in with Christian.

Dr Sanaa knows that my dad took Sol to Ghana without me. She knows that in my dreams I wished I was there with them and that I really wanted to be friends with Alessandro and Bea and Finlay and Sienna. She knows that Sol used to say that I 'use' my Addison's disease when it suits me. And that I held a knife up to his face when he came too close to me. She knows what Sol wrote in my birthday card and that when my dad left, I felt that Sol blamed me. Dr Sanaa knows that when my dad moved out, I discovered a beast inside me. I don't know its name and I have never seen its face. She knows that when it is not hibernating, it thrashes against the bars of its cage. And that it is loud and uncontrollable and angry. She knows that my bus fell forty feet off a bridge and that the bus was going to burst into flames but Miss Wilks saved me. She knows about the time my mum was late to pick me up from behind Morleys and I thought that I was going to die.

Dr Sanaa understands how hard it is when you have Addison's disease and what it feels like to have to take tablets three times a day. I tell her what it was like when I lived with my dad. That he thought I was 'insolent' and 'disrespectful'. I tell her about the time he poured hot water from the sink all over me and I had to run as fast as I could with hot water and palm oil and spinach in my hair. I tell her about the time he did WWF wrestling on me without saying 'ready, steady, go', and choke-slammed me into the wardrobe. I tell Dr Sanaa that when my dad was angry, it was like lightning and thunder and hailstones.

Dr Sanaa knows that when my mum was pregnant with me, my dad pushed her down the stairs and she had to go to hospital in an ambulance. She knows that the reason I know all these things is because my mum told me about it so many times when I was just a child. Dr Sanaa knows that my dad didn't beat Sol, or my mum when she was pregnant with him. I tell Dr Sanaa about Coral, that I never got to meet her, and that we never talked about her after she was still-born.

*

Dr Sanaa knows that before I knew the poem about magpies, I touched wood three times and made the sign of the cross. She knows that I blinked when I said 'Amen', to say 'pretty please' to God. Dr Sanaa knows that I touched wood because I didn't want anything bad to happen to my family, especially my mum, and that I had to do this to protect her. She knows about the butterflies in my chest and how long they've lived there. She knows that I wanted to stop touching wood and making the sign of the cross because I didn't want people to ask me what I was doing, and I didn't want to tell them. It was a private thing between me and God. Dr Sanaa knows that I was able to stop touching wood when I met The Girls and they became my best friends.

Dr Sanaa says that when I was a child, I touched wood and made the sign of the cross to try to find safety in a world filled with trauma. It was the way I tried to create control and stability amid violence and chaos. Dr Sanaa says that repetitive behaviours can also be called 'compulsions' and that touching wood, making the sign of the cross and saying 'Amen' is a form of 'compulsion' that I developed in response to the overwhelming and constant fear I had that 'something bad' was going to happen to me or my mum. It was my way of trying to reduce the risk of that bad thing happening, a 'mental ritual'. Dr Sanaa says that obsessive compulsive disorder, or OCD, is common in adults who have experienced childhood trauma.

I have gone from touching wood to looking for magpies.

I did not see a magpie before I boarded flight BA 0081 from London Heathrow to Kotoka airport for Sol's wedding in Accra – before I saw my dad and the wheelchair. I wish I had seen it so I could have been prepared.

Dr Sanaa says that I have made an association between seeing magpies and certain events that have happened in my life. For example, seeing a magpie and being diagnosed with Addison's disease. That association strengthened my superstition and encouraged my compulsive behaviour. Dr Sanaa wants me to start challenging the link between seeing one magpie and a bad thing happening; what is the evidence to link the sight of that magpie to that particular event? She wants me to think like the lawyer I am. She wants me to decide how much power I am going to give this bird.

The next time I see a magpie, I have to count to ten before I start looking for another one. That's going to help me introduce a delay between seeing the magpie and engaging in my impulsive response. I am also going to take deep breaths.

I think Ghanaians are superstitious, generally speaking, yes. But Ghanaian superstitions generally have some kind of underlying rationale. Children used to be told not to sing in the shower because dwarves would come and get them, but it was really to protect them from ingesting the harmful ingredients used to make soap. It has evolved into a superstition over time, but it started out as a way for parents to protect their children.

What does it look like, the magpie? Can I describe it? The magpie's tail is a unique blend of green and blue, and as long as its body. Its plumage is black and white. Its wingspan is distinct in colour and form, an arrangement of white and blue feathers. It is as iridescent as it is loud. Its black beak, foreboding, when alone in sight. But paired with a partner, the magpie gives the gift of assurance and hope.

'It is a beautiful bird, actually.'

What else do I think of when I see those colours, apart from the magpie?

'My carnival headdress. It was beautiful.'

Dr Sanaa would like me to do some research on the origin of the magpie superstition before our session next week. Where does it get its name from, 'magpie'? Does it represent different things in different cultures? If so, what?

Dr Sanaa wants me to remember that the magpie is a bird. It is just a bird, a bird of beautiful colours. I can say that to myself too.

GRIEVING

I am thirty years old and I am not living the life I dreamed for myself. I want to be in a healthy relationship. I'm not sure I know what one looks like. I want to love and be loved and to have my own family. I want to have a baby, Dr Sanaa, a baby girl, so I can show her what it is to be loved and honoured and cherished.

I don't want to wonder what it would have been like if Nurse Florence had been my mum instead of the tired nurse who came home after long shifts with her beloved babies. And who, or what, I would be if Papa hadn't sent *bofrot* and *kele wele* to 37 Military Hospital so my mum would marry his second-born son in London.

I don't want to wonder why Efua Simpa sent lightning pain flashing through my dad's body when he was only three years old or who he would have become if she hadn't. I don't want gravel to sit at the pit of my stomach every time I think about him in that wheelchair. I don't want to feel guilty about it or him. I don't want the idea of his vulnerability to invade my thoughts. Or to wonder if he needs my help while he dribbles on a different continent. I don't want to will his right hand and mouth to do the things he used to do to me, just so

I know he can. And I don't want to think about his orthopaedic shoes. Jesus.

I don't want to worry about what will happen to Sol, and his marriage if he doesn't process his trauma. Or what kind of father he will be to his unborn child.

And I don't want to spend my life grieving for my baby sister Coral and wishing I had only just seen her face.

I feel like someone or something inside me has died.

I am grieving.

For my dad. For his right eye that used to stare at mine and make me look at my shoes or the floor. For the right side of his mouth that used to call me 'insolent,' 'defiant' and 'disrespectful'. The same mouth that made people laugh and laugh and laugh at Ghanaian functions. I am grieving. For his right hand, the hand that used to beat me. I am grieving for the old softness of his hands and the shade of brown that used to be his skin. I am grieving for the dad that Sol used to have. The dad he loved so much. The dad he still loves.

My mum. I am grieving for Nurse Florence. The fact that I only met her once. That she never came to my house or confronted my dad. That she never advocated for herself and didn't know that she could walk away until she did. That it took her so long. I am grieving for the choices she had to make. That she couldn't hold her head as high at home as she did at work. I am grieving for the time I spent resenting her for it and the example she didn't show me. How much I wanted to not be like her. I am grieving for the idea that she never knew true love. I am scared that the same thing will happen to me. I am scared that my life will mirror hers.

Sol. I am grieving for the childhood he had and for the pain he has buried. I am grieving for the fact that he couldn't fulfil his dream of playing the drums because the sound of the cymbals made his heart betray him. That he didn't know what it was to be part of a family until he married Sienna. I am grieving for his battle with guilt and failure and inadequacy as a brother to me. I am grieving for the lost opportunities that he may never again enjoy with his dad. I am grieving for his feelings as well as my own. I grieve for the siblings we could never be and the family we never had. I am grieving for the journey he must now embark on.

For Christian. I am grieving for the love we had. Our relationship and lives together. I am grieving for the companionship I have known and lost. The meals we cooked and ate. The walks we used to take. I am grieving for the father that Mai has lost and the family we no longer have. I am grieving for the future I had hoped for and dreamed of with him. For our unborn child and what she would look like. For our children. I am grieving for the fact that he removed the choice from me. That he left me with no option but to walk away. And the fear that I will never love again.

Together, Dr Sanaa and I consider Christian's weekly alcohol consumption against NHS guidelines. I calculate the units on my phone. Dr Sanaa helps me to understand that Christian consumed, in one day, in excess of the national weekly guidance. I could never have brought up the subject of his drinking. Not without enraging him. I tried once but he shut me down. Is that the sign of a healthy relationship?

Together, Dr Sanaa and I consider the role that Christian's procrastination played in our daily lives. My inability to communicate with him. His looking for another job, abstractly mentioned, never seriously pursued. I wanted to encourage him from a place of love and support but I didn't know how – without angering him. Is that the sign of a healthy relationship?

Together, Dr Sanaa and I talk about when I fell down the stairs – when he pushed me down the stairs – and how I felt as I cowered at the bottom with red wine in my hair. We talk about the way I felt when he shouted at me, when he stood over me and roared. We talk about the day he took the strawberry from my hand to stop me eating it and the day he threw the remote control at my head. We talk about physical and emotional domestic abuse and the different forms it can take.

We talk about how hard it is for me to say those words out loud – 'he *pushed* me down the stairs' – and what that meant about him and for our relationship.

THE EMPTY CHAIR

I am unlovable.

Dr Sanaa says that I have been through a lot in my life. She wants me to 'think like the lawyer I am'. What does it mean to be 'unlovable'? We talk about The Girls and their role in my life. They are always at the end of the phone and were by my side in my darkest moments. We are forever brunching and lunching and laughing together. They are good people with kind hearts. Would they be friends with me if I wasn't the same?

My inner voice.
　　Before I met Dr Sanaa I wasn't aware of my inner voice. I didn't know what it was or that I had one but she has helped me to identify it. Who is it? What does it sound like? What type of things does it say to you? Is it an angry voice? A gentle voice? A kind voice? Does it laugh at you? Does it encourage you? Is it consistent? What is its tone? My inner voice is my dad. He is in my head all the time. He tells me bad things about myself in case I forget: all the things I don't know and cannot do, all the things that are wrong with me. He tells

me how bad I am at my job. What a burden I am as a person. That I don't deserve happiness. That I will never find peace.

I recognise my most wise, compassionate and courageous self as the friend I am to The Girls and the girlfriend I was to Christian. The Girls reciprocate the same qualities. Christian did not. I do not know how to reflect that person inwards, towards myself. It's not that I don't want to 'challenge' my inner voice, I just don't know how to.

Dr Sanaa tells me that I can control my inner voice, which makes it sound like I am stronger than I feel and more powerful than I am. I don't feel that there are many things in my life that I can control. She teaches me how to turn down the volume and that I can. She shows me a way to hug myself when I need to practise 'self-love'. I can wrap my arms around myself and give myself a gentle, reassuring hug. It can help me feel calm.

I can edit the ends of my nightmares. By creating the endings I choose. We practise together: I close my eyes. I am at Nursery Road trying to get home to West Norwood to my haven, my flat. I get on the bus outside H&M. I tap in on my Oyster card and take a seat on the lower deck. I listen to 'Superstition' on Spotify and try my best to internalise Stevie Wonder's wise words. I get off at West Norwood station stop and walk through the park to get home. I see Bev, Queen of the Park. She gives me a big cuddle. It is Tinker Bell's birthday. She will save me a slice of birthday cake and drop it round for me later. I do not look for magpies to determine my fate or fortune. I don't even care about them in the ending to the dream I am creating. I get to my front door and take out my keys. I put them in the door and turn them to the right. I am home. Mai is waiting for me. She is so happy to see me. I take off my shoes and put the kettle on. I am home.

There is no evidence to suggest that I am unlovable.

I love. And I am loved.

*

Dr Sanaa tells me about 'the empty chair exercise'. I'm going to ask you to imagine that your dad is sitting opposite you in a chair: your real dad, The One You Used to Know, and you are going to say to him all the things you would have liked to say to him as a child but couldn't because you were scared or because you couldn't touch wood. And then we can start to have a think about the things that adult Stella would like to tell The Man Who Used to Be Her Dad but can't after his stroke. Shall we give it a try?

Dr Sanaa asks me to face an empty chair in my living room and to think of something I would like to tell my dad. I close my eyes to imagine him. It is harder than I thought. I see my dad in front of me, his height concealed by his seated stance. It is too hard to look at the black of his pupils. He has no difficulty looking at mine. I can feel his gaze aimed like a laser on my forehead. He has changed out of his blue overalls into house clothes of grey trousers and a dark blue jumper. His arms are crossed at the chest, his fingernails are oil-stained. He looks indestructible and menacing. He is waiting and listening.

I remember the time you took me and Sol to a football match to watch Ghana play Nigeria. It was a day trip for the three of us. Uncle Papafio was supposed to go instead of me, but he was sick, so you took me instead. I remember in the car you told Sol that Ghana and Nigeria were West African rivals. That every Nigerian person you meet will tell you that Nigerian jollof rice is the best jollof rice in the world and that any Ghanaian person who hears that will just laugh because we know it isn't true. Nothing beats Ghanaian jollof rice. You said that Ghanaian people don't like it if you think that they are Nigerian because they are not fraudsters. That made me really want Ghana to win.

You explained that the Ghanaian football team were called 'The Black Stars' and the Nigerian team were called 'The Super Eagles'. I remember that the Ghanaian fans were waving colours of red and yellow and green, the colours of the flag. The Nigerian fans were on the other side of the stadium waving their colours of white and green. On the Ghanaian side, there were trumpets and drums and percussion instruments. It was like a concert. The Ghanaian fans were singing a song. Me and Sol listened carefully so we could learn the words: 'We will put *peppeh* in your eyes, you will see, we will score you!' We sang it over and over again to the Nigerian players and their fans, so they knew we meant business. When we won by three goals to two, I felt like being Ghanaian was the best thing in the world. I was so happy that you took me to the football match with you and Sol that day.

I remember the time you carried me on your shoulders at Auntie Baaba's wedding. I felt like I could almost touch the sky. That is my earliest memory, not just of you, but of life. It is my best memory of you. My other memories are different.

Dr Sanaa says that is enough for today when my tears make it hard for me to see my dad in the chair or say anything more to him. To finish today's session, she wants me to think about something.

'If adult Stella could say anything to child Stella, what would she say?'

'I think she would say, it's not your fault.'

'Well done, Stella. You're doing really well. You should feel very proud of yourself.'

STELLA

20 April 2020. It is my birthday and I am thirty-one years old. I should be on holiday with Christian, somewhere beautiful and warm, sunset snorkelling or paddleboard surfing, but I am alone in West Norwood with Mai, my faithful dog. The hot water of the shower distracts me from my tears and I make my face up to conceal myself from the outside world. That is a good thing about being a woman-girl, you can always make your eyelashes bigger and your cheeks a little rosier. I team a loose-fitting green dress with leopard-print trainers and a Stella McCartney cross-body bag that Eimear convinced me to get when she was dizzied by the bright lights of the city, 'an investment piece'. I felt guilty when I bought it. So much money on a bag. I cannot escape the red letters from Sudbourne detailing unpaid school fees or my mum's bank statements. How did I get to this place from whence I came?

He calls in the morning. I take it as a sign that he cares. That I didn't dream it or imagine his love. He has not erased me entirely from his memory. I do still exist. He is sorry that he stood over me and roared the colour red. I do not pick up. Because to pick up is to go back.

That he called is enough for me for now.

Kemi opens the door to Farah's house. The familiarity of her face, her smile and her voice provides the kind of comfort that only a friend of twenty years can offer. She gives me a kiss on the cheek and a big squeeze to help with my hurt.

'Happy birthday, Stella. You look amazing!'

Farah interrupts her pretence at domesticity to smother me in love. She is waving a bouquet of flowers in my direction. They are beautiful.

'You've lost weight, Stella.'

'I know. Every cloud, eh?'

She gives me a hug, for strength.

The kitchen is filled with helium balloons of rose gold and pastel pink, and latex confetti balloons in heart and pear shapes. The numbers 3 and 1 are centred on the island with ribbon and weights. Croissants, pains au chocolat, strawberries and freshly squeezed orange juice carefully arranged around them. A pot of just-brewed coffee blesses the air. They have laid on a beautiful birthday brunch. Eimear joins us from Connemara on FaceTime.

'Happy birthday, Stella-Star! I wish I was there with you!'

She asks me to remember everything that I have achieved: I am a barrister. I have bought a beautiful home. I have incredible friends. A gorgeous dog. She tells me that I am amazing and that she loves me very much. 'We all do.' She is always telling me things like that. By the time they reach me, the words have usually lost their meaning. Dr Sanaa's words in my ears tell me that maybe she is saying it because it is true.

'Thank you.'

Kemi presents a birthday cake of strawberry and elderflower Victoria sponge. My favourite. 'It looks delicious, thank you so much.' A cue for Eimear to announce my gift:

'Stella, for your birthday, we are going ... to Iceland! Not this weekend – next. A Girls' Trip!'

I have always wanted to go. Eimear is going to fly from Dublin and meet us in Reykjavik. We are going to explore the rugged landscape. Together. Visit the Blue Lagoon and black sand beaches. Together. We are going to stand under waterfalls and gaze at the Northern Lights. Together. So romantic.

'Me, you, Farah and Kemi. We have an itinerary and we are going to have the best time! How excited are you?'

My heart pumps gratitude and warmth and love all around my body.

'Thank you so much. I don't know what to say.'

Before Eimear goes.
Can Farah just remind us.
One more time.
Please.
About the time.
You went to Thailand.
And Stella ate that
Beef massaman curry?

The reference cannot but force orange juice, croissant and straw-berry infused laughter across the well-decorated island. The type that makes eyes crease, breath shorten, and tears stream. Laughter that insists on lingering long after it is time for calm.

My friends remind me that I am loved and supported, that I am not alone.

They help me look forward.

To think about tomorrow.

ACKNOWLEDGEMENTS

Thank you, Katie Hernon, for creating a peaceful place for me to write and for inspiring me to put pen to paper. Nina Harvey, thank you for encouraging me to believe, reflect and continue; for being my first editor and reader. Laurie Wilks, thank you for your laughter, friendship and monosyllabic feedback. Elizabeth Smaller, for your wise counsel and constant support, thank you.

I could not have published this book without the belief of my wonderful agent, Juliet Mushens. Thank you for taking a chance on me and for being the ultimate Hype Girl. To my publisher, Juliet Mabey, your wisdom, perception and vision for this book encouraged me to go further than I knew I could. Thank you to you, my copy-editor Tamsin Shelton and everyone at Oneworld Publications who has played a part in bringing this book to life.

Thank you to my mum for inspiring me in a myriad of ways. To my brother for accompanying me on this journey of life. And to my family for making me the woman I am today. Thank you to Yvette Selormey for being my sister and supporter. To Barbara Yankah for being my fairy godmother extraordinaire. And to Jada-Rose, my partner in crime.

To my girlfriends for supporting and loving and celebrating me within an inch of my life: Ruki Ware, Bunmi Kelekun, Sally El-Boghdadly, Helena Chow, Eleanor Ashby, Lydia Lee, Oniz Suleyman, Becky Butler and Fani Gamon. To Tora Hutton, Charlotte Langman and Harriet Johnson for the gift of your friendship. To Laura Goodman, Natalie Dowle and Erin Thompson for the role you have played. To Kiki Cofie and Bibi Cofie for making me laugh like no one else can. To Ama Sogbodjor for being the original and the best. To Shade Saint James for your example, for your forgiveness. To Sophie Sellu and Jamz Supernova for walking alongside and inspiring me. To Nana Antwiwaa Wireko-Brobby for being my girl on the ground. To Charlotte Bateson-Hill and Ruth Morris, my oldest and first friends.

To my beautiful nephews: Musa, Eesa and Ibby; and my godsons: Zachy, Freddie and Basta for the love and joy you bring to my life.

I am grateful to the Society of Authors for the John C Laurence award. And to my dog Blue. I'm sure there was life before you, I just can't remember it.

MARIE-CLAIRE AMUAH is a British-Ghanaian barrister special-ising in white-collar crime. She studied English and French at the University of Nottingham before embarking on a legal career. She is also a trustee of Black Cultural Archives, a national heritage charity dedicated to collecting, preserving and celebrating the histories of African and Caribbean people in Britain. She received the John C Laurence Award from the Society of Authors to support the writing of her debut novel, *One for Sorrow, Two for Joy*. She was born, raised and currently lives in South London.